CW00385381

POSSESSED

Elise Noble

Published by Undercover Publishing Limited

Copyright © 2019 Elise Noble

v6

ISBN: 978-1-910954-96-6

Edited by Nikki Mentges at NAM Editorial

Cover art by Abigail Sins

www.undercover-publishing.com

www.elise-noble.com

Most of us have far more courage than we ever
dreamed we possessed.
- *Dale Carnegie*

CHAPTER 1 - NICOLE

I DIDN'T EVEN have to open my eyes to know something was wrong. The bed was too cool, the room too quiet. Carlton's limbs always flopped over to my side, and he had a habit of snoring quietly in the early hours. So where was he? The bathroom? I listened carefully for the sound of running water through the paper-thin walls, but the whole house was silent apart from the quiet snuffling of George and Templeton, my pet rats.

I had to do it. I had to look, which was easier said than done when it felt as if my eyelids had rusted shut. That was what happened when I stayed up until after midnight writing a research proposal that had to pass muster with Professor Fairchild. And Carlton had definitely been home last night. He'd arrived back from work just after two, made mugs of cocoa for me and Lulu, our housemate, who'd stayed awake to give me moral support and check for spelling errors, then he'd helped me upstairs to bed.

But now the room was empty in the grey morning light. What time was it? I rolled to check on my phone, but it wasn't in its usual place on the nightstand.

"Where's Carlton, boys? And where's my phone?"

No answer, but the rats did twitch their whiskers at me.

Had I left the phone downstairs? Since Lulu was a neat freak, our three-bedroom house in the Mission District of San Francisco was scrupulously tidy, and when I stumbled into the kitchen, my textbooks were stacked neatly on the fold-up dining table in the kitchen. But my phone wasn't with them.

A house in San Francisco, you ask? How could we afford that on our definitely below-average incomes? Well, firstly because I was almost certain our landlord used his rentals business as a front for money laundering and we didn't ask awkward questions, and secondly, due to the fact it was one step away from being demolished. The back wall moved if you leaned on it hard, wind whistled in around the ill-fitting window frames, and Lulu scrubbed mould off the ceilings every other day. And did I mention how tiny it was? I slept on a futon-slash-sofa—one barely wide enough to be called a double—that folded up to give me room to dress in the mornings.

But there was still no sign of Carlton. Not even a note. He worked the late shift at Jive, a bar three streets away, so he never got up early.

Perhaps I'd put the phone in my purse? Yes, that was a possibility. Except when I went looking, I couldn't find the purse either. And didn't we have a TV yesterday? My addled brain had just begun to realise there was something very, very wrong when I caught sight of my reflection in the mirror over the sofa and gasped. No, not because my brown hair was sticking out in a thousand different directions or because the dark circles under my eyes could have been drawn on with a Sharpie, but because of what was missing.

My necklace.

The gold necklace I'd worn every day since my eighth birthday. My mother had fastened it around my neck right before she started explaining about our birthright and what life had in store for me, and now it was gone. Suddenly, nothing else mattered. I ran up the stairs two at a time and scrabbled around in my bed, pulling off the covers and shaking the pillow, but it was pointless. The necklace had disappeared.

"What's up?" Lulu asked from the doorway, rubbing her eyes. "Why are you tossing things around?"

"My necklace is gone. Carlton's gone. My phone's gone."

"Huh?"

"Everything's gone!"

"Wait, wait, back up..." She yawned and glanced at her fitness tracker, which doubled as a watch. "It's six o'clock in the morning. Too early for this."

But I was wide awake now, angry and scared at the same time. Was Carlton playing some sort of sick joke? It was mid-June, not the first of April, and he didn't have much of a sense of humour anyway, so I quickly ruled that out.

Slowly, the only likely explanation sank in. Carlton was missing. So was my phone and my solid gold necklace. In a daze, I walked to the chest of drawers, and when I found the fifty bucks I kept stashed under my socks for emergencies had vanished as well, I didn't know whether to cry or throw something. My boyfriend had robbed me. Okay, so the relationship hadn't been all that serious, but it still shocked me that he'd stolen my freaking stuff!

"I can't believe this," I mumbled, walking out of the room. I had a nasty feeling what else I'd find downstairs. Or rather, what I wouldn't find. "My laptop's gone."

Lulu had trailed after me, and now she shrieked from the doorway to the living room. "Where's the TV? It's the final of *Cruising for Love* today, and I need to know whether James picks Britney or Yolanda."

A more thorough check of the house revealed Carlton's stuff had vanished too, as had Lulu's iPod, the blender, and my e-reader.

"He's even taken the damn chargers," she said. "I'm gonna kill him."

"You'll have to get in line. Although I still can't believe it. *Carlton*?" Then I had another thought. "What if it was somebody else? What if he tried to stop them and got hurt?"

"Then where is he?"

"I'll check outside."

"Not on your own, you won't."

"It's daylight now, and one of us needs to phone the police. Since I don't have a phone..."

"Be careful, okay?"

"I will; I promise."

Being honest, I didn't want to go outside alone either, but I had an ulterior motive. One person would know for sure whether Carlton had done the dirty on me, and that was Herman. And when I say person, I mean ghost. Herman had once been a person, but ever since he'd gotten run over by an out-of-control Buick in 1967, his spirit had been hanging out on the sidewalk in front of our house.

Before you write me off as a lunatic and book me straight into the nearest asylum, I should probably explain. Remember that birthright I mentioned earlier?

Well, this was it. Like my mother, and her mother before her, and her mother before that, and her mo—you get the picture—I had a direct link to the spirit world. I could talk to them, and they could talk to me. And since ghosts never slept and were tethered to the spot where they died, it stood to reason that if Carlton had walked out of the apartment carrying our TV in the early hours of the morning, Herman must have seen him.

The only problem was how to ask the question without passers-by thinking I'd lost my mind. Usually, I pretended to be on the phone, but today, that was a problem. Instead, I squatted down behind the rickety fence that bordered our front yard and pretended to look for something in the weeds. Lulu's tidy streak didn't extend outside, and there was so much greenery, I was surprised conservationists hadn't slapped a preservation order on us.

"Herman?"

"What did you drop?"

"Nothing. I just need to talk to you."

"Where's that phone of yours?" He chuckled. "Broken? Modern technology's not all it's cracked up to be, is it? Back in my day, phones were built to last. Big chunky things that—"

I didn't need yet another lecture on the sixties. "No, I think it got stolen. Did you see Carlton come out of the house during the night?"

"Couple hours ago. Carrying a duffel bag and a TV, which I thought was mighty strange."

The last bit of hope that Carlton wasn't an utter dog leached away. Actually, that was an insult to dogs. Carlton was more of a skunk. No, worse. A flea on a skunk. An amoeba on a flea on a skunk. That TV had cost me almost four hundred bucks on sale, and I'd saved up for months because I wanted to watch the box set of *The X-Files* Lulu gave me the Christmas before last on a decent screen.

"Did you see where he went?"

"He had his car pulled up to the kerb, that old Ford, and he headed off towards Potrero. He needs a new muffler. You should tell him that."

If I ever caught up with him, I'd ram his rusty muffler up his thieving behind. "On his own?"

"Yup." Herman tilted his head to one side and leaned forward a few inches. "You look upset. Did that boy of yours do summat he shouldn't have?"

"You could say that."

"Nicole?" Lulu called from the door. "What are you doing down there? Did you find something?"

Yes, but not my sense of judgement, which had obviously gone missing when I let Carlton into my bed.

"Just a footprint. Big, like Carlton's tennis shoes."

"He took my hair conditioner too, the little worm. The expensive stuff."

"I'm so, so sorry."

Lulu stuck her feet into a pair of ballet pumps and started outside. Oh, crap. I clambered to my feet, knees cracking, because of course there wasn't a footprint and I couldn't let her see that. Luckily, I managed to meet her halfway, and she threw her arms around me.

"Nicole, I'm the one who should be sorry. Here's me complaining about hair conditioner when you lost your boyfriend and your laptop."

"I just want my necklace back," I mumbled.

And truly that was the only thing that mattered.

Sure, the electronic stuff was expensive and I had precious little money to spare, but my research work was all backed up to the cloud, as were my phone contacts. Everything else could be replaced with a bit of time and effort, but I couldn't afford to lose that necklace. It was priceless, not just to me but possibly to mankind, if my mother's vague explanation was to be believed.

"And I want to give Carlton Hines a solid kick in the crotch with my teal boots. You know, the ones with the pointy toes?" Lulu said. "From both of us. I can't believe he did that. I mean, he seemed so nice."

Yes, he really did. Lulu and I had been renting our narrow little house for the past four years, ever since we met at university. Chalk and cheese, or so the saying went, but we'd been friends from the start. At twenty-five, Lulu was a year younger than me, and originally, she'd planned to be a dancer. But three years into her stage career, a knee injury left her heartbroken and out of work, and she'd signed up to study dental science at UCSF instead. She still kept fit, still turned heads, and still got mistaken for a cheerleader every time we went out for drinks together.

Me? I was the frumpy sidekick to her Bond girl, and I owned more lab coats than dresses.

After moving to California for my undergrad degree, I'd stuck around to study for my PhD in genetics, more fluent in geek than girl talk. The only reason we'd met at all was because the elevator was out of order. Lulu had just survived another operation on her knee, and the stairs were a nightmare with her crutches so I stopped to help. By the time we'd made it to the sixth floor, I'd discovered that Lulu had recently split up with her boyfriend, and he'd stiffed her on the rent so she needed a new roommate ASAP. And I'd also learned that one of Lulu's dental hygiene lecturers had gotten caught in a cupboard with the dean's personal assistant doing something they shouldn't have been doing since both of them were married. If gossiping were an Olympic sport, Lulu would have won gold every time.

But I didn't mind that so much. I rarely had anything interesting to say, at least to humans, so her cheerful chatter filled the silence. I'd also spent the whole of the previous day trying unsuccessfully to get my landlord to do something, *anything*, about the mouse infestation in my rented apartment, and the idea of moving into a rodent-free home—apart from George and Tempi, of course—filled me with indescribable joy. I loved animals, don't get me wrong, but those freaking mice chewed everything.

Carlton was the fourth person to rent the box room-slash-cupboard next to mine over the years. Lulu and I could just about manage the rent between the two of us, but long-term, it was a stretch, and Lulu hated having to curb her social life to pay for a room we didn't use anyway. Carlton had come via Craigslist after an ad on the university noticeboard offered up only a guy whose "special skill" was eating spaghetti through his nose and a girl allergic to cleaning products who clearly wasn't a good match for Lulu. And Carlton had seemed so sweet. Gentle. He'd even remembered to put the toilet seat down.

His migration from the box room to my bed had been a natural progression, one that started off with a shared love of nature documentaries and moved via lazy weekend brunches to him taking the virginity I'd inadvertently hung onto well into my twenties.

Red flags should have waved when he didn't like George and Tempi. More than once, Carlton had suggested moving their cage downstairs, onto the high shelf above the TV. Never mind the mould above it or the fact that the sun beat down there in the afternoons. And Carlton would never let me get the boys out to play if he was home.

In all honesty, I hadn't seen him as a partner for life, more of a friend with benefits, but I hadn't expected this...this betrayal. He'd stolen my most precious possession as well as leaving me feeling like an idiot. How could I ever trust a man again after this?

At least I still had Lulu.

"I don't have any pointy boots, but I'm with you on the crotch thing. I'll freaking castrate him, but I've got to get my necklace back first."

"Don't worry; I've got a pair of boots you can borrow."

Well, that was something at least. "But how the hell are we gonna find him? Did you speak to the police?"

"Yes, and they said they'd send someone to take a statement, but we're clearly not a priority."

Disappointing, but not surprising. In the last two or three years, crime in San Francisco had risen to unprecedented levels, and as previously safe neighbourhoods became dangerous to walk through at night, the SFPD had been stretched to its limit. A simple theft with no injuries would be way down the list. But that didn't stop Lulu from grumbling.

"I had to spell my name twice, and even then I'm not sure the guy on the phone wrote it down right. Why do we bother paying taxes?"

"Because otherwise, the murder rate would be twice as high."

"It's already horrific. Did you see the news last night? They found a headless body in Buena Vista Park."

"No, I didn't." And I didn't particularly want to think about it either. Guess I'd never be visiting Buena Vista Park again. "Can we change the subject?"

"Okay, sure. Did Carlton say anything about where he might have gone? Mention a trip? Drop any hints?"

"No, nothing." This had come totally out of the blue. "He always said he liked living here. The only place we ever spoke about going was Alaska to see the Northern Lights, and it's the wrong time of year for that."

"What if he went to Alaska anyway?"

"With his hatred of being cold? He only wanted to do a one-day visit."

In winter, he and Lulu had bickered constantly about the thermostat setting. It was the one subject that brought disharmony to an otherwise peaceful household, and in the end, he'd solved the problem by agreeing to meet her halfway on the temperature, wear a sweater downstairs, and pay an extra twenty bucks a month towards the heating bill.

"Okay, so that's a fair point. We'll have to start at Jive. Maybe he mentioned his plans to someone at work?"

"You think he discussed stealing from his roommates with a colleague? I know Jive can be a bit edgy, but..."

"No, I meant his plans to leave the area."

Of course. Right now, my brain wasn't functioning properly. The lack of sleep was part of it, for sure, but what if there was another reason for the grogginess? Carlton had made us cocoa last night, something he hadn't done in weeks. What if he'd slipped an Ambien into it?

"I suppose he might have spoken to someone," I said.

"What time does Jive open? I've never gotten there before eleven p.m."

"Seven this evening."

"Then we'll be there." Lulu yawned again. "Although I don't know how I'm gonna stay awake that long. I've never felt so tired."

Lulu was the perkiest person I'd ever met, even when she was sleep-deprived, but today, she seemed oddly lethargic.

"I think Carlton doctored our drinks last night."

It took a few moments for that to sink in, then Lulu's blue eyes flashed with anger.

"He's gonna be sorry when we catch up with him. Hell hath no fury like two women who've been screwed over by a spineless asshole."

My raging fires still needed kindling. I felt numb inside. Frozen. Looking back, I think I was still in shock, torn up inside from the breach of trust. But I nodded anyway.

"Tonight at Jive. Yes, he'll be sorry."

CHAPTER 2 - NICOLE

"HE TOOK YOUR necklace?" Professor Fairchild asked.

Despite my exhaustion, I'd struggled into university because the deadline to submit my research proposal wouldn't suddenly move forward just because my ex-boyfriend was a lying toad. Professor Fairchild had been my supervisor for the past three years, and despite our obvious differences—he was a sixty-seven-year-old widower from Berkshire, England, who enjoyed fossil-hunting in his spare time and thought Twitter was what birds did—I counted him as one of my closest friends.

"And my laptop. Can I borrow yours to finish my funding application?"

"You don't even need to ask." He waved me over to his desk and pulled out his chair so I could sit down. "If you don't mind my saying, you look terrible."

"I know."

"How about I get you a cup of coffee?"

A groan escaped. Professor Fairchild might have been at the forefront of genetic research, but he'd never have gotten a job as a barista. The workings of the coffee machine were beyond him, so he used instant, which he insisted on tipping in straight from the jar. I'd once seen him fill a quarter of the mug with coffee granules. And it was a toss-up whether you got no milk, the right amount of milk, or far too much milk. But today? I needed the caffeine like a junkie needed their fix.

"Coffee sounds good."

"You're sure it was Carlton?"

"It was definitely him. Herman saw him carrying the TV out to his car in the middle of the night."

"Old Herman, eh? How is he these days?"

"Bored. And he hates the new model Nissan. Says it looks like a coffin on wheels."

Professor Fairchild was the only living person who knew my secret. I'd never intended to tell a soul other than my own child, if I ever had one, which—let's face it —seemed unlikely given my track record with men. But everything had changed the day the professor's wife died.

I'd been with him when the police came to the lab late one November evening two and a half years ago, although I didn't find out the details of what had happened until the next day. Darlene was still in the hospital when the news came, with medical staff trying to revive her, which was pointless since she'd died at the house. In the dining room. That was where her spirit remained, hovering in the narrow gap between the antique mahogany dining table and the front window as blood seeped from a gaping chest wound.

A robbery gone wrong, detectives said. A confrontation with an armed man high on drugs who'd been looking to fund his habit. Perhaps if she'd just handed over her valuables, she'd have lived, but she threw a brass candlestick at him and paid the ultimate price.

I'd first met her almost three weeks later when the professor didn't turn up for work two days running. Day one, he'd called in sick, but on the second day, he didn't answer the phone. I'd felt nauseous myself as I rang the bell with my lab partner, Damien, standing behind me. Though neither of us voiced the words, we'd been expecting to find a body, the remains of the broken man who'd barely spoken since the funeral. But instead, we found Professor Fairchild riddled with a cold and hungry because he didn't know how to turn the stove on.

So we'd come up with a plan. Damien visited on Monday nights to do the laundry, while I got Thursdays and the cooking—dinner for two plus six reheatable meals for the freezer. Rosaria from the cleaning agency came on Wednesdays and did the ironing too.

And that first Thursday when we'd sat down to eat, there'd been a third person at the table—Darlene—although she couldn't use a chair because she'd have fallen straight through it.

"It's you! One of those... What did the spirit guide say the name was? Electos?"

Electi, but I couldn't correct her, not with the professor picking at his spaghetti bolognese right opposite me.

"You're here to avenge my death? Because I must say, I wasn't expecting you to show up quite so quickly. The guide said it'd take a while for my turn to come around since there are only four of you."

No, I wasn't there to avenge her freaking death. Okay, so technically that was my job, but one I'd been trying my very best to resign from for my entire life, hence the research into genetics.

What's with all this death avenging, I hear you ask? Well, the whole reason spirits remained stuck in place was to help the Electi to find their murderers, at which point, we were supposed to banish the killers' nasty black souls from the face of the earth, thereby freeing the spirit to continue to the afterlife or wherever they went to join the line for reincarnation. Except this was the twenty-first century, and we couldn't simply go around executing people.

Sadly, nobody had updated the spirit guides on this, and they still went through the same spiel as they had for the past...thousand years? Two thousand years? Five? Ten? Who knew how long we'd been around? So many details of our history had been lost in the sands of time.

And even if I'd wanted to do my duty, Darlene's killer was safely locked up in police custody after he'd tried the same trick the following week, only that time, he'd picked on a lady with a slightly more accurate pitching arm. I could hardly break into jail and hold a pillow over his face, could I?

It wasn't until the professor headed to the kitchen to fetch more Parmesan that I'd been able to reply.

"Yes, I'm one of the Electi, but we don't work like that anymore." Well, the others might—I had no idea—but I figured it was better to present a united front. "We leave justice to the court system now, and the good news is that the man who shot you's been caught."

Her hopefulness turned to confusion. "But how do I get free, then?"

Uh, yes, about that... "I'm afraid you don't. But you do get to stay in the same house as your husband, so there's that."

"How do I talk to him? He hasn't been right since... since I...since I died"—Darlene made a little choking sound—"and I'm worried about him."

"You can't talk to the living. That's not possible, I'm afraid."

"But I'm talking to you."

"I'm different."

"You look the same, other than that weird blue glow."

Ah, the glow. That was how the ghosts recognised us. Apparently, I shimmered in shades of blue from the palest tint to almost navy, and the air crackled when I got near. Whoever blessed me with those particular traits must have been a special kind of sadist, because otherwise, I could have snuck around incognito and avoided a hell of a lot of awkward conversations.

"I get that, but there's no way of you speaking directly with...with...Professor Fairchild."

"His name's Geoffrey."

"Okay, Geoffrey."

"But he needs me. We met when we were ten years old, did you know that? My daddy worked in England for a while. Geoffrey lived next door but one, and when the time came for my family to move back home, I stayed. Then we came to San Francisco together. We *need* each other. And Geoffrey's so absent-minded around the house. If I'm not here to remind him to eat and sleep and pay the bills, he clean forgets."

A month passed. Two months. Even though I cooked for him, the professor lost weight, and his once-healthy frame turned gaunt. He withdrew into himself. He fell asleep in the lab, and his research projects went nowhere until one day, Damien overheard him talking to the dean.

"Fairchild's gonna quit," he whispered the moment I walked into the lab. "I heard him telling Cato half an hour ago."

"But he can't quit. We need him here."

"Nicole, we need the old Professor Fairchild. Since Darlene died, he hasn't been all there, and I like the guy, you know I do, but I need a proper supervisor, one who provides support instead of staring into space from dawn to dusk."

Truthfully, so did I, but I also didn't want to give up on the professor. He hadn't given up on me. Soon after we met, I'd sprained my arm when a drunk cyclist mowed me down on a crosswalk, and I ended up almost destitute because I had to quit my part-time waitressing job. The professor had loaned me five hundred dollars, then spent countless evenings helping me to fill in grant applications and scholarship forms until I got enough money to fund the rest of my studies.

Now, he may have been technically past retirement age, but until Darlene's murder, his mind had been sharper than those of men fifty years his junior. And he had so much knowledge locked up in his head, knowledge we couldn't replace by simply slotting another supervisor into his vacant lab coat.

But helping him would mean taking a huge chance. Opening myself up to questioning and possibly ridicule, both of which I'd avoided by keeping my damn mouth shut. My mother had kept quiet about her abilities too, but my grandma had been more open as a young woman and gotten labelled a freak for her honesty. Eventually, she'd moved to a new town to start afresh, away from the vicious rumours and wagging tongues.

Could I really risk that happening to me?

I got my answer at dinner that Thursday night. The professor barely ate, just sat there stirring the chicken salad into a mess on the plate, chicken salad I'd spent a half hour preparing.

"Would you rather I made something else?" I asked.

"Oh, no, this is delicious." A pause, and the fork clattered onto the plate. "I'm sorry, Nicole. I know how much effort you've put into helping, but I just can't go on like this."

Sweat popped out on the back of my neck as I got a bad, bad feeling about whatever he had to say. "Like what?"

"Living in this house, surrounded by memories. The bad ones..." He glanced over at the spot where Darlene had fallen. "And the good ones. They hurt too. I'm planning to move away."

Move away? Away from Darlene? Oh, shit.

Chapter 3 - Nicole

BEHIND THE PROFESSOR, Darlene stiffened, and she would have gasped if she'd still been breathing. As it was, she pressed her palms to her chest, hands over a heart that no longer beat.

"Stop him! Please, you have to stop him. I'll be left here alone, and Geoffrey, he'll be on his own too. I realise he doesn't know I'm here, but I still talk to him all the time just in case a miracle happens and he hears me."

"Where are you planning to move to?" I asked her husband.

"I've been looking at a retirement community near Walnut Creek. You and Damien shouldn't be wasting your time on an old man like me."

"I don't mind."

"But I do. Don't worry; I'll make sure I hand you over to an appropriate supervisor. And I must apologise for being so terribly ineffective lately. Losing Darlene knocked me for six."

"Geoffrey'll hate living in a retirement community," she told me. "Can you really imagine him playing golf? Or doing Tai Chi? He's never been keen on the great outdoors other than those damn fossils."

I had to agree with her. While I understood why the professor wanted to leave this place, I had a horrible suspicion he'd regret his decision later on. And whether he realised it or not, he still had a lot left to give the world of science.

So I did it. I laid myself bare, metaphorically speaking.

Deep breaths, Nicole. "So this is gonna sound crazy. I don't even know where to start..."

I'd been bottling my secret up for so long I felt like a carbonated drink sitting on a vortex shaker. Now it was about to come fizzing out.

"Some of the world's greatest scientific breakthroughs were once considered crazy," the professor said. "When Heinrich Hertz first demonstrated the existence of radio waves, he was incredulous whenever anybody suggested they might one day travel around the earth. And when Röntgen discovered X-rays, he only told his wife because he feared people would say he'd gone out of his mind."

"But those discoveries were easy to prove compared to..." I trailed off, wishing I'd never started down this path.

"Whatever you've got to say, I promise I won't judge, Nicole. I'm an old man. In my lifetime, I've seen the impossible become a reality, and the future will bring even more miracles."

"I can see ghosts," I blurted. "Darlene. She's right here."

Until then, I'd been worried about the professor's suicidal thoughts, but as he pressed a palm to his chest in a mirror of his wife's earlier move, I feared his heart might give out instead. Especially when he turned as white as...snow. You thought I was going to say "white as a ghost," right? Well, ghosts weren't actually white.

They stayed the same colour in death as in life, complete with vivid additions like bloodstains and sometimes harsh make-up. A snapshot of their final moment.

But now the professor stared at me. Then at the three-quarters-full glass of wine beside my plate—no, I'd barely been drinking. Slowly, he smiled. But it wasn't the happy smile of a man who could now communicate with his wife in the afterlife. No, it was the same wary, overly sympathetic expression of the elementary school teacher who'd once caught me talking to an "imaginary friend" and referred me to the guidance counsellor.

"Have you talked to anybody about this?"

"Until you? No."

"I see. And how long has this been going on?"

"Since I was eight years old."

"Did you experience a traumatic event at that time? Because sometimes that can trigger an unexpected emotional response."

Not a traumatic event, more of a gradual transfer of powers from my mother to me. "That wasn't it."

The professor opened his mouth to speak again. Closed it. His brow furrowed. This was the face of a man unaccustomed to dealing with anything he couldn't see under a microscope or on the gel matrix of our electrophoresis apparatus, no matter what he might quote about Hertz and Röntgen.

Fortunately, Darlene stepped in to help.

"Tell him that the dry-cleaning ticket he was looking for this morning is in the kitchen drawer next to the microwave."

"Uh, this might sound odd, but were you looking for

a dry-cleaning ticket this morning?"

"How do you know that?"

"Because Darlene just told me you were. It's in the drawer next to the microwave."

He didn't take his eyes off me as he backed into the kitchen, and sure enough, the ticket was exactly where Darlene said it would be. But even with that proof, he struggled to believe me.

"What did you do?" he asked, looking wildly at the ceiling, his eyes darting from side to side. "Fix up a hidden camera? Because that's slightly disturbing, Nicole."

Now do you see why I avoided telling anyone about the whole Electi thing?

"No, I didn't. If you don't believe me, that's fine. I was only trying to help."

"Geoffrey wasn't always closed-minded like this," Darlene called from the next room. "Remind him that when we were eleven, he thought he saw a ghost in the woods behind his grandma's house and ran home so fast one of his shoes fell off."

I duly repeated the tale, and this time, I was afraid the professor might join Darlene, the way he clutched at his chest again and sagged back against the counter. Would it count as murder if the shock killed him?

"But...but...nobody else knew what happened that day. She swore she'd never tell a soul."

"And she kept that promise until now." He didn't look too steady on his feet. "Perhaps you should sit down again?"

"I don't understand what's happening here."

"Neither did I at first, but I've had years to get used to the problem."

The professor shuffled back through to the dining room, dazed, pausing only to slop Scotch from the bottle on the sideboard into a tumbler.

"This can't be real," he mumbled, more to himself than to me.

"That's exactly what he said when he got his scholarship to Stanford," Darlene told me.

"Darlene says that was your reaction when you got your scholarship to Stanford."

Now he believed. I saw it in his eyes, but it wasn't easy for him. On the one hand, he wanted my abilities to exist because it would bring him closer to his wife, but on the other hand, it went against a lifetime of scientific training. That evening, I'd called everything he thought he knew about life into question.

It had been a turning point for both of us.

Like the scientists we were, we'd joined forces to research, research, research. In the evenings, after we'd put in the hours on our official projects, we analysed me, Darlene, a handful of ghosts who lived near the research institute, and even Herman at one point. The professor borrowed all sorts of equipment from his friends, and we found that ghosts emitted low levels of high-frequency electromagnetic radiation. Barely detectable from a single phenomenon, as the professor had taken to calling them, but put a group of them together and he got quite excited.

A metallurgist friend of his had gotten involved, and from the chemical composition, he concluded that the talisman on my now-missing necklace dated back around five thousand years to ancient Egypt. They'd extracted their gold from quartz veins, apparently, which meant it was never pure—rather, it contained some silver and other trace elements that could be measured and compared. Which had been created first? The Electi or our gold charms? Right now, I couldn't answer that question.

And what about me? I now knew more about my genes than ever. Three months ago, I'd found a piece of non-human DNA lurking among my chromosomes, the genetic recipe for an ancient virus. A human endogenous retrovirus, to be precise, or HERV. Right now, I didn't understand much about it—whether it could replicate or what, if anything, it did—but I'd never seen it in another person before, and neither had the professor. How did it get there? Well, many years ago, a virus had inserted a DNA-based copy of its own RNA genetic material into my genome, and it got passed down from my ancestors all the way to me.

Was it linked to my strange abilities? Without samples from the other Electi to compare my DNA to, it was difficult to be certain what made me different. The professor's area of expertise was ageing, specifically work around the Hayflick limit—the theory that each human cell could only divide around fifty times before it deteriorated. How did the cells count? Well, each chromosome had a protective cap at the end, a telomere, and with each division, the telomere shortened. When it disappeared—voila. No more division, and welcome to old age.

His research centred around telomerase activators, compounds that repaired the DNA strands at the end of chromosomes and extended cellular function. Sounds great, huh? In theory, yes, but at the moment, it was hit and miss whether the activators caused cancer or prevented it.

Why was all that important? Because my ultimate goal, the reason I'd signed up to study genetics in general and the human genome in particular, was to identify whatever cosmic hiccup had left me glowing as I walked down the street and find a way to *turn it off*.

The professor theorised that the activation of my abilities as a child coincided with the shortening of my telomeres, and if I could find a way to extend them again, that could be the magic bullet I'd been looking for. All of which had led me to this moment, sitting at Professor Fairchild's desk drinking a mug of really bad coffee while I cursed Carlton Hines and my own stupidity.

"You've called the police?" the professor asked.

"Yes, but they still haven't visited, so I guess a missing trinket isn't considered a priority. Lulu and I are going to look for Carlton ourselves."

"Is that wise? Remember what happened to Darlene when she tangled with a criminal."

"I don't think Carlton's dangerous, and besides, I don't have a choice. Mom told me the necklace was important and that I should never take it off. Even if we don't know *why* it's important, I can't let it disappear forever."

"Is there anything I can do to help?"

"Not right now." I managed a faltering smile. "Are we still on for dinner tomorrow? I thought I'd make Darlene's meatloaf recipe."

"Of course. I'll make sure to buy the ingredients after work. And you can tell me how Darlene's been getting on with that new TV show."

Ever conscious of his wife, the professor had squashed a sofa and TV into the dining room and now spent most of his spare time in there. When he went to work, he put on HGTV so she didn't get bored, and on the weekends, he redecorated according to her latest inspirations.

"Sure. The one on indoor gardening, right?"

"That's the one."

I didn't watch TV obsessively like Lulu, relying instead on second-hand accounts from her and Darlene, but I was still angry Carlton had stolen my flat-screen. Oh, just wait until I got my hands on him...

Chapter 4 - Nicole

"YOU CAN'T GO to Jive in that outfit," Lulu said. "You'll never get past the velvet rope."

"What's wrong with it?"

"Navy-blue ballet flats, grey jeans, a top a nun would love—you're fifty shades of boring. Don't you have *any* blingy jewellery?"

I just stared at her.

"Oh, yes. Right. Sorry." Her perky smile popped back. "Never mind, you can borrow mine. I've still got a faux sapphire necklace that'll match your eyes perfectly. And I'll lend you the top I got in the Macy's sale a while back. Nobody's bought those yet."

Lulu had read some self-help book a couple of months ago, and since then, she'd been on a mission to declutter the house, which included selling anything that didn't "speak to her" when she touched it. Lucky old me, getting to wear the dregs.

She didn't mean to make me feel inadequate. Lulu had a heart of gold, but occasionally, she was a little short on tact. And it didn't help that my usual idea of going to a nightclub was attending a late meeting of the Scientists of the Future society. Sometimes, we really let our hair down and brought cupcakes and wine.

"Will the top fit?"

Lulu had boobs. I didn't.

"It's got a draped neck. You'll look amazing."

I'd much rather have curled up on the sofa with a book, but reading wouldn't get my necklace back. Which was why, at seven, I found myself at the back of the line outside Jive, trying to block out the high-pitched yapping of the girls standing in front of us. Blondie to the left couldn't decide which of her boyfriends to bring tonight, so in the end, she'd opted for neither in the hope of meeting a better model. Perhaps I could set her up with Carlton? They deserved each other.

I'd only been to Jive once before. Two months ago, Carlton had snuck me in through the staff entrance because some band he liked was playing a set, and I'd taken four fifteen-minute bathroom breaks in an attempt to avoid the writhing mass of bodies on the dance floor. The heat, the noise, the lack of respect for personal space—it had all left me feeling queasy, and he'd insisted on introducing me to half of his colleagues, so I had to pretend to be sociable. Judging by the crowd already waiting outside, tonight wouldn't be much better.

"You two, you can go in," the doorman said, his attention firmly fixed on Lulu. I couldn't even blame him since she'd left her blonde hair loose and worn a skirt that stopped two inches below her ass. And thank goodness she'd dressed up because the sky had turned a horrible black colour, and I could've sworn I'd felt a couple of spots of rain.

She blew him a kiss as we ducked under the rope. "Thanks, honey."

Sometimes, I wished I had her confidence. Not necessarily her wardrobe, just her "I don't care" attitude. She saw the silver lining in every cloud, and she was already looking at new iPods. This time, she wanted one with more features and an armband so she'd be able to wear it jogging.

I kept quiet until we got inside, and then I could hardly hear myself speak. What sort of damage was this doing to my hearing? The music—an electronic wall of noise with no words and no distinguishable melody—thumped as we elbowed our way across the dance floor towards the bar, but the other patrons seemed to be enjoying themselves.

The bar itself was the focal point of the club, gleaming metal that stretched from one side to the other, lit up by strategically placed neon lights that flashed in time to the beat. Between that and the strobes above the DJ's booth, the place was an epileptic's worst nightmare. My worst nightmare too. I might have looked the part thanks to Lulu, but I felt like an impostor as we lined up for drinks. Half a dozen bartenders scurried around shaking cocktails and pouring shots, and I began to realise what a dumb idea coming to Jive had been. I didn't recognise a single staff member from my visit with Carlton, and how were we supposed to ask questions when they never stood still and nobody could hear a conversation over the music?

Lulu must have read my mind. "Don't worry; I've got a plan." She leaned forward to speak to the nearest bar girl, a pretty brunette with half a dozen piercings in each ear who didn't look old enough to drink. "Two Hellfires," she yelled.

The girl's brows knitted. "Huh?"

Lulu pointed at a bright orange concoction a girl

nearby was drinking and held up two fingers. "Two of those."

This? This was her plan? For us to drink something that, judging by the colour of it, would probably irradiate our insides? At that moment, I didn't mind so much that Carlton had taken my money, because at least it meant Lulu was paying for the vile little concoctions.

The bar girl pushed a glass in my direction, and I gingerly took a sip. Yes, it was every bit as bad as I'd feared. Synthetic orange flavour fought with the burn of cheap vodka, and I quickly swallowed before I got tempted to spit it out.

"This is horrible."

"Yes, but they're two for the price of one tonight, and we've got to drink something or it'll look weird."

"What's wrong with water?"

"Nicole, this is a *nightclub*."

Yes, unfortunately it was. Why did people come to these places voluntarily?

"You're enjoying this, aren't you?"

"It's important to make the best of things. Besides, I haven't been out to a club in ages."

True. Lulu had spent most of her evenings online lately, checking her listings on eBay and hunting for a part-time job that paid better than waitressing, sending email after email while reality TV played endlessly in the background. Occasionally, she went on a date, but she hadn't seemed particularly enamoured with any of her recent suitors.

"What's the rest of your plan? Tell me we can go home soon."

"Simple." She leaned in close enough to shout in my

ear. "We hang out by the bar and wait for one of the staff to take a break. Then we follow them to the bathroom or the smoking place or the rest area or whatever."

Simple, if the bar staff hadn't all been workaholics. Simple, if I'd had any practice at "hanging out." Simple, if I hadn't felt like an awkward dork when I tried dancing alongside Lulu. I stumbled, stepped on the foot of the poor guy next to me, and would have ended up on my ass if his friend hadn't held me up. After that, I squashed myself into a dark corner and chugged back the drinks Lulu brought me until it was time for...for action, I guess.

Boy, I was so not cut out for this espionage stuff.

Almost two hours passed before the brunette who'd first served us waved at one of her colleagues and slipped through a door marked *private*.

"Her?" I asked Lulu. She'd been flirting with a bartender, a blond guy with chunky plastic-framed glasses and a hipster haircut, and I'd secretly been hoping he was our target. No man could resist Lulu's charms.

But she shrugged as her gaze tracked the girl. "Worth a try."

Nobody stopped us as we followed our target into the staff area. The music was blessedly quiet there, and I quickly realised some of the throbbing in my head was from the alcohol rather than the incessant *thump, thump, thump* of the bass. Oops.

In front of the customers, the bar girl had been smiling, full of energy, but once we got into the staff area, we found her sagging against the wall with her eyes closed.

"Are you okay?" Lulu asked.

"Who the hell are you? You shouldn't be through here."

"We're looking for Carlton Hines."

"Hey, join the club. If I ever find him, I'll kick his scrawny ass from here to Texas."

"What did he do to you?"

"Skipped work for two nights running. Have you seen how busy we are out there?"

"He skipped out last night?" I asked. "But he said he was working."

"Well, he wasn't working here. How do you know Carlton?"

Lulu got in first. "She was dating him until he stole a bunch of our stuff and disappeared."

"He was nice until then," I added weakly.

"Yeah, he was always nice," the girl said. "Kinda shifty, but nice."

"Shifty?"

"Hung out with the wrong people, always had too much cash or none at all, used to take phone calls outside and clam up if anyone got too near. Yeah, shifty."

A chill ran through me. I really hadn't known Carlton as well as I thought, had I?

"I never saw that side of him, not once. Do you have any clue where he might have gone?"

"Sorry. We've got a good team of people working here, but Carlton mostly kept to himself."

"What do you mean, he hung out with the wrong people?" Lulu asked. "We need to find him. One of the things he stole had sentimental value, and Nicole here wants it back."

The bar girl ticked off on her fingers. "Ramon Cool, local fixer. Shane—I don't know his last name—he swears he doesn't deal drugs, but everyone knows he does. And Jerry, who tells everyone he's a cab driver, but how many cab drivers do you know that carry a matching pair of pearl-handled revolvers?"

Guns? Great. "I think I'm gonna be sick."

The bar girl pointed to her left. "Bathroom's through there."

"She's drunk too many Hellfires," Lulu told her.

Maybe so, but that wasn't why I wanted to puke. "It's got nothing to do with the drinks and everything to do with the fact that Carlton's an asshole. How could I have misjudged him so badly?"

Lulu put an arm around me and squeezed, which only made me feel worse. Now I remembered why I stuck to water and the occasional glass of wine.

"We both misjudged him," she said. "Okay, so probably we want to avoid the killer cab driver, but how do we find Ramon Cool and Shane?"

Freaking hell. That line belonged in a bad B-movie, not my life.

"Ramon keeps a table at Cheech's," the bar girl said. "You know, the diner down the road?"

Lulu nodded. "The place with the cheap coffee?"

And the multiple health violations. I always thought Cheech's looked as if aliens had beamed it up from the Midwest, then accidentally dumped it back in the wrong place.

"The burgers are good too," the girl said. "Just don't ask what's in them. Anyhow, Cheech lets Ramon use the table in the back corner as a sort of office. He's there most evenings."

"Is Ramon Cool his real name?"

"It's the only one he uses."

"And Shane?"

"Who knows? I just see him around from time to time."

So we had one lead to follow up on at least. And if Ramon didn't know where Carlton had gone, perhaps he could tell us where to find Shane?

Another of the bar staff poked his head around the doorjamb. "Hey, Donna, it's chaos out there, and your break's done." He gave Lulu the once-over, then broke into a smile. "Do I know you?"

"They're looking for Carlton," the bar girl told him.

"Popular guy. You with that other dude who came in on Monday?"

Lulu and I looked at each other.

"What other dude?" I asked.

"Big guy. Blond hair, forgot to shave. Kind of evasive when I asked why he wanted Carlton."

"Ramon?" Donna the bar girl asked.

"Nah, Ramon's fat, and he hasn't bleached his hair for months. This was a white guy, all muscle. When I phoned Carlton, he sounded kinda nervous."

Nervous? "You told him someone had been asking questions?"

"Figured he should know. Nobody wants any trouble in here." The bar guy took a step forward and peered at me, head tilted to one side. "Hey, I recognise you. You're Carlton's girlfriend, right?"

Could that be why Carlton had left so suddenly? Because a stranger was after him and he'd been warned by his buddy? For a moment, I felt relieved that it wasn't me who'd scared him off, but then the relief gave way to a twinge of fear. What had Carlton done that meant he needed to run in the first place?

"Ex. I'm his *ex*-girlfriend. Do you have any idea who the big guy was? Did he mention his name?"

The barman shook his head. "Just said he'd come back later in the week. Donna, hurry up. The crowd's stacked four deep out there."

And I felt properly sick now. No, I wasn't kidding. The mix of too many nasty little cocktails and the news that the man I'd been involved with had a hidden dark side made my stomach backflip like an Olympic gymnast.

"Excuse me."

I only just made it to the staff bathroom before thirty bucks' worth of alcohol made a reappearance. A horrible experience, but judging by the unnatural orange colour, it was better out than in.

"Are you okay?" Lulu asked from outside the stall door.

"No."

"Sorry, stupid question. D'ya want a breath mint?"

This was what my life had come to. Popping breath mints while I leaned over a nightclub toilet. Hello, rock, have you met bottom?

"I'm never drinking spirits again."

"Suit yourself. So, what do you want to do now? Go to Cheech's and find Ramon?"

Good question.

"I'm not sure. Who the hell is this other guy?"

"The blond beefcake? No idea. But perhaps we should hang around and find out?"

The wistfulness in Lulu's tone made me pause, and I remembered that looks-wise, her biggest weaknesses were muscles and designer stubble.

"Do you have an ulterior motive there?"

"Uh..."

Busted. But sometimes people made the right decisions for the wrong reasons, and sticking around to look for the blond-haired stranger could make sense. We knew where to find Ramon, but we didn't have the first clue about our man of mystery, and if we missed him when he returned to the club, we might never find him. Of course, that was assuming he hadn't located Carlton himself and left town already.

But then again, what if we wasted time hanging out at Jive when Ramon could lead us straight to my errant ex?

For a brief moment, I considered splitting up so we could cover both bases, but did I really want to handle either task alone? No, I didn't.

"How about this?" I suggested. "We go to the diner and speak to Ramon, then come back here. How long will that take? An hour?"

"Less if we walk quickly."

"Okay, let's do it. That's a good plan."

Yes, it *was* a good plan. Except like so many other things in my life, it didn't work out quite the way I'd hoped.

CHAPTER 5 - NICOLE

WE MADE IT halfway to the door, but not before I'd had my ass groped and gotten a drink spilled on me.

"Ouch!" Lulu squeaked in my ear.

"What's wrong?"

"Some bitch just elbowed me in the side."

Remind me again why people came to this place for fun? Jive was oppressively hot, and I was gasping for breath when I saw Donna waving from behind the bar. Were her frantic gestures aimed in our direction? I checked behind us, but I couldn't see any other likely candidates.

"Hey." I grabbed Lulu's hand. "I think we need to go over there."

"What? Why?"

"I don't know yet."

My toes had been stomped on three times by the time we reached the bar, and I hoped whatever Donna had to say was worth it. At that point, I'd have given my new centrifuge to be able to turn the clock back to a point where I'd never met Carlton Hines.

"I thought you'd gone," Donna said when we got within shouting distance. "Shane was here."

"Was? He's left already?"

So near, yet so far.

"He went out to the smokers' corner ten minutes

ago, and I haven't seen him come back."

"The smokers' corner?"

"Through the fire exit to the alley. All the nicotine addicts hang out there."

Not tonight, they didn't. When I gingerly pushed open the door, the spots of rain I'd felt earlier had turned into a deluge, and neither Shane nor anybody else was in sight. A single dim bulb above the door cast a yellow glow over the narrow passageway, and rivulets of water ran along the dirty concrete, carrying with them the detritus of city life—a pizza box, an empty beer can, a crumpled candy wrapper.

"Yeuch," Lulu said, backing inside. "No way am I going out there."

And I wouldn't have gone either if it hadn't been for one thing: the filmy cloud that rose from behind a dumpster to my right. An indistinct shimmer with the vague shape of a human and shadows instead of facial features. Any normal person would have mistaken it for smoke or steam or fog, but the weather suggested otherwise and it moved too quickly, too precisely, along the alley and around the corner of the next building.

I'd only seen that peculiarity once before, outside a supermarket in Noe Valley on the day a middle-aged couple had the mother of all arguments in the parking lot and the guy ran his wife over with a Suburban. The wheels went right over her freaking head, and it popped open like a watermelon. A clear-cut case of wrongful death, and the spirit guide had shown up within minutes to explain the ins and outs of the afterlife to her. I'd seen it arrive. The same wispy haze that had just appeared from behind the dumpster.

Ah, shit.

I had to look. If there *was* a fresh corpse behind the dumpster, I couldn't just leave it there while the rain washed the evidence away.

"Wait! Where are you going?" Lulu asked as I tiptoed out into the storm.

My clothes were soaked within seconds, and the puddles slopped over the tops of my shoes. Lightning flashed, and there she was. A blonde girl around my age, her lifeless remains slumped in a heap against the dumpster as her worried-looking spirit hovered alongside.

"Are you...?" she started, but she was cut off by Lulu's scream.

"Ohmigosh, ohmigosh, ohmigosh! Is she... Is she dead?"

"Uh, why don't you go back inside?"

I was surprised Lulu had followed me out in the first place. Her mascara was already starting to run.

"She *is* dead, isn't she? What should we do? The cops... We should call the cops."

Lulu fumbled in her purse, only her phone slipped out of her grasp and landed on the concrete. Even with the puddle to break its fall, the screen still smashed into a spider's web of tiny cracks.

"Dammit," she cursed.

Great. "Does it still work?"

"I don't know. I don't know!"

"Are you one of those Electi people?" the dead girl asked.

What now? I couldn't exactly have a deep and meaningful conversation because Lulu would think I'd lost my mind. The best I could manage was a nod while she doubled over and puked.

"I'm dead. I'm freaking dead! I mean, I've got college tomorrow, and I'm supposed to be taking exams next week, and I've spent the whole month revising and I wanted one day off, just one day, but I came out here for a cigarette and some asshole shot me. Can you believe that?"

"Yes" probably wasn't the answer she wanted to hear, but with blood leaking out of her body at my feet, I absolutely could believe it. Unfortunately.

"Fuck! What happened?" a man asked from behind me.

Hurrah, now we had an audience.

"We just found her like this. If you've got a phone, could you call the police?"

"Is she dead?"

"Sure looks that way."

"You've checked?"

Think, Nicole. Think! A normal person would have checked her vital signs by now because they wouldn't have been relying on the victim's departed soul to provide evidence of death. Reluctantly, I crouched beside the girl and felt for a pulse, just for show.

"Can't feel anything."

"What the hell are you doing?" she asked. "I literally just told you I'd died."

"Yes, but I'm supposed to be incognito here," I muttered.

"Like an undercover detective? I love cop shows. Tonight's the final episode of... Aw, now I'll never find out who did it."

I gave another slight nod as the guy called 911 behind me. A small crowd had gathered now—a dozen or so morbid onlookers. Lulu was crying, and I didn't know whether to comfort her or pretend to give the dead girl CPR or take a cab to the nearest airport and fly far, far away.

"You need clues, right? My name's Macy Sheldrake, and I came here with my friend Karen because it's her birthday. I guess she's still inside, and she's gonna totally freak when she finds out what happened, because she hates blood and..."

Get to the point. Macy was one of those overly talkative spirits. I knew a girl like her in real life once, an undergrad at university, and she'd chattered so much I'd been forced to wear earplugs in the lab.

"Anyhow, I came out here for a cigarette, like I said, but me and Karen were supposed to be quitting together, so I hid behind the dumpster so she wouldn't see me if she peeped out. She's gotten really sanctimonious, even though she uses, like, seventeen nicotine patches at the same time and chews the gum constantly."

Clues. Macy had mentioned clues. And right now those were all washing away as the rain fell harder still.

"Has anyone got an umbrella we can hold over her?" I asked the crowd. "Or a jacket? Something we can use to preserve the evidence?"

"Move over, CSI," Lulu muttered.

"How about this plastic?" a teenager asked, pulling a piece of sheeting from the next dumpster along. It looked like the kind of stuff they wrapped furniture in. I didn't know where the kid had come from—no way was he old enough to drink at Jive—but I was grateful for his presence.

"Perfect. Can you hold one end? We need another volunteer."

A black guy stepped forward, hesitant, and I knew how he felt. But he helped anyway. Meanwhile, Macy was still talking at double speed.

"So I bummed a cigarette off this guy I was dancing with, and I still had a lighter in my purse even though I thought at first I'd taken them all out because I figured they'd only lead to temptation and... Hey, where *is* my purse? I definitely had it earlier, but now I can't see it."

Hmm... Had Macy been killed in a robbery gone wrong?

"It's Louis Vuitton. Well, almost. The V's more of a U, but it only cost fifteen bucks so I couldn't be too fussy. You need to find that because it's got my phone in it, and Karen and me had this whole WhatsApp chat about her two boyfriends, and they don't know about each other, and—"

"Macy," I hissed, leaning in closer so the rain drowned out my words. "Who shot you?"

"I'm not totally sure. Before it started raining, this bunch of guys came outside, and they were talking about—"

The sound of a siren at the end of the alley cut her off. The police had arrived, and at the most inopportune moment. Or opportune, depending on how one chose to look at it. After all, I had no intention of trying to solve Macy's murder. I just wanted to find Carlton and get my damn necklace back, not play Nancy Drew.

"Everyone stand back," the nearest cop said.

There were two of them, one in his twenties with a moustache that he had to have grown for a bet, and an older guy who'd gone pudgy around the middle. It was the younger of the pair who did the talking.

"What happened?" he asked.

I so didn't want to get involved in this. A shrug seemed appropriate.

"We just found her like this," Lulu said, echoing my earlier words.

"Who's we?"

"Me and my friend Nicole."

She nodded towards me, and the policeman turned to stare. Yes, I looked like a bedraggled rat, but there wasn't much I could do to fix that right then.

"Did you see anyone else out here?"

We both shook our heads.

"It was raining," Lulu added, as if that wasn't obvious.

"Has anybody touched the body?"

"I did," I told him. "I checked for a pulse, but that was all."

The group behind him edged closer. Why did people get so interested in others' misfortune? One guy was videoing the scene, for YouTube or Twitter or Facebook no doubt, and another girl turned to take a selfie of herself with the body. What had happened to the concept of dignity? It seemed to have flittered away on the wind around the time social media was invented. Did I partake? No. Lulu had tried setting me up with accounts, but apart from a few paranormal-orientated forums that I'd joined long, long ago under an alias with a vague hope of getting a lead on the other Electi, I steered well clear. And I'd long since given up on those forums too.

"I'll need your details, and everyone else's who's here." The moustachioed cop started corralling the crowd into the space between a rusted washing machine and a stack of soggy cardboard boxes while his colleague radioed for backup. "This is a crime scene now, so you'll need to keep out of the way. And stop with that filming."

Then I saw him. A silent guy, standing a good four inches taller than anyone else in the crowd. But it wasn't just his height that got my attention—he was big all over. A muscular physique, just like Donna's friend had said, and he had dirty-blond hair too, although there was no sign of stubble tonight. Could this be the man who'd been looking for Carlton? How many other big guys frequented Jive? Not many, according to Lulu, who constantly complained that all the hot fitness models hung out on Instagram rather than anywhere near the Mission District. And this man was certainly magazine-spread-worthy.

Yes, I know I spent most of my time locked up in a lab, but I wasn't blind. And trust me, the guy had good genes. His personality? Perhaps left a little to be desired. He looked me up and down, not just undressing me with his eyes but peeling a layer of skin off too. That gaze was *intense.*

I nudged Lulu, who was looking decidedly green around the edges.

"What do you think of that guy over there?"

She slowly turned her head. "A ten."

"I meant, do you think he could be the person Donna said was looking for Carlton?"

"Oh. I guess he might be." The older cop shone his flashlight over Macy, and Lulu gagged again, but this time only bile came up. "How do they do it?"

"Who? What?"

"The cops. How do they sleep at night after they see

dead people every day? I couldn't live with myself."

Yes, it was difficult. But with no cure for my affliction in sight, I just had to close my eyes and block out all the spirits. Maybe one day, I'd be able to rest a little easier, but that would take a miracle.

CHAPTER 6 - NICOLE

AN HOUR LATER, Jive had closed early, and everyone who'd been out in the alley was clustered around the bar drinking complimentary glasses of tap water. I still felt fragile, but seeing Macy had sobered me up in a hurry.

Even though it was almost eleven o'clock—way past my regular bedtime—there were over a dozen of us hanging around, waiting to be questioned. The big guy —Lulu had christened him Thor because he looked like a scruffier version of the movie character, albeit in a leather jacket and jeans—was among those still to speak to the police. He leaned against the bar at the far end, keeping to himself, the only person in the whole place who looked relaxed despite the situation.

Lulu wasn't the only one who'd thrown up outside. The alley had been awash with garishly coloured liquids and diced carrots—why was it always diced carrots?— and the cops had sidestepped the mess as they cursed the heavens and muttered about forensics. At least we'd gotten a thank-you for our efforts with the plastic sheeting.

I hadn't managed to speak to Macy again, and I had to confess to being slightly intrigued. Why would someone risk shooting her in a public place like that, and at nine o'clock in the evening? Yes, the alley was dark and hidden away behind the club, but it wasn't exactly deserted, and all it would've taken was one stray nicotine addict to meander out and there'd have been a witness. A live witness. Would the culprit have shot them too?

A chill ran through me. Because of the spirit guide's presence, I knew Macy hadn't been dead for long when we got there. What if Lulu and I had gone out after Shane two minutes earlier? Would we have been lying next to Macy in the rain?

And where had Shane gone? Had he been involved? Donna was busy being questioned by the police, so presumably she'd mention his presence.

"What's wrong?" Lulu asked. "Why did you shudder?"

"I was just thinking that if I hadn't needed to puke, it could have been us lying behind the dumpster with Macy."

"Macy? Who's Macy?"

Oh, hell. Why couldn't I have kept my big mouth shut? Tiredness. That's what it was. My brain didn't function properly after the moon rose.

"Uh, the dead girl?"

"How do you know her name?"

"Someone in the crowd said they thought they knew her. Although they might just have been speculating, so probably we should keep quiet in case they got it wrong."

Lulu bobbed her head. "Keep quiet. Yes. Good idea."

Too late, I realised Thor had crept up behind us. For a big guy, he sure knew how to move stealthily.

"Macy, huh? Did her friend mention a surname?"

I screwed my eyes shut, a pointless move if there ever was one because when I opened them again, he was still right there, his chest filling my field of vision. I had to tilt my head back to look at his face.

"Not that I heard."

Funny how we were all made of the same stuff, wasn't it? The base pairs—adenine and thymine, cytosine and guanine, suitably arranged into DNA then chromosomes then the human body. Carbon, oxygen, hydrogen, nitrogen, calcium, phosphorus... And yet through some witchcraft, the magic of evolution had produced both Thor and the weedy little man currently leering at Lulu.

Thor didn't leer. He held my gaze and sucked the breath out of me. *Focus on his face, Nicole. Don't look at the body.* Oh, and now he was smiling. That was... That was... Unfair? Dangerous? Definitely not sexy.

"Can you recall who it was that knew Macy?"

His accent was Californian, but I'd certainly never seen him around town. Lulu hadn't either. How did I know that? Because she'd never have stopped talking about him.

"Sorry. I think it was somebody behind me."

"You found the body?"

"Unfortunately."

He leaned in closer and sniffed. What was he, a dog? Okay, so I might have snuck an inhale too, and Thor smelled of leather and musky cologne with a hint of sweat underneath. The kind of aroma that made a woman want to rub up against him like a cat.

Freaking hell.

It was official. I'd gone crazy. One glimpse of his muscled chest, and I'd lost my damn mind.

Don't be a pussycat, Nicole. Be a hedgehog instead. Or perhaps a porcupine. Something prickly to get rid of this man who'd clearly been sent by a higher power to complicate my life.

"Is there a problem? Don't you understand the concept of personal space?"

"You don't smell like a smoker."

"So?"

"Why were you in the alley? Only the smokers and the addicts go out there, and you don't look high either."

"Maybe I just didn't get a chance to shoot up yet."

Lulu stared at me, and I clapped a hand over my mouth. What was I even saying? It's as if I were determined to make the cover-up worse than the crime.

Fortunately, Lulu came to my aid with a high-pitched giggle. "She's only kidding. Neither of us do drugs. Okay, so I tried weed once, but I coughed so much I thought my lungs were gonna come up." Nice visual. "We were in the alley because we were looking for someone."

Thanks, Lulu.

"Really? Who?"

"My boyfriend," I said, then glared at Lulu. "But I'm sure Mr... Mr... Whatever, he doesn't want to be bothered with that."

"*Ex*-boyfriend," Lulu said. "They split up. Nicole's totally single now."

Please, stop talking.

"Nicole?" Thor held out a hand. "Beckett Sinclair."

Oh, great. Now I had the choice of being rude or touching him, and as my hand inched towards his, I had a strong desire to run as fast as possible in the other direction. But with the police blocking the door, I had to stand my ground.

"Yes, Nicole. And this is Lulu."

"Lulu? Is that short for Louise?"

"Luciana, but nobody calls me that." Now she moved into flirt mode, something that came as naturally to her as putting on mascara in the mornings. "Do you live around here, Beckett?"

"I live near Sacramento."

"And you came all the way to San Francisco to visit Jive?"

He laughed, and my insides did a funny little clench and release. I never got stupid over men. *Never.* Five months, I'd known Carlton, and not once had he ever made my knees go weak. Five minutes near Beckett, and I needed a stool.

"I'm here for the same reason you are. I'm looking for someone."

Lulu's fingernails dug into my arm, but she didn't look at me. "Really? Who?"

"Corey Harmon."

Thank goodness. We'd got it wrong. Beckett wasn't after Carlton at all. Either the barman had gotten confused, or there were two giant blond men hanging around in the Mission District this week.

"What for?" Lulu asked.

"He skipped bail."

Her eyes saucered. "You're a bounty hunter?"

"Technically, I'm a bail fugitive recovery agent." He hit her with that smile. "Yeah, I'm a bounty hunter."

Really? I thought those guys only existed in movies. And didn't California change its bail system a while back? Instead of people paying to get released, a court would assess a person's likelihood of leaving town based on a bunch of computer algorithms and either let them go or hold them in jail depending on the results. Technology-based progress, according to the presenter, which seemed fitting for the state that brought us Silicon Valley.

"Wait. I thought California got rid of cash bail? I'm sure I saw a TV program on that."

"Then I guess you missed the sequel where the new governor changed it back again. Turned out computers weren't so good at second-guessing the criminal mind. The jails ended up overflowing, and half of the people they let go didn't turn up for their court dates."

Oh. "I didn't realise."

"Have you looked at the statistics lately? California's crime rates have skyrocketed, and the other states are having serious problems too."

And America wasn't the only country going to hell in a handbasket, as the professor said. Every day, the news was full of horror stories. Genocide in Africa, mass murders in Europe, a plague of home invasions in Australia... The other night, after a particularly gruesome true-crime special, Lulu and I had talked about moving to Antarctica, and we were only half joking.

"Okay, I believe you. Can you spare us the lecture now?"

"What did Corey Harmon do?" Lulu asked. "Are you allowed to say? Or is it a secret?"

"Felony DUI. Hit a lady on a crossing while he was twice over the limit in a vehicle he shouldn't have been driving."

"He stole the vehicle?" Lulu asked.

"Borrowed it. But he didn't have a driver's licence. At least, not a genuine one. It got suspended."

"What for?"

"Speeding."

"Is the lady gonna be okay?"

"She died. Now her little girl's got to grow up without a mom."

My heart seized because I knew how it felt to lose a parent, although my mom hadn't died until the eve of my eighteenth birthday. Instead of celebrating, I'd entered adulthood alone and in tears, unable to stomach the cake she'd bought for me. Even now, my eyes prickled when I thought of that day, of the moment the policewoman had shown up on our doorstep and delivered the devastating news, but I refused to cry in front of Beckett.

Lulu had a kind soul, and her mouth formed a little O in shock. "And you think Corey Harmon came to Jive?"

"So I've heard. Do you spend much time here?"

"Not really." Lulu lowered her voice. "It's not that good, and the drinks are expensive."

"Did you ever run into a guy called Carlton Hines?"

I'd made the mistake of taking a sip of water, and now it went down the wrong way. Lulu thumped me on the back as I coughed and spluttered all over Beckett. Had the barman been right? Was Carlton somehow connected to Corey Harmon?

"Why?" I asked once I'd recovered. "Were they friends?"

"Not exactly. At the moment, I'm working on the theory that they're the same person."

Luckily, I'd vomited up the entire contents of my

stomach already. Carlton, the man I'd been sleeping with for most of this year, was a felon on the run? No way. I mean, he didn't even drink. Not so much as a glass of wine with dinner. And I'd seen his passport in his sock drawer when I put his laundry away, and his driver's licence and his gym membership card too. They were definitely all in his name with his photo, although he never actually went to the gym.

And more significantly, when we witnessed a car accident downtown, a young girl who stepped off the kerb too early and got clipped by a delivery truck, he'd comforted her and her mom until the ambulance arrived. If he'd been guilty of a similar offence, surely his reaction would have been slightly iffy?

No, Carlton may have been a thieving rat, but he wasn't Corey Harmon.

"You're wrong on that."

"Then you *do* know Hines?"

"He was our roommate."

Beckett raised an eyebrow. "Was?"

Now Lulu joined in again. "Yup, until he stole a bunch of our stuff and disappeared early this morning."

"And he was also your ex?" Beckett focused on me, and I wanted to wither and die. "You think he was here tonight? He was the person you followed outside?"

"No, that was someone else," Lulu said. "A friend of his."

"*Maybe* a friend," I said. "We don't know that for sure. It's just hearsay."

"Male? Female?"

Did I want to tell Beckett about Shane? Lulu glanced sideways at me, and I gave my head a tiny shake as I took a moment to weigh up the pros and cons—once a scientist, always a scientist. Analytical thinking was ingrained in me, at least when overly attractive bounty hunters didn't turn my brain into mush.

Yes, Beckett might be able to find Carlton faster than us because he'd undoubtedly had practice at this, but that didn't alter the fact that he was looking for the wrong man. And if he waded in with his giant feet— what were they, size twelve?—he could scare Carlton off, and my necklace would be lost forever. No, we needed to tread softly.

"Does it matter? He wasn't there, anyway."

"He might have a lead on Harmon."

"Well, Hines isn't Harmon, so you'd be wasting your time."

"Let me be the judge of that."

"I was dating the asshole for nearly four months. Do you really think I wouldn't have noticed if he was an escaped felon?"

Beckett's roll of the eyes answered in the negative.

"Gee, thanks."

"What makes you so sure they're the same person?" Lulu asked.

"A buddy of mine saw Hines here in San Francisco and called me."

"So you haven't seen him yourself?"

"Not yet."

"What if your buddy was mistaken?"

Beckett shrugged. "Then I'll keep looking. If you're so convinced I'm wrong, why don't you help me out and give me the name of this friend?"

"I'll save you some trouble—Carlton's a slug, but he's not a murderer. He even steps over ants on the sidewalk."

At least as a member of the Electi, I only had to deal with humans. Can you imagine if I were responsible for animals too? If I had to wade through trapped insect spirits until I found the people who'd stomped on cockroaches or meted out arachno-revenge with a rolled-up newspaper? I wasn't sure whether animals lived by similar rules and another team of justice seekers got the pleasure, but either way, it wasn't my problem.

Beckett? *He* was my problem.

"Why are you protecting Carlton Hines if he stole from you?" he asked.

"Because I know him better than I know you. How can I be sure if you're even a bounty hunter?"

Silently, Thor extracted a piece of paper from his pocket, unfolded it, and handed it to me. Two photocopied certificates, side by side, showing that Beckett Joseph Sinclair had completed a Bail Fugitive Recovery course and a Powers to Arrest course.

"You just happen to be carrying this around?"

"Legally I have to."

Oh. "Well, it still doesn't make a difference. You're... You're..."

"I'm what?"

"Intimidating."

Now his smile faded. "I don't mean to be. Not with you, anyway."

Lulu reached out and squeezed his biceps. "It's because of your size. Right, Nicole? Do you go to the gym a lot?"

"I have a weight stack at home, but we're not here to talk about me."

"There you go, being all gruff again," Lulu said. "You should smile more often."

I think he tried, but it came out as more of a grimace. "And your friend should do her civic duty and help get a killer off the streets."

Thanks for the guilt trip. "I keep telling you—"

A cop walked over to us. "Nicole Bordais?"

Fantastic—now Beckett knew my surname. "Yes, that's me."

"Time to give your statement."

Saved by the Old Bill, as they'd say in England. Sometimes, I liked to watch overseas police dramas when I couldn't sleep, although that would be tricky now since I had nothing to watch them on. Maybe in a few years' time, I'd look back and laugh at this episode, but right now, I felt like crying. Carlton's betrayal, my missing belongings, Beckett and his arrogance... It was too much.

More than ever that evening, I wanted my life to be normal.

CHAPTER 7 - BECKETT

WHAT WASN'T NICOLE Bordais telling me? First, she'd tried to protect Corey Harmon, then she'd given me the brush-off. And that bullshit about overhearing Macy's name? Nobody in the crowd had known who she was—I'd asked them all while Nicole was messing around with plastic sheeting and muttering to herself. Granted, she'd been switched on when it came to forensics, but other than that, she came across as scatty and evasive.

And tired. Last night when I'd followed her home, she hadn't even noticed.

Did she really believe that Harmon and Hines weren't the same person? Or was she just covering for her boyfriend? Or ex-boyfriend... Something about this story didn't add up. If he really had stolen from her, why didn't she want help with finding the asshole? And Harmon was an asshole, no mistaking that. A contact in the Sacramento PD had shown me the crime-scene photos after Harmon ploughed into Alicia Thomas, and even after everything I'd seen during my eight years in the US Army—three years in a regular infantry unit followed by five in special forces—her mangled body still gave me nightmares. If I'd been her husband, the father of her baby, Harmon would have been rotting in the ground by now.

But as it was, he'd been let out on bail, and now he'd disappeared. Since I avoided watching the news whenever possible, I'd only heard vague rumours of the incident until my Aunt Tammy dropped Harmon's file in my lap.

"Find him," she'd said.

Tammy Jo Browder was my mother's younger sister, fifty-three years old and owner of Browder Bail Bonds. Nobody argued with her, especially not my uncle.

I'd flicked through the file. "A DUI? Can't Eric deal with it?"

Eric was the main recovery agent at BBB, or Triple-B as the locals called it. I only got stuck with what he couldn't handle, the tricky stuff, and Corey Harmon sure wasn't that. No priors other than his collection of speeding tickets, no weapon, no need for me to get involved. Some men might have relished getting tough with escaped felons, but not me. I'd seen enough danger during my military career. An easy life, that was my thing now, at least until Aunt Tammy sent me on a guilt trip.

"Eric's been looking for him for the past five months and gotten nowhere. We've got less than a month left before the bond's forfeited." California law allowed us one hundred and eighty days to hunt down assholes who skipped bail and return them to court. "Now it's your turn."

"What makes you think I'll do any better?"

"Firstly, because you've got good instincts." A rare compliment from Aunt Tammy. "And secondly, because Janie Gruber's grandson swears he saw Harmon working behind the bar at a club in San

Francisco last week. You remember they went to school together? Janie called me right after Matthew mentioned it."

"Well, if you know where he is, then why can't you send Eric?"

"Because Eric's looking for Jean Birkin, and baby Lafayette's due right about now. You wouldn't want him to miss the birth of his first child, would you?"

See what I mean about the guilt? And let's not go into the fact that Eric and his wife had decided to name their kid after the park she'd apparently been conceived in on a wild weekend trip to LA.

"What's Jean done this time?"

"Indecent exposure."

Say what? Jean Birkin was at least eighty years old and only came up to my chest even in her chunky orthopaedic shoes.

"You're gonna have to elaborate."

"She went to Frances Engleman's wake at Mulder's Funeral Home with Bethy Fincher three weeks ago, only Bethy parked in a no-parking zone. Jean tore up the ticket in front of the cop who wrote it, and when he said it still stood, she mooned him and told him to bite her ass."

"Did Mr. Mulder serve his home-made wine?"

"I believe so. But that still doesn't change the fact that Jean failed to appear in court, she's out on bail for a misdemeanour, and she's not answering her door or her phone."

Failure to appear. An FTA. That was what we called them when they decided to try running. Fortunately, that didn't happen often because few people in the town of Abbot's Creek wanted to deal with the wrath of

Aunt Tammy.

"Has Eric checked out the bakery on Mulberry? She used to buy cannoli there every morning."

I'd gone to school with Reggie Birkin, and he ate *all* the cannoli. Now, he made his money moderating online chat sites from the sanctity of his mom's basement, only emerging into daylight when he ran out of Pepsi.

"Eric said he looked there."

"How about the lawn bowling club? The quilting circle? Bethy's house?"

"She's not at any of them. He spotted her in church last week, but he said he couldn't arrest her in God's house, and she snuck out the side door."

Fuck me. My cousin had been outsmarted by an octogenarian. Impending fatherhood had fried his brain, which was yet another reason not to get involved with a woman. They didn't just screw with your dick; they screwed with your head.

And if Eric was busy buying diapers and baby clothes and cribs and shit, then yeah, that left me with Corey Harmon. I flipped through the file again. Bail had been set at sixty thousand bucks, and I'd get ten percent of that when I caught him. Not the best paycheck I'd ever earned, but it'd pay off the loan on my truck and, more importantly, keep Aunt Tammy off my back. Nobody got away from Browder Bail Bonds— it was a point of pride for her. Sure, she got collateral for every bond, but in this case, she held the title to Harmon's mother's house. Since Mrs. Harmon had a lung condition that left her breathing from an oxygen tank, Aunt Tammy would look like the world's biggest bitch if she evicted the lady. And while Tammy Jo

Browder cultivated her reputation for getting tough on criminals, she hated being trash-talked by the women in town.

Which was why I was currently sitting outside the tired little house Nicole Bordais shared with Luciana Moreau and, until recently, the man calling himself Carlton Hines. Right now, she was my only lead to the FTA, and from her caginess last night, I suspected she was hiding something. Not money, or she'd have kept the front yard better maintained, but she definitely knew more than she let on.

I thought back to what she'd said last night. Was I really intimidating? Yeah, I liked to scare FTAs, but not potential witnesses. How did the saying go? Nothing to hide, nothing to fear. Perhaps the two girls had only been nervous because they were guilty of something?

The front door opened, and Nicole came out, pausing to check it was securely locked behind her before she shuffled towards the sidewalk. She didn't look as though she'd gotten much sleep, and I might have felt sorry for her if she'd been more cooperative last night.

She almost walked into my truck before she saw me. I'd considered covert surveillance, but in the end, I decided rattling her cage would be the best way to get fast results. Last night, I'd run a background check, and Nicole Bordais was smart. She'd landed a full scholarship to the University of San Francisco, graduated magna cum laude, and now she was one of the Institute of Human Genetics' shining stars. If I gave her space to think, she'd find it easier to stay one step ahead of me, but if I kept on her tail, she might make a mistake.

I'd also checked out Carlton Hines. Since he came to San Francisco, he'd kept a low profile, and nobody I'd spoken to had seen him in public outside of his shifts at Jive. But finding information here was harder than back home. I didn't have much of a network outside the Sacramento area, so I'd been reduced to trading favours with other recovery agents that I'd have to pay back at some point. In Abbot's Creek—population five thousand and change—Aunt Tammy knew everyone, and I was friendly with local law enforcement as well as being familiar with the darker side of life in the small town.

So far, I hadn't come up with much here in San Francisco, but now that my contacts had a new alias to work with, I was hoping for some movement. Carlton Hines must have made friends or at least acquaintances during his time in the city. Nobody was an island. But while I waited for news, that left me to spend the day with Nicole.

"What are you doing here?" she asked, half-angry, half-nervous. A combination that shouldn't have made my dick twitch, but it did. Perhaps it was the way she flitted about, so small and dainty like an animated china doll. No, not a doll. A water sprite. When I first saw her in that dingy bar, she'd been wearing a pale-blue top that shimmered when she moved, almost ethereal, like something from another world.

"Sun's out. What better day to visit the Mission District? Want me to buy you breakfast?"

"No, I do not. I want you to go back to Sacramento or the sewer or wherever it was that you came from and leave me alone."

"Hey, you were the one who started talking to me."

"Stalking's a crime. Do you know that?"

"Yup. Penal code section 646.9. Any person who wilfully, maliciously, and repeatedly follows or harasses another person and who makes a credible threat with the intent to place that person in reasonable fear for his or her safety, or the safety of his or her immediate family... But I'm not making any threats, and I've got no malicious intent. I'm just a man doing his job."

Nicole tossed that shiny brown hair of hers and huffed. "No, you're not. Because if you were doing your job, you'd be looking for an escaped felon, not hanging around outside my house."

"Guess we'll have to agree to differ on that."

Another exasperated sigh—good, I was getting to her—and she strode off along the street. I'd been prepared for that seeing as she didn't appear to have a car and she had to get across the city to college, so I hopped out of my truck, locked the door, and strolled after her. One advantage to being tall—it didn't take much effort to keep up.

"Are you planning to follow me all day?" she asked over her shoulder.

"Yup."

She opened her mouth, but either she couldn't think of a sharp comeback or she didn't consider me worth the effort because she closed it again and headed for Potrero Avenue. I allowed my gaze to drop to her ass for a second. Nice. Hey, a job's gotta have some perks, all right? Especially since I didn't want to be in San Francisco chasing after a two-bit criminal like Corey Harmon in the first place.

For a moment, I considered calling Aunt Tammy and telling her to find someone else to go after the slimeball, but on reflection, I decided I valued my hearing too much. My uncle had the right idea—be quiet, do what he was told, and keep out of her way. At least if I was a hundred miles from Abbot's Creek, she couldn't nag me constantly.

I sighed and kept walking.

CHAPTER 8 - NICOLE

"DAMMIT!"

THE TEST tube hit the floor, and little slivers of glass flew everywhere. At least it had been empty.

"Are you okay?" Damien asked.

No. No, I wasn't okay. Beckett Sinclair had followed me all the way to the lab building, and when I went out at lunchtime to get a sandwich, he'd been lounging on a bench outside, feet crossed at the ankles, eating a burger that was bigger than my head.

And he'd had the cheek to grin and wave.

Asshole.

But I didn't want to burden Damien with my troubles, or admit how stupid I'd been with Carlton, so I smiled and shook my head.

"Just a little tired."

"Got much left to do?"

"Not really."

In fact, I'd been finished an hour ago, but I'd been hoping that if I hung around, Beckett would get bored and crawl back into his hole. On any other day, I could have asked Professor Fairchild to go outside and check whether Beckett was still there, but the professor had gone to LA to give a talk this afternoon and been invited for an impromptu dinner by the host. He'd called somewhat sheepishly at five to ask if I'd mind postponing our weekly get-together until tomorrow night, and I assured him it was fine and that Darlene would understand. Like me, she wanted him to go out and meet new people rather than moping around the house.

But that left me at loose ends. If Carlton hadn't stolen my cell phone, I'd probably have called Lulu to see if she wanted to grab something to eat at the diner down the road, the one that didn't mind catering to her nut allergy. Luckily, Lulu's phone still worked after its tumble in the alley, but I hadn't gotten around to buying a new one yet—lab work had taken priority, as it always did—so all I had in my borrowed purse was a loan of fifty bucks, an almost-empty tube of ChapStick, my emergency chocolate bar, and a well-thumbed paperback copy of Jane Austen's *Pride and Prejudice*. Reading it was like putting on a comfortable old sweater, and although I still hadn't entirely given up on the hope of meeting my Mr. Darcy, it seemed unlikely to happen anytime soon.

Why? Firstly, because I shied away from serious relationships while I searched for a cure to my affliction. It was hereditary, you see—any child of mine would gain the ability to see spirits, and I hated the prospect of placing that burden onto them. Twenty-seven years ago, my mom had faced the same agonising decision, and I was the result. While I didn't hate her for bringing me into the world—far from it, I'd had a wonderful childhood, and she'd done her best to help me to cope with the horrors I witnessed every day—I still wanted to prevent my own offspring from being hounded by the dead for their entire lives.

And secondly, the Mr. Darcys of this world didn't

spend much time hanging out in genetics labs.

"Why don't you go home?" Damien asked. "I'll clean up the mess."

How about Damien, I hear you ask? He was kind, considerate, and understood a woman's needs. Believe me, I'd had the same thought a hundred times, mostly when I watched him climbing into his boyfriend's Ford Focus at the end of the day. If Mr. Darcy had a gay brother, Damien would certainly have fitted the bill perfectly.

"No, it's fine. I can manage." A shard of glass lodged underneath my fingernail, and I yowled in pain. "Dammit!"

Damien pulled the splinter out with a pair of tweezers, blotted up the blood, and wrapped a BandAid around the end of my finger before picking up my purse and marching me to the door.

"Enough, Nicole. You're tired, and you're stressed. Go home and treat yourself to takeout and a nice bubble bath. You deserve it after what that douche did to you."

I'd told Damien the basics of Carlton's betrayal, but not the details. If he knew about my necklace, he'd try to help, probably by buying me a new one because he didn't understand the importance of what I'd lost.

"I'm going."

He fished around in his wallet and pulled out a twenty-dollar bill. "On second thought, dinner's on me."

See?

"Damien, you don't need to—"

He tucked the cash into my pocket and gave me a little push. "Go."

"But—"

The door closed behind me. *Oh, Damien.* I'd make it up to him somehow, but guilt over his kindness wasn't my biggest problem this evening. No, that was Beckett Sinclair, who was loitering outside the building when I got downstairs. Thankfully, I saw him before I stepped fully outside the door, and since he wasn't looking in my direction, I was able to back away inside and take evasive action. Or in other words, sneak out of the fire escape. Yes, technically we weren't supposed to do that, but people had been using it as a shortcut for years, and the building manager turned a blind eye.

And taking the rear entrance meant I could cut through next to the Mount Sutro Reserve, then pick up the Muni—the San Francisco Municipal Railway—at Laguna Honda Boulevard without a certain bounty hunter seeing me. With any luck, he'd spend the whole night waiting outside the lab building while I enjoyed my dinner, courtesy of Damien. What did I want? Mexican? Italian? A burger and fries? After the trials of the last two days, I deserved a milkshake at least.

A light drizzle was falling as I left, and that soon turned into proper rain as I hurried along the sidewalk. Mount Sutro's overhanging trees sheltered me from the worst, but water still splashed up my legs from the fast-forming puddles. The perfect end to a perfect day.

When I first came to San Francisco from Vermont, before I met Lulu, I'd spent hours walking the woodland trails around Mount Sutro. The towering trees reminded me of my place in the world, that no matter what my mother might have told me, I really was just an insignificant little dot on the face of the planet. And weirdly, that gave me solace. I didn't want the responsibility that came with my abilities.

But tonight, as dark clouds rumbled overhead, the trees were more foreboding than comforting, and when a bush rustled behind me, I almost jumped out of my skin. My heart pounded as I spun around, only to find an indignant raccoon staring back at me, cocky in a way that only an oversized rat could pull off. I had to force down the bubble of hysterical laughter that threatened to escape.

"Stop being so stupid, Nicole," I chided myself.

I should have brought a coat, but the weather had been perfect when I left home this morning. Hindsight was a marvellous thing. With hindsight, I'd have braved Beckett and taken the direct route home. Or camped out in the lab overnight. Or just curled up in bed all day with the quilt over my head.

A twig cracked, and I whipped around again, but nobody was there. Fear crawled up inside my chest with spidery legs as I quickened my pace to get away from the deserted side street and back to civilisation. Damn my nervousness. Damn Beckett and his pushiness. Damn Carlton for ever existing.

How did I first know something was seriously wrong? Because I caught sight of the spirit of a young girl in front of me, and her eyes didn't light up with the usual excitement of a dead person meeting their designated saviour. No, instead she looked past me, and her mouth dropped open in... What was that? Surprise? Horror?

I'd barely had time to process the question when I heard footsteps behind me, coming fast. This time, I only had time to turn halfway, scarcely a second to register the blur of a man hurtling at me. A giant.

Was that...? "Beck— Oof!"

The air rushed out of my lungs as he shoved me sideways into the forest and slammed me against a tree trunk. No, it wasn't Beckett. This was worse—much worse—a stranger with glittering black eyes and a malevolent smirk. The scar running down one cheek told me this wasn't the first fight he'd been in, but if I didn't get away fast, it might be *my* last.

"Where is he?" the stranger hissed.

What? "Who? Where's who?"

"You know who."

"I don't! I don't know what you're talking about."

I opened my mouth wider to scream, but an arm across my throat cut off the sound before it could escape. The man leaned closer, pinning me with his weight, and minty breath washed over me.

"Answer the question."

Last fall, Lulu had dragged me along to a women's self-defence class, more because she had a crush on the instructor than out of a burning desire to learn how to look after herself. Being honest, I'd spent more time worrying over a project deadline than listening to the instructions, but I did remember one important tip: when all else fails, go for the gonads.

My knee came up on instinct, and when it connected, my attacker's piggy eyes widened and he grunted like a wounded beast. His grip loosened long enough for me to break free, but panic and fear and a really, really bad sense of direction led me deeper into the woods rather than back to the street.

I tripped on an exposed root and slammed one hand into a tree trunk. Pain shot up my arm, but I couldn't stop, not for a second.

"Help me!" I screamed on instinct, but who was there to hear? The foliage muffled my cry, and what kind of crazy person would risk venturing into the woods to save me, anyway?

Should I try to hide? I could already hear Scarface crashing through the undergrowth on my tail, and the chances of me outrunning him were slim.

"Are you in trouble?"

Who was that? I caught movement to my right and saw a pale face in the gloom, watching me from the middle of a bush. How long had she been there? Time enough for the branches to grow up around her and hide everything but her head. Another year, and that would vanish too.

"A man's chasing me," I whispered. "Which way is the road?"

"Wait, you're one of those Electi, aren't you? The guide told me—"

"I need to get out of here!"

"So do I. I've been stuck for at least ten years. Probably fifteen. It's not easy to keep track of time when—"

"Where's the damn road?"

"There's no need to be so rude."

"Sorry. I'm sorry. Please, just tell me where—"

A truck rumbled past to my left, and I didn't stop to finish my sentence, just ran towards the sound. As fast as my feet would carry me, straight into... Ah, rats.

This time, Scarface kicked my legs out from underneath me and pressed me into the ground. He leaned down, sneering, as I struggled to move beneath his weight.

"You little bitch. I oughta slit your throat for that

trick."

His colouring said he had foreign heritage, and his accent was a strange mix of Spanish and New York gangsta, as if he'd watched *Goodfellas* over and over in his attempts to learn English.

"Get off me!"

"Talk."

What the hell did he want me to say? I could barely breathe, let alone form a coherent sentence. Muddy water seeped through my clothes, and Scarface's fingernails dug into my skin. He leaned in closer, and I closed my eyes as his gaze bored into me.

"Don't try to resist, bitch. Just give me—"

Suddenly, I could move again. The weight lifted, replaced by a rush of air and a meaty thump. What the...?

My eyes flew open in time to see Beckett's fist collide with Scarface's jaw, and the sickening crunch made me shudder. Where had Beckett come from? I didn't know, and at that moment, I didn't care because he was definitely the lesser of two evils. And with him tackling Scarface, I could run.

Or at least, I could stagger. A bolt of red-hot agony shot through my ankle as I clambered to my feet, and I almost fell again. My sense of direction had malfunctioned once more—no surprises there—and a whimper escaped as I stumbled forward, trying to put as much distance as possible between the two men and me.

It didn't work.

"Nicole!"

I got swept off my feet again, this time bridal-style, and I found myself plastered against Beckett's muscular chest as Scarface crashed through the forest to get away.

"Put me down."

"No."

What an arrogant... I opened my mouth to complain as Beckett stooped to pick up my purse, but then I thought the better of it. Perhaps staying where I was for a few moments was sensible, but the instant we reached the road, I'd be telling Beckett where to go in no uncertain terms. True, he'd helped me out, but he was also the reason I'd gotten into this position in the first place.

Fat drops of rain fought through the canopy above and plopped onto my face, mixing with the tears I failed to hold back. Two days ago, I'd had a quiet, pleasant, if slightly unusual life, but now? Now I had two men after me and not in a good way, plus a third on the run with my most prized possession.

Boy, did I need a glass of wine and a cupcake.

Chapter 9 - Beckett

FUCK. I'D WANTED to irritate Nicole, but I'd never intended for her to get hurt. And worse, the asshole who attacked her had gotten away clean. Given the choice between helping her and pounding the teeth out of him, I'd opted to check she was okay. And she wasn't. The physical damage didn't look too bad, but she was shaking like a dog shittin' razor blades, and damn, there were tears.

That didn't stop her from giving me attitude, though.

I ignored the demands to put her down because she'd most probably land in the mud again, and I wanted to get her out of the storm sooner rather than later. My truck was parked on a side street near the university, and getting to it would take long enough without pausing for an argument.

Why had that guy been after her? I wanted to believe it was a coincidence, that he'd spotted a lone female and decided she was an easy target, but my gut said it was something more. Especially after what I'd seen outside the science building. Or rather, who.

I hadn't been the only one hanging around today. There'd been someone else, a weedy guy who had either a bad cold, allergies, or a drug problem. Reminded me of a rodent, so in my head, I'd nicknamed him Pinky out of the cartoon. To be honest, he looked more like the Brain, but after following him to the store at lunchtime and watching him try to pull a door that clearly said "push," I wasn't convinced of his intellect.

He'd spent the afternoon sitting on a bench, pretending to read a paperback. And I say "pretending" because in three hours, he'd only turned through a handful of pages of the dog-eared Spanish thriller.

Even when the building began to empty, he stayed put, paying more attention to the door than his cover story. If there were an award for most obvious surveillance in a supporting role, he'd have won the prize hands down. And where was I? I'd borrowed a toolbox and a reflective vest from the old army buddy whose floor I was sleeping on at night—he'd dropped the kit off along with my truck a half hour after Nicole arrived at the university—and spent the day polishing the little brass signs on the outside of the lab building. Nobody paid the slightest attention to janitorial staff, not even the other janitors. One smiled and raised a hand in greeting before he trudged inside, and another ignored me completely.

Pinky had taken a bunch of calls during the day, but when his phone rang again just before eight, he sat up straighter. Who was calling? From his posture, I'd put money on the boss. Pinky's focus shifted from the front door to the side of the building, and when I followed his gaze, I caught a glimpse of a woman remarkably similar to Nicole disappearing towards a path in the distance.

Fuck. She'd gone out of another exit.

I abandoned the toolbox and followed, hanging back so I didn't spook her. It was then that I saw the third guy. Just for a second or two, a dark form slipping along behind her like a wraith, but I was fucking sure I hadn't imagined it, no matter what the army shrink might have had to say about my psychological state. And worse, Nicole's new shadow had one arm raised as if he had a phone pressed to his ear.

Was this guy working with Pinky?

She wasn't hanging around, and she moved with the haste of a woman afraid of being followed. When she darted down a cut-through, I thought I'd lost her, and there was no sign of her pursuer either. At least, not until I heard the scream.

Other than to see he was almost as big as me, I hadn't got much of a look at the new guy before he took off, and now, as I carried Nicole back towards the university, I cursed myself for being so damn stupid. I should have realised she'd try to give me the slip, should have anticipated that there was danger out there. Now she'd been hurt, and if she'd just left through the front door as usual, she'd probably be riding the bus home in cramped comfort instead of sniffling in my arms.

"I'm sorry," I muttered under my breath, and she tilted her head back to look at me, brows pinched. "For being an idiot," I clarified.

Shit, was that a bruise forming on her neck?

Even though Nicole was tiny, my back began to ache, but I wasn't putting her down. Not when I'd contributed to this. No, I'd carry her the whole way to the truck, then repair the damage with Advil later.

But not all of today's damage could be fixed with a few pills. A tear rolled down Nicole's cheek, and my chest tightened. Aw, hell. Back when I lived at home and my little sister got upset, I'd bribed her with candy and she snapped out of it, but Rosalie was seventeen now, and I couldn't remember the last time she'd cried. I had a feeling a package of Reese's Pieces wouldn't work with Nicole. Wine? What about wine? Or perhaps I could buy her dinner...

I set her on her feet momentarily so I could open the door to the truck. Was there a good takeout place nearby?

Hold on, what was I thinking? We needed to report the attack to the police first. Of course we did. This was a defenceless woman, not a big lump like me who was used to sorting out his own problems. Where was the nearest—

"Ow! What was that for?"

My shin throbbed where she'd kicked it, and her glare would have cut through steel.

"Get off me!"

My hand dropped from the small of her back like it had been burned.

"Sorry, I—"

"I'm not getting in your truck. Thank you for saving me from that...that freak, but I can take care of myself now."

"I'm not leaving you here. I'm taking you to the police precinct, and then I'm gonna make sure you get home safely."

"I can call a cab. Or... Dammit." Another tear fell.

"What?"

"I don't have a cell phone at the moment."

"You took a secluded shortcut alone without a phone?"

"I didn't have much choice, did I? Carlton stole it,

and you won't leave me alone."

She pushed me with surprising strength, but I stood my ground. "We need to talk about Carlton." Because if Pinky and his cohort had targeted her, fifty bucks said he was the reason. I couldn't imagine a girl like Nicole being mixed up in any nefarious scheme, whereas her ex... "And what kind of man would I be if I abandoned you here?"

"Slightly less of an asshole than usual?"

Okay, so I probably deserved that.

"Look, let's go inside. You can tell one of your science buddies that some asshole named Beckett Sinclair's gonna take you to make a police report, and then they'll know who to come after if anything bad happens to you."

"If anything *bad* happens to me? What the hell do you plan on doing?"

"Nothing bad's gonna happen. It was just a figure of speech. I plan on playing chauffeur then buying you dinner on the way home."

"Oh, no, no, no. You do *not* get to bribe your way out of this."

"Fine. You can pay."

"You're a dick."

"Sure am. And right now, I'm a dick who's gonna drive you to the police precinct. Do you need to tell someone where you're going? You can borrow my phone."

A little of the fight went out of Nicole as she sagged against the side of the truck.

"If I call Lulu and tell her what happened, she'll freak out."

"So, tell her in person later." Nicole's bottom lip

quivered, and that sent a fresh wave of guilt through me. "If you don't want to ride with me, I'll pay for a cab. How about that? I'm not letting you go home alone, not with that guy still on the loose."

"Scarface," she whispered, running a fingertip up her left cheek. "He had a scar here."

"Yeah, I saw that too." Just a glimpse, and now he had a bruise to go with it. "We'll tell the police. If he's mugged anybody else, they may be able to link the crimes."

I didn't think it was a random attack, but I also didn't want to scare her more. My plan didn't work. Her shoulders trembled, then a shudder jolted her whole body. Now what?

"You okay?"

"It wasn't a mugging." She spoke so softly I had to lean closer to hear the words. "He was after me personally. I think… I think because of Carlton."

Tears turned into sobs, and this time, she didn't protest when I lifted her into my truck. My fears had been confirmed: I wasn't the only man searching for Corey Harmon, and whoever else wanted to find him wasn't afraid of hurting people to get what he wanted. I cursed Harmon under my breath for being a first-class cretin, cousin Eric for not knowing how to use a condom, and Aunt Tammy for giving me a job I'd never wanted in the first place.

"What makes you say that?" I asked Nicole.

"B-b-because when he was holding me on the ground, he said, 'Where is he?'"

"He didn't mention Carlton's name?"

She shook her head then winced. "No, but I don't know who else he could have been talking about."

"Sore neck?"

"A little. He slammed me into a tree and held my throat."

"Do you need to go to the hospital?"

"No, I just want to go home."

"Via the precinct, right?"

"I guess."

"You can't seriously be thinking of not reporting this?"

"I didn't get a good look at the guy, so I bet it'll be a waste of time. The police still haven't sent anyone to talk to Lulu and me after Carlton stole our stuff, and the officer who interviewed us in the club the other night for all of five minutes basically told me they're so overworked that they don't even have the manpower to investigate a murder."

She wasn't wrong. Every night, the news anchors pasted on grave expressions as they read their stories and offered false reassurances that the police would soon catch the perpetrators of the latest murder or robbery or rape. They rarely did, and the platitudes offered by the governor and chief of police did nothing to put the brakes on what was turning into an epidemic. Good for Aunt Tammy, but not so good for Nicole.

And worse, I couldn't give the best description of Scarface either. His head had snapped back when I punched him, so the image in my mind was kinda blurry. But how about the fourth person in the forest? What did they see? I'd put my army training to good use and approached quietly, keen to have the element of surprise on my side, and I'd heard Nicole talking to somebody before Scarface found her again.

"What about the other person who was there?" I asked as I pulled away from the kerb. "Did you get a better look at them?"

Another hesitation. "W-w-what other person?"

Nicole's voice had been sounding stronger, but now the tremor came back, and when I glanced over, she'd turned a few shades paler.

"I heard you speaking to someone. Asking where to go."

"You must have imagined it."

A quick answer, and one I'd grown accustomed to. I gave my head a shake to clear the memories of my time in the hospital, a time that had haunted me for the past four years. What I'd seen. Who I'd heard. The derision whenever I mentioned it to anybody afterwards. But this time, I was certain my mind hadn't been playing tricks. Why would it conjure up a totally bogus conversation?

Nicole was hiding something, that much was clear. First with her refusal to discuss Corey—and if he really *had* ripped her off, I couldn't see why she'd cover for him—and now with her denial of events in the forest. How could I get her to spill her secrets?

I had two choices: strong-arm her into talking or try to gain her confidence. Since I wasn't about to sink to Scarface's level with a woman who'd been through enough shit already this week, that left the second option.

I'd play along.

For now.

"Guess I must have, but you still need to file a report. That guy belongs in jail."

And having him out of the way would make my job

a hell of a lot easier.

"What if the police link Scarface to Carlton and start looking for them both? I don't want to scare Carlton off. He..." She paused yet again. "He took something important from me."

Was that why she wouldn't talk to me either?

"What did he take? A purse? A laptop?"

"Yes, but I don't care about those. Well, I do, but they're replaceable. It's a necklace my mom gave me that I need to get back."

"Okay, so don't tell the cops everything he said." That suited me too. If the cops found Corey before I did, I wouldn't get paid, and worse, Aunt Tammy would remind me of my failure every Thanksgiving and Christmas for the next decade. "Just say you got attacked and give the best description you can. The man's dangerous, Nicole."

"If I go, will you leave me alone?"

"No."

She whipped her head around, and a lingering tear flew through the air and landed on my hand. "No?"

"I need to find Harmon." The *tick, tick, tick* of the clock made me channel Aunt Tammy and send Nicole on a guilt trip. "I've got two weeks and five days to get him into police custody, or his mom'll lose her home."

A cute little gasp escaped her lips. "Really?"

"She put it up as collateral for his bail bond."

And Mrs. Harmon was a sweet lady. Even though Corey had graduated from Creekside High seven years previously, she still baked cakes for each school fundraiser, and until her health problems made it difficult for her to leave the house, she'd chaperoned every one of Rosalie's field trips. Corey hadn't just destroyed the future of the lady he'd mown down while under the influence, he'd fucked up his mom's life as well. Yet another reason I had to stick around and find the little worm, ASAP.

"Gonna have to make a decision, Nicole." And hopefully the right one.

She snatched at the seat belt and clicked it into place. Folded her arms. "Fine. You win. Take me to the police station and get it over with."

CHAPTER **10** - NICOLE

NORMALLY, IT WAS satisfying to be right, but today the taste of victory wasn't so sweet. The police had questioned Beckett and me and taken photos of my bruises, and we'd given the best descriptions we could, but when neither of us could tell them much, it had turned into more of a box-ticking exercise than anything else. Or at least that's what it felt like. Sure, the detective who did all the talking had said the right words and looked sympathetic in the right places, but the constant glances at his watch and the grumble of his stomach told me he had other priorities. A mugging gone wrong, that was what he said, and I had to nod and agree because I didn't want him to know the truth. Thank goodness Mr. Sinclair had just happened to be passing.

In a strange way, I was relieved about their blatant disregard. You probably think that's crazy, huh? But at least the police wouldn't be asking questions that might send Carlton deeper underground. If he disappeared forever, I'd never find my necklace, and that was my priority in all of this. Hard to explain, but it was a part of me. My soul ached without it.

"So..." Beckett said as he held the truck door open for me afterwards.

"So."

"My offer of dinner still stands."

"I'm not hungry."

"Your choice, but we need to talk. I'm not dropping this, and either we work together to find Corey Harmon, or we carry on annoying the shit out of each other."

"I told you before, I don't know—"

He cut me off by slamming the door. What a gentleman.

When he slid in behind the wheel, he had his phone in his hand. I thought he planned to make a call, but instead, he passed it over to me.

"What's this for?"

"Look at the screen."

"Why have you got a photo of Carlton?"

"Look closer."

I did so, even though it was so late my eyes didn't want to stay open. I'd never been much of a night owl, late-night deadline-induced panics excepted. In the picture, Carlton looked as if he felt the same way. Tired. Ticked off. Uh, wait a minute.... What was that board with the lines on it in the background? Little beads of sweat popped out on the back of my neck as I realised where I'd seen that pattern before.

"Is this a mugshot?"

"Yes. Of Corey Harmon. If you'd listened to a word I had to say, I'd have shown it to you before."

"But... But..." Oh, holy hell. Not only was my ex a low-down dirty thief, but he was also a killer? I couldn't... I didn't want to... "This can't be happening."

Beckett's voice softened. "I'm sorry he turned out to be such a prick. But he's been lying to you for months, and now I really, really need your help to track him down and get him back into court where he belongs."

Messy thoughts flipped and flopped around in my head, and the overall effect left me feeling queasy. Carlton—Corey—had used me as his cover story, and Lulu too. I wanted to stuff his testicles through a meat grinder for that. But he hadn't seemed like a bad person, and what if he was trying to change? He'd never touched alcohol in all the time I knew him, not once. And he'd helped around the house. Unblocking the sink, repairing the door handle, that sort of thing.

He still stole your freaking stuff, Nicole. Was I merely trying to shape the past to justify my own bad decisions?

I didn't like Beckett much either. True, he'd come to my rescue tonight, but he was pushy and rude and arrogant, and so, so stubborn. But he also wanted to help a lady to keep ahold of her home. Gah! Was it too late to quit university and become a lab assistant? Say, in Canada or even England?

This was all such a shambles. My life had been torn apart by a guy so unspectacular that he hadn't even managed to find my clitoris when I literally printed out a diagram showing him where it was, and now the bothersome cousin of a Norse god had shown up to help me patch things back together again.

"But I don't know anything. That's the whole problem."

"I bet you know more than you think. And you sure know San Francisco better than I do." Beckett flashed me a smile, and I hated the way my heart sped up. "If you help me to find Harmon, I'll help you to get that necklace of yours back. Deal?"

Well, it wasn't a great offer, was it? But when the

only leads Lulu and I had were a fixer, a drug dealer, and a gun-toting cab driver, it struck me that working with a giant bounty hunter might be better than trying to do this alone, if only to have some muscle backing us up. And with Scarface involved too...

"Deal," I muttered, but my sigh said I wasn't happy about the situation.

Beckett, of course, ignored the subtext. "Dinner?"

"No."

He ignored that too and turned into the parking lot of a fast-food joint.

"Why ask if you're just going to do whatever you please?"

"Because I'm hungry, and the only thing I've eaten since breakfast is a cold cheeseburger on account of spending the whole day waiting around outside your building. If you'd said yes, I'd have stopped someplace where the food doesn't come in styrofoam boxes, but you didn't, so here we are. I'll drop you at home then eat when I get back to my buddy's apartment."

Oh. "Sorry."

"Can I order now?"

I nodded, and he rolled down the window. "A double cheeseburger with everything, a large fries, chicken wings, and a side of coleslaw."

The speaker crackled. "Anything to drink?"

"Gimme a root beer."

Root beer? Ugh. The man had no taste whatsoever. When his meal arrived, he caught me watching as he took a long sip, then held out the cup.

"Want some?"

"No, I do not."

But the smell of fried food made me realise I was

hungrier than I thought. Pride wouldn't let me change my mind about dinner, but as Beckett paused at the exit of the parking lot with his turn signal on, my traitorous stomach gave me away with a loud gurgle.

And Beckett, the ass, nestled the bag in the centre console and opened the top so he could dig into the fries while he waited for a gap in the traffic. The three or so weeks we had to find Corey promised to be the longest days of my life.

"Still not tempted?" Beckett asked as the glorious aroma of carbs filled the cabin.

Dammit, I had no willpower. "Maybe just one or two fries."

He chuckled to himself as he pulled out onto the road, but instead of driving towards my house, he swerved back into the drive-in entrance and stopped next to the speaker again.

"A large order of fries, a cheeseburger, and a Diet Coke."

"You're that hungry?" I asked.

"They're for you. Otherwise you'll eat half my dinner by the time you get home."

Chapter 11 - Beckett

FRIDAY MORNING FOUND me back outside Nicole's house, except this time, I was invited. Okay, so perhaps not invited, but she'd grudgingly agreed to my presence.

Fuck, my back hurt after yesterday's exertions. I popped the top on the bottle of Advil I kept in the glove compartment and swallowed a couple dry. Where was Nicole? She wasn't due at the university until half past nine, but we were supposed to discuss our next move on the Harmon case over breakfast first, and I needed coffee and some sort of food. I was a big guy with a metabolism that would turn a supermodel green with envy, which meant I ate more or less constantly. Think that sounds good? Well, try taking a look at my grocery bill.

While I waited, I scrolled through my emails. Aunt Tammy had requested an update, and I filed that in the "later" folder along with a reminder from the veterinarian to take my dog for his booster shot and a message from my attorney to call him. With no sign of Nicole, I opened up the *Unexplained* forum and clicked on the "Spooks & Spirits" noticeboard. There were only a few new comments since I checked in last night, and a quick scan showed those were all most likely from kooks.

Think *I* was a kook for reading that stuff? Fifty bucks says that if you'd seen what I saw four years ago, you'd believe in ghosts too, and you'd damn well get curious the way I did.

A door slammed, and Nicole hurried along the short path towards my truck as my stomach let out a loud growl. I figured she could use a good meal too—she'd weighed next to nothing when I picked her up yesterday.

"Ready?" I smiled, but she didn't return it.

"Let's get this over with."

In the truck, she flicked strands of her shiny brown hair out of the way as she did up her seat belt, and I caught sight of the bruises on her neck. Shit. Although it wasn't my hands that had choked her yesterday, it might as well have been. She'd only walked home that way because I'd been outside the lab building, wading into a mess I didn't totally understand with my battered size-twelve boots.

For the second time in my life, I'd gotten a girl hurt through my own selfishness, and although the outcome this time hadn't been as tragic, it still shouldn't have happened at all.

"Where's good to eat?"

"Who knows? I usually skip breakfast."

She glared at me, arms folded. Good start, but I deserved it.

I'd spotted a kitsch little café three blocks back, one of those places with mismatched tables and a hundred kinds of coffee that most women loved. Which probably meant Nicole would hate it, but in the absence of a better idea, I swung the truck in that direction.

For a June morning in California, the atmosphere

sure was frosty, but if I opened my mouth, the wrong thing would undoubtedly have come out of it. So I stayed quiet until I'd reversed into a kerbside parking spot, then walked around to open Nicole's door. See? I wasn't a complete Neanderthal.

Inside was every bit as bad as I'd feared. Gluten-free muffins lurked behind salted-caramel cronuts, and I wasn't even sure who worked there because every fucker had a beard and dressed exactly the same. I was about to tap the nearest clone on the shoulder when a tattooed pixie appeared from nowhere with an order pad in her hand.

"Can I help?"

I gestured at Nicole. "Ladies first."

She paused. Bit that bottom lip the way she did when she was nervous. "There's no need to give me special treatment just because I wear a skirt occasionally. Haven't you ever heard of equal opportunities?"

I might have written her off as a feminist, but her nervous glance towards the blackboard on the wall told me the real reason for her touchiness. She didn't understand the ridiculous menu either. Fine, I'd play.

"Can I get a coffee?"

"What kind?" the pixie asked.

"Black."

"And which beans?"

"Surprise me."

"Micro, fat, mega, or Goliath?"

"The largest you have."

"Syrup?"

I just stared at her.

"Okaaaaaay, no syrup. Anything to eat?"

"Do you serve pancakes?"

"Of course. Spelt, buckwheat, or teff?"

My eyes rolled all of their own accord. "Don't you have normal flour?"

"You mean with *gluten*?" She whispered the word as if I'd asked for herpes, eyes wide in horror.

"Yes, with gluten."

"We do, but nobody ever orders those."

"Then I guess today's a memorable day. I'll have a portion of plain ol' regular pancakes with bacon and maple syrup."

"Low-sodium bacon or hickory smoked or... Shall I just write down 'classic'?"

"You do that."

First time ordering a meal took longer than eating it. The pixie turned to Nicole, who quickly straightened her face.

"And for you?"

"I'll have the same as he's having."

The only free table had a top fashioned out of a giant copper tray, an armchair on one side, and a stool on the other. Since I didn't want to get my head bitten off again, I waited for Nicole to pick her seat first, and she opted for the stool. Which left me to sink so low in the chair it put us at eye level for the first time.

"So..." I started.

"So."

"How are you feeling? After yesterday?"

"Sore."

Had I really been expecting anything else? "I'm sorry I—"

"Can we stop talking about it? I'm not interested in your apologies. All I want to do is find Carlton, or

Corey, or whatever his name is, and you promised you'd help." She gave her head a little shake. "I can't believe I was stupid enough to get tangled up with him."

Having made a monumental fuck-up in that department myself, I had sympathy for her, but I needed to put that to the side and focus on the case. Goal number one—find Corey Harmon. Goal number two—avoid Nicole getting injured again.

With Anna, I hadn't had that second chance. With Nicole, I was determined not to fuck it up.

"I did promise to help. And I've been asking around, but—"

"Lulu and I got three names when we went to Jive, and I need you to go with me to talk to them. You know, act as muscle."

"Muscle? Have you been watching too many action movies?"

Those high little cheekbones turned pink. "Shut up. Will you come or won't you?"

"Who are the three people?"

"First, a guy called Ramon Cool. He's supposed to be some sort of fixer, and he hangs out at a diner near here."

"I think I've heard his name mentioned."

By Joel—the friend I was staying with—when I complained about my back last night. Apparently, Ramon could get me the good stuff, but I'd declined the offer. More than once, the docs had prescribed me something stronger than ibuprofen, but despite the aches and pains, I nearly always tossed the pills into the trash. I'd seen too many of my former colleagues get addicted to painkillers, and I refused to walk that path.

From what Joel said, Ramon was a night owl whose office hours started when the sun went down and ended when he'd made enough cash to feed his movie-memorabilia habit. The guy collected everything from a replica Batmobile to Forrest Gump's sneakers.

"Really?" Nicole asked. "You know him?"

"Know *of* him, but not because of this case. How about we go visit him this evening?"

"I'm supposed to be having dinner with my supervisor tonight."

Great. Another delay. "I thought you wanted to get your necklace back?"

"I do. But the professor gets lonely, and..."

"And what?"

"Nothing. What if I finish work early? Could we visit Ramon first?"

"No, because he won't be awake, but we can go after dinner. Deal?"

"Okay."

The pixie had long since disappeared, but a bearded man with an ear gauge dumped our breakfast on the table and walked off without a word. Service with a smile. I may have come from Hicksville, but at least Mary-Kate at the diner asked how my day was going.

"What's this?" Nicole asked, poking at a pink slab of meat with her fork.

"I think it's the bacon."

"But it's not crispy. Bacon's supposed to be crispy."

And the syrup was supposed to be on the pancakes, not served up in a tiny jug with no handle.

"Next time, I'll do the research and take you somewhere with proper bacon, okay?"

"Next time?"

I couldn't fucking win, could I? "Tell you what—I'll buy you a package of bacon and you can cook it however you want. These two other people you want me to visit with you, who are they?"

"A drug dealer called Shane, and a cab driver called Jerry who's apparently quite fond of his guns."

Guns? Next time Aunt Tammy tried to strong-arm me into a job, I'd tell her to shove it. I'd had enough of getting shot at overseas without it happening in my own backyard.

"Do you know where to find either of them?"

"Sorry. I was hoping you might be able to help with that too. Don't bounty hunters have contacts in the criminal underworld?"

"The criminal underworld? You've definitely been watching too much TV."

"I don't have a lot of money to go out, okay? And this is your *job*."

"I've got a few contacts, but remember, I came here to find a jerk with a DUI, not a hardened crime lord."

Her fork clattered onto the plate, and I blew out a long breath. *Don't act like an ungrateful ass, Sinclair.* Nicole had given me three leads, which was three more than I'd had before.

"I'll ask around while you're in the lab, okay?"

"If we're going to find Shane, then we'd better do it quickly because the police'll be looking for him too. He was in the alley right before Macy got murdered."

"I thought you didn't see anybody?"

"I didn't, but one of the bartenders from the club told me he went out there."

Just keep piling the shit on, why don't you? "Make

sure you're ready when I come to pick you up from the lab later. What time will you be finished?"

"What makes you think I want a babysitter?"

"I know you don't want a babysitter, but if you think I'm gonna let that asshole with the scar near you again, I've got news—until we catch him or Harmon or preferably both, I'm your shadow, sweetheart, whether you like it or not. And you can protest and snipe and complain about bacon all you want, but I hate seeing those bruises on your neck, so you're not getting more of them. Any other questions?"

"Just one."

"Yeah?"

That porcelain veneer cracked to reveal a tiny smile. "What the heck is teff?"

Chapter 12 - Nicole

I WANTED TO hate Beckett Sinclair, I really did, but he made it difficult when he dropped me off at the professor's house with a family-sized package of streaky bacon and a reminder to call him when I was ready to be picked up. I even felt a little guilty for my outburst this morning. Okay, outbursts.

But inside, I was still shaking from the encounter with Scarface, and my whole thought process was seriously impaired.

"What's this?" the professor asked when he opened the door. "I thought we were having chicken?"

Dammit, I should've stuffed the bacon into my purse. Lulu's purse. It was her favourite, one of the few things that had survived her recent clear-out, but she'd insisted I borrow it.

"We are. I, uh, I thought I'd wrap it around the fillets."

He gazed past me. "Who's that? A new friend?"

I turned to see Beckett's truck still idling at the end of the drive, and he gave me a wave so I couldn't even pretend he was just a random passer-by.

"Yes. I mean no. Sort of. It's a long story."

"Well, there's plenty of time to tell it over dinner, and I'm sure Darlene can't wait to hear it too."

Who else did I have to talk with? Only Lulu, and

she'd insist on doing my hair and make-up before shoving me into Thor's car. Lulu was a firm believer in rebound flings. A true convert. Right now, she was on a rebound of a rebound of a rebound of a rebound, and each fling had gotten shorter and shorter until she'd switched to rebound one-night stands. At least the professor and Darlene might offer a more balanced viewpoint, one that wasn't overshadowed by blond hair and muscles.

Or so I thought.

"If I were still alive, I'd shut that young man's testicles in a nutcracker," Darlene said. "Carlton, not that nice bounty hunter."

"Well, uh..."

"Tell Geoffrey to give you the spare TV from the kitchen. He never watches it anyway."

"I can't do that."

"Of course you can, dear. And you'll have to, seeing as I can't speak to him myself. Get him to hunt out the nutcracker for you too. It's in the drawer by the refrigerator, or at least that's where it always used to be."

"I don't even know where Carlton is."

"What's she saying?" the professor asked. "Can't the police find Carlton? He should be in a jail cell."

"Darlene wants you to give me the spare TV and the nutcracker, but I really don't need them."

"Of course you can take the other television. I can't recall the last time I so much as turned it on. But I thought you never ate nuts because of Lulu's allergies?"

"I don't." Having to rush her to the emergency room with anaphylaxis once was quite enough. "But I really miss them. Especially those brazil nuts with the chocolate on them that my mom always used to eat at Christmas. And maple pecan— Wait! That's not what this is about. And no, the police probably won't find Carlton. Not only has he been on the run from the cops in Sacramento for months, but Lulu also reported the theft to the police right after it happened, and they still haven't come over. They don't seem the slightest bit interested in solving it."

Or in solving the mugging, but I'd decided not to mention that to the professor and Darlene. Why didn't I just tell them the full story? Because they'd both been through quite enough in their later years. I mean, Darlene was dead, for goodness' sake. I didn't want to give either of them anything else to worry about, so I'd worn a turtleneck to hide the bruises, and now sweat dripped down my back. Apparently, nobody in England used AC, so when the professor's broke last year, he'd never gotten it fixed. Finding a repairman was on my to-do list, but after the first one I booked failed to show and the second gave an outrageous quotation, I'd sort of given up since the professor didn't seem bothered by the heat.

"What are you going to do?" he asked. "I know how much that necklace means to you. I've got savings— perhaps we could hire a private detective to hunt Carlton down? I never did like that shifty little toad."

Ever had somebody do something so kind it makes you want to cry? Well, that was me, blinking back tears in the professor's dining room. I couldn't take his retirement fund, no way, but the very fact that he'd offered it made me well up. But what did he mean, he'd never liked Carlton?

"You thought he was shifty? Why didn't you say

anything?"

"Because you seemed happy, and I didn't want to rock the boat. Now, about that detective..."

"Tell him Betsy Mae Finnegan knows a private investigator," Darlene said. "She hired him when her cat went missing, and it turned out one of the ladies from the church choir had catnapped Purdie in revenge after Betsy Mae invited Reginald Marks over for iced tea. Quite the scandal, it was."

"Thank you for the offer, but I'm not taking any money."

"But your necklace..."

"Beckett Sinclair's offered to help. He's not exactly a detective, but his job is to find people, so I'm hoping he'll get lucky."

"Like a modern-day knight in shining armour," Darlene said. "Riding in to save the day."

"Beckett's no hero. If he hadn't stirred this mess up by coming to San Francisco in the first place, I'd be sitting at home, watching my TV and typing on my laptop."

And dating a felon. Okay, so there was a small flaw in my reasoning.

But I'd have my freaking necklace, and its loss was the worst part of this whole ordeal. Every time I touched my throat and found it missing, my breath caught.

"The man's only doing his job," the professor reminded me. "If Carlton did kill that poor lady, he should go to prison. Was Beckett that muscular young chap who dropped you off in the truck?"

"He insisted."

"And so he should with Carlton on the loose. If he

wasn't driving you around, I would be."

"There's no need—"

"A muscular young chap? Do you have a photograph?" Darlene asked, and I couldn't help rolling my eyes. "What? I may be old and dead, but I'm not blind."

Old and dead and married, but I refrained from saying that out loud because it would only invite awkward questions from the professor.

"No, sorry, I don't. Hey, let's have dessert." I pushed my seat back before anyone could argue and scurried through to the kitchen. Thankfully, I'd reminded the professor to take the apple pie out of the freezer earlier, so all I'd had to do when I arrived was put it into the oven. The sweet smell of pastry drifted towards me as I searched for a tea towel.

"Is he giving you a ride home this evening?" the professor asked from the doorway.

"Who? Beckett?"

"Unless you have another chauffeur you're not telling us about."

"Uh, sort of. We're supposed to be going out after dinner to look for Carlton."

The professor sucked in a breath. "Are you sure that's wise, you going along?"

"Carlton took my necklace, and I want it back. And I don't think he's dangerous. He got arrested for DUI, which was really, really stupid but it's not as if he set out to hurt anyone."

And quite honestly, the safest place for me right now was by Beckett Sinclair's side. If Scarface came after me again and I was alone, I didn't want to contemplate the outcome.

"Promise me you'll be careful."

That was something I *could* do. "I promise. Can I borrow your phone to call him?"

"You don't even need to ask."

***

I'd been to Cheech's Diner a few times with Lulu, but always in the morning for coffee. In daylight, the place looked old and run-down, a narrow space with a row of faded plastic stools in front of the counter on the right-hand side and booths on the left. At night, shadowed corners and the neon glare from the beer signs on the walls masked some of the imperfections, but they couldn't hide the cockroach that skittered across the cracked linoleum in front of me.

"Yeuch!" I clutched at Beckett's arm before I realised what I was doing, then let go just as quickly.

"Don't look down," he muttered as we stopped by the register. "Or up."

"Why?" I followed his line of sight and saw the spider on the ceiling. "Oh."

If Mom's necklace hadn't been at stake, I'd have run past the row of prostitutes sipping milkshakes at the counter and straight out onto the street, even though there was a group of tattooed men hanging around outside the door. Don't get me wrong, I thought tattoos were cool, just not when they were on somebody's face.

But before I could suggest to Beckett that we might want to come back after we'd bought some hand sanitiser, a bottle-blonde waitress in her mid-forties sashayed up to us and gave him a gap-toothed smile.

"What can I get you, hun?"

"Two coffees, a bacon cheeseburger, onion rings, and two portions of fries."

"Coming right up."

"You're *eating* in here?" I asked once she'd moved out of earshot.

"Always did have a strong constitution. When I was in Afghanistan, we fried the roaches up and dipped them in chilli powder."

"That's disgusting."

"Yeah, well, it didn't kill me."

"Why were you in Afghanistan? Were you in the military?"

"The army."

"And they made you eat bugs?"

"Sometimes there wasn't much else."

"What about the canteen?"

A friend of Damien's was an army cook. I'd talked to him at one of Damien's famous Saturday-night parties, and while I may have had a bit too much to drink that evening, I was almost certain he hadn't mentioned serving up arthropods.

"A lot of the time, my unit wasn't anywhere near the chow hall."

"Why not?"

All I got was a wry smile.

"Oh, I get it. You could tell me, but then you'd have to kill me?"

"Something like that. If the roaches don't do the job first."

I shuddered, then tried to cover it up by running a hand through my hair when a scantily clad lady turned to stare at me.

"Can we get this over with? Is Ramon even here?"

Beckett gave a barely perceptible nod towards the furthest booth, where a black man took up the whole of one side, spread out across the cracked vinyl seat like a melted ogre. Dark little eyes watched us as we waited for the waitress to pour our coffee.

"That's Ramon?"

"I recognise him from the description I was given."

"By who?"

"An acquaintance."

An acquaintance. Huh. What a great arrangement this was—I told Beckett everything, and he told me almost nothing.

"So what now? Do we go talk to him?"

The waitress handed a mug of coffee to Beckett, then shoved a second across the counter in my direction.

"Take the weight off your feet, hun. I'll bring your food over."

"Stay beside me," Beckett muttered. "Right beside me."

Up close, Ramon looked more like an oil slick. Malevolent and kind of greasy. Stay beside Beckett? I wanted to hide behind him.

"Ramon Cool?"

"Who's askin'?"

"A guy with a problem."

Pudgy sausage lips parted to reveal a set of surprisingly white teeth. Something glinted in the neon lights, and before I caught myself, I'd leaned forward to take a closer look.

"It's a diamond," Ramon said. "For my late Momma."

I wasn't about to question why he thought sticking

a stone to his teeth was a fitting tribute. "Looks nice."

"Good teeth are important. Wanna know my secret?"

"Uh, okay?"

"You gotta brush with activated charcoal every night. Gets rid of the coffee stains."

"I'll definitely remember that."

"So what's this problem?"

Beckett took over again. "Ever hear of a guy named Carlton Hines?"

"What if I did?"

"He's disappeared."

"Tell me somethin' I don't know."

"He rented a room from my friend here, and when he skipped town, he took a bunch of her stuff with him. She wants it back."

"Take my advice: quit lookin' and write it off as a loss."

"Can't do that. One of the items belonged to her mother—a necklace—and sentimental value isn't something you can replace."

"I get where you're coming from, brother, but if Carlton Hines don't wanna be found, you won't find him. Believe me, I bin lookin' myself. That asshole stiffed two of my clients on their deposits, and now I gotta cover that."

"Deposits for what?"

"Who did you say you were again?"

"We didn't. But this is Nicole, and I'm an old friend of her late brother." He held out a hand to Ramon. "Beckett."

Wow. I didn't know whether to be impressed by how smoothly Beckett lied, or concerned. But I couldn't blow his cover story.

"That's right. I didn't know who else to turn to."

"You got any recording devices?"

"Of course not." Who did he think we were? Undercover detectives? "I don't even have a phone because Carlton stole it. I was dating him, okay? And yes, I'm quite aware of how stupid I was, so you don't need to tell me."

Ramon looked me up and down, and I took a step back. This was worse than walking through one of those giant metal detectors and finding you'd forgotten to take the coins out of your pocket. I half expected an alarm to go off.

But finally, Ramon nodded. "New driver's licences."

"I'm sorry?"

"The deposits. They were for new driver's licences."

"Care to elaborate?" Beckett asked.

"Carlton Hines sells some of the best fake documents around. Passports, driver's licences, birth certificates. He'll even get you a new social security number for an extra five grand. The man's got more identities than a schizophrenic, and he's probably in Tahiti by now. Only thing you can be certain of is that sure as shit, his name ain't Carlton Hines."

Carlton was a forger? An actual criminal? I mean, I knew he was a wanted man for the car accident, but selling counterfeit documents was premeditated and most definitely illegal. That was a whole other level of wrongdoing, and one that left me feeling sick to the pit of my stomach.

Which meant that when the waitress brought Beckett's food over, I almost puked.

"Where are you sitting, hun?"

Ramon gestured at the bench seat opposite, and I had little choice but to slide in first, sandwiched between the grubby wall and Beckett's massive thigh.

"Here." He shoved one portion of fries in my direction. "I thought you might be hungry."

After the cockroach conversation?

"I already ate." I pushed them back towards him. "Help yourself."

Beckett covered everything in ketchup—burger, fries, onion rings, even the pickle. Did he believe it had antibacterial properties? Hopefully, his constitution was as strong as he claimed, because if he came down with food poisoning, I'd never find my necklace.

"So," he said. "Back to Carlton."

"Already told you that you're wastin' your time, bro. Buy the girl a new necklace." Ramon paused a moment, then dug into his pocket. He held out his closed fist and waited until I opened one hand. "In fact, take this one. You deserve it if you dated that motherfucker."

Something small and slinky tumbled into my palm. A delicate gold chain with a sparkly red pendant. Were those rubies?

"That's real kind of you—"

"But she can't accept." Beckett took the gift and put it on the table. "We just need to find Hines, and we've heard two names mentioned. A cab driver named Jerry and a drug dealer named Shane."

"Which Shane?"

"There's more than one?"

"Around here? Three. Four if you count Dr. Shane, but he only deals in pharmaceuticals. You got a picture?"

"No picture." Beckett turned to me. "How about a

description?"

"Sorry. But I could go back and ask."

"Can you give us the details of all four?" Beckett asked Ramon. "Then we can check them out ourselves?"

Ramon's meaty jowls flopped around as he shook his head. "No can do, brother. I shouldn't even give you the details of one. People value their privacy."

"In that case, we'll have to get back to you on the description. What about Jerry?"

"Heard he skipped town last week. He's got a sister in the Midwest."

"Why'd he leave?"

I understood what Beckett was asking—did Jerry's disappearance have anything to do with Carlton?

"A problem with his girlfriend's husband, or so I've heard. He hooked up with some biker's old lady. Jerry always did have more guns than brain cells."

"Do you have a surname for him?"

"Nah, he's like Madonna. Never uses it."

Beckett stuck a greasy onion ring in his mouth and chewed. "Except without the pointy bra, right?"

Ramon chortled, and all of his chins wobbled. "I like you, man. And if you find Hines, I'll like you even more."

"I'll find him. But in case he does try to sell Nicole's necklace on, I'd appreciate you keeping a lookout."

"You got a picture of that?"

"They were all in my phone. The data's in the cloud, but until I get a new one... Would it help if I drew it in the meantime?"

I did my best with the waitress's ballpoint on a napkin, sketching out the asymmetrical gold medallion with one curved edge and a hole in the centre. It looked as if it had once been part of a circle, and if I had to guess, I'd say the other three Electi each had a similar piece. Symbols decorated the surface, worn with time—some ancient language I didn't understand plus two thick lines that radiated out from the hole in the centre.

Ramon nodded and took Beckett's number, but as we headed for the door, I glanced back in time to see him wad up the napkin with my drawing on it and wipe a stray smear of ketchup off his chin.

Great. Another possible lead: dismissed. Apart from Lulu and the professor, Beckett was the only person who'd actually helped so far, which meant I had to be grateful even though he irritated me.

"Where to now?" I asked.

"Jive. We need to ask your barmaid friend about Shane."

CHAPTER 13 - NICOLE

"DONNA'S NOT HERE," the barman at Jive said. "Day off."

The music shook my insides, stirring up the nausea in my stomach. Thank goodness I hadn't touched those fries.

"Will she be back tomorrow?"

A shrug. "Can I get y'all a drink?"

I just wanted to go home, but my throat was dry from shouting to Beckett over the music.

"Uh, a sparkling water and..."

"Two beers," Beckett said, leaning over the top of me to be heard. I was already quite hot enough without being sandwiched between him and the wooden bar, but he didn't seem to care as he caged me in with his arms. "Unless you want something stronger."

"I already ordered water."

Didn't he ever listen? Maybe I should have taken a leaf out of his book—he'd gotten close enough for his lips to brush my damn earlobe as he shouted.

"You'll stick out like a whore in church if you drink water in here."

"I don't want to get drunk." Even if he was admittedly right about blending in.

"It's one beer, and I'll carry you home if it comes to that."

"You're not carrying me anywhere."

"Suit yourself. I can call you a cab if you'd prefer."

"Just hurry up and ask your questions, okay?"

"*Our* questions."

"Whatever."

The good news was that Beckett sure did find it easy to talk to people. Women, mainly, but some of the men asked him for gym tips. The bad news? Of the two people who knew Carlton, neither recalled him hanging out with anybody called Shane.

"Now what?" I asked Beckett two hours and three beers later. My feet hurt, and a piggyback didn't seem like such a bad idea after all. "This is hopeless. The only thing we know is that Shane was in here two days ago, and now he's vanished. He might as well be a ghost."

Of course, if he were a ghost, that would have made life so much easier. But as it stood, I only had one option left—to sneak back to the alley and talk to Macy in the hope that she saw Shane and could give me a description. Although if he *was* the person who killed her, memorising his eye colour was probably the last thing on her mind.

Rather than answering, Beckett steered me through the club with a hand on the small of my back. Which I probably should have slapped away, but by then, I was too tired to care.

"Where are we going?"

To the alley, it turned out. Tatters of yellow crime-scene tape still hung from the handles of the dumpsters, but apart from that and the lack of a body, it didn't look so different from when I'd first seen it. Smelled just as bad too. And it was raining again.

"Why are we here?" I asked. Macy waved

frantically, her head only just visible above her dumpster, but I had to ignore her from my spot in the doorway. "I don't have a jacket."

Beckett's blue T-shirt turned almost black on the shoulders as he stood in the drizzle, looking skywards. I leaned forward a little and twisted to follow his gaze.

"What is it?"

"It's too dark to see properly."

"What are you looking for?"

"Cameras. They're everywhere nowadays. If Shane was in this alley, then ten bucks says he didn't walk back through the club after a girl got killed. If we follow the routes he could have taken, I bet he got caught on tape somewhere. We just need to find the footage."

"To show to Ramon?"

"Exactly. I already asked the manager about cameras inside the club, but the system's been malfunctioning for months, and they've got nothing."

I lost my balance as I yawned, and when I clutched at the doorjamb, I got a wad of used gum stuck to my fingers.

"Yeuch!"

"Tired?"

"You've only just noticed?"

"Let's come back early tomorrow when we can see better."

Tomorrow... Usually, I volunteered at the animal sanctuary on Saturdays, but finding my necklace would have to take priority this week. Cindy who ran the place would understand, but the dogs would miss out on their walks, and that made me furious at Carlton all over again.

Beckett mistook my quiet seething on the walk back

to his truck for exhaustion, and when we arrived, he lifted me inside and did up my seat belt. The only good thing about that evening? It turned out being carried into my house wasn't as bad as I thought.

***

The alley looked even worse in daylight. Eerie tendrils of the marine haze that drifted across the city most mornings swirled in the breeze, and I zipped my sweater right up to my chin in an attempt to ward off the chill. Vomit pooled to the right of Jive's fire exit, drying into a lumpy mess, and the only colour came from the piles of trash beside the dumpsters. Was it really that difficult to lift the lid and put it inside?

"Anything?" I asked.

Beckett pointed above my head. "One camera, but see the wires at the back?" Presumably he meant those little frayed ones hanging out. "We won't get anything from that."

"What are you doing?" Macy asked. "And why did you ignore me last night? That's super rude."

I cut my eyes to Beckett and shrugged, but she didn't take the hint.

"How are you supposed to fix this if you won't even answer?"

"I'll come back later, okay?" I muttered.

"What did you say? Can you speak louder?"

No, I freaking couldn't, but I sidled closer on the pretence of studying the area around a rusted fire escape.

"He's helping me to find Shane."

"Shane? Why? Do you think Shane killed me? Are

you crazy? Shane can't even kill a spider. Like, there was one in his bathroom once, and he refused to shower for three days and peed in the sink."

This was what my life had been reduced to? Hunting for a guy who peed in the sink?

"Then who *did* kill you? Do you know?"

"Some ugly dude with a scar on his face."

A...a *scar*? My heart stuttered. No way. Could it be...? How many men with scarred faces and murderous tendencies were running around San Francisco in any given week?

"What's up?" Beckett asked. "You look as if you've seen a ghost."

"A ghost?" I forced a laugh that sounded mechanical and high pitched to my own ears. "Of course not."

"I take it you don't believe in them?"

"I'm a scientist. I like to see evidence with my own eyes before I commit to having a strong opinion."

"Don't you ever wonder what happens to a person after they die?"

"I can't say I've spent much time thinking about it, but I guess there's the choice between burial and cremation."

"I meant what happens to their soul. That spark that makes a person a person rather than just a collection of molecules."

"There's no proof such a thing exists."

"So because you don't know how to measure it in the lab, it can't be true?"

Wait a minute. Why were we even having this argument? I of all people knew Beckett was absolutely right in this instance, and thanks to my work with the professor, I also knew that rudimentary measurement of the soul was possible too. Although we hadn't yet worked out how to introduce that to a sceptical world without getting written off as charlatans.

"I'm open-minded."

"Really? Because you don't sound that way."

"Why are you so touchy? Do... Do *you* believe in ghosts?"

Answer a question with a question. Many years ago, Mom had taught me how to deflect awkward inquiries back to safer topics.

Beckett shrugged. "Yeah."

What? He admitted it, just like that? I stared at him, and now it was his turn for the gawky laugh.

"Don't write me off as a kook, okay?"

Oh, please. I was the least likely person to accuse him of being kooky. Well, one of the four least likely, but seeing as I had no idea who or where the other three were, that didn't help much in the current situation.

"Huh? I mean, why? Why do you believe in ghosts?"

"Because I saw one. Kind of. But is this really the right time to be having this conversation? We've got an FTA to find."

No, it wasn't, not in a filthy alley under the watchful eyes of Macy, who seemed to find the whole conversation amusing judging by her giggles. I suppose I should have been grateful that she was smiling after everything she'd been through in the last few days, but it did add another layer of discomfort. A double helping of awkwardness.

But now that Beckett had knocked me for six with a revelation I totally hadn't been expecting, I couldn't let it go. Instead, I shifted back half a pace to put some space between him and me, then grimaced when my Converse squished into something nasty.

"I'm not sure when we'd have a better opportunity."

"Forget I said anything."

"No way. You can't make a statement like that then just brush it away. When did you see a ghost? Where?"

Was it possible that somebody besides the Electi had a link to the supernatural? Or... Or could *Beckett* be one of us? I discounted that possibility almost as soon as I thought of it—Mom always said that fate would bring us together one day, but she also said the other three were female. Unless Beckett was trans... No, he wasn't a member of the Electi. Otherwise he'd have been chatting with Macy by now.

"In Afghanistan. When I died. Can we drop this now?"

"You *died*? I mean, I'm sorry for all the questions, but...but..."

"If I tell you, will you stop staring at me like I'm a freak?"

"Sorry. Yeah, of course. I didn't mean to."

This was like some weird kind of role reversal. Usually, I was the one who got gawped at for saying or doing something stupid in the presence of spirits, but oddly, it didn't feel any less uncomfortable the other way around.

"I fell through the floor of a building while I was hunting down terrorists. The noise brought out the bad guys, and I got shot up pretty bad, but the guys from my unit got me back to base in time for me to die in the hospital."

"But you're still here now." I reached out to prod

him in the chest, which was like stubbing my finger into a brick wall. "And you're definitely not a ghost."

"Technically, I was dead for three minutes and twenty-eight seconds, but they brought me back."

"And that was when you saw the ghost?"

He nodded. "Ghosts, plural. First, I saw myself, lying on the operating table while I stood in the middle of my own body. Then I realised four other people were there too, all of us squashed together in the same space, and I was stuck fast. Couldn't fucking move. I recognised two of the figures, and my arm was *in* Sergeant Dawkins. Then this *thing* appeared, like a grey mist with a woman's face. And she looked pissed, the same way my first girlfriend did whenever I wanted to check out the guns in Walmart. As if I was taking up her valuable time and it was far more important than mine."

The spirit guide. I'd never met one personally, but I could imagine they were kept quite busy since they had to chat with every single person who passed over.

"And what happened?"

"Dawkins told me to get my ass back into my body because otherwise I'd be stuck staring at his ugly mug for all eternity unless our saviour arrived. And then I woke up two days later in the ICU." He opened up the gap between us to six feet. Ten. "Have you heard enough now? We need to work our way along the street and look for anywhere that might have security cameras."

He began walking away, and I tripped over my feet trying to catch up.

"Wait. Wait! Did you talk to any of the others? And what about the spirit guide? Did *she* say anything?"

"What did you call her?"

"The spirit— Oh. Shit."

"Why'd you call her a guide? Because that was what *she* called herself."

"Uh... I don't know? Maybe I heard someone use the term sometime."

"I thought you didn't have any interest?"

"I don't. But Lulu often watches reality shows— *Search for a Spectre, America's Most Haunted Houses,* that sort of thing." Thank goodness the professor had donated his spare TV, otherwise she'd have been squinting at reruns on YouTube. "So, what else did they say? The ghosts, I mean?"

Beckett had seen freaking ghosts. Only for a few minutes, but that was more than anyone else I'd ever met except for my mom. I didn't believe anything on those TV shows for a moment. I'd even glimpsed a piece of string they forgot to edit out on *Search for a Spectre.*

"For a girl with no interest in ghosts, you seem remarkably curious."

"Well, uh..."

"Let's make a deal—if you tell me the truth about why you want to know, I'll tell you the answer."

How did he keep backing me into corners? "Are you accusing me of lying?"

"Every time you fib, you bite your lip, like when I took you home after Scarface attacked you and you said you were fine. I was worried you were gonna draw blood."

Did I really do that? I ran my tongue over my lip and felt the little row of dents from my front teeth. Dammit.

"You'll think I'm crazy," I muttered.

"I already think you're crazy. There's not much you can say or do that'll make the situation worse."

Gee, thanks.

"Oh, just tell him," Macy said. "At first, it was fun watching you dance around each other, but it's getting boring now. You should be solving my murder, not arguing in an alley with Shazam's hotter cousin."

"Shazam?"

"You're not a comic-book fan?"

Now Beckett was looking at me funny. Funnier.

"Who are you talking to?"

This was a nightmare. I lost my damn mind when he was around. "Nobody."

"Nicole..."

Macy rolled her eyes. "Just. Tell. Him."

"I can see ghosts," I blurted, then sucked in a deep breath as if I could swallow the words back down. "Did I mention I've been drinking this morning? I had vodka for breakfast."

"Bullshit." A pause. "You can see ghosts?"

He sounded incredulous, and after the sob story he'd just given me, I couldn't help feeling annoyed.

"You just complained about people writing you off as a kook, and when I say I've also seen ghosts, you do exactly the same thing? Do you realise how much of a hypocrite that makes you?"

"Yeah. I mean, sorry. I..." He scrubbed a hand through his already messy hair. "I don't know what to say."

"I was talking to Macy, okay? She's over there laughing at us."

"You two are hil-ar-i-ous. This is way better than

that couple who had the screaming match yesterday after they realised they'd both been having an affair with the same guy."

"This isn't funny."

"Are you serious?" Beckett asked.

"Unfortunately."

"And in the forest the other day? Were you talking to a ghost then?"

I nodded. "But she wasn't very helpful."

"This... Whoa. This is deep. You see ghosts every day?"

"They're everywhere."

"But... But..." Beckett was speechless, which was a real novelty. "Wait. The only reason I saw ghosts was because I died. Yet you're..." He reached out to prod me. "Alive?"

"Thanks. That hurt."

"Sorry."

"Yes, I'm alive."

"Then how does this all work?"

"It's a long, long story."

"You can tell it to me over breakfast."

"You have to stop buying me food."

"But you're too thin. You should eat more."

"Okay, so sometimes I forget to eat lunch when I'm busy, but I'm fine the way I am. And I don't have time to go for breakfast. My research paper won't write itself."

Macy interrupted again. "She's totally right. You don't have time to eat when you're supposed to be looking for my damn killer. Grab a sandwich to go or something."

"You know he can't hear you, right?"

"Is that a ghost talking again?"

"The same ghost. Macy."

"What's she saying?"

"That we shouldn't go for breakfast because we should be solving her murder instead. And, by the way, it wasn't Shane who killed her. It was a guy with a scar on his face. Sound familiar?"

"Fuck."

"But she knows Shane."

"Holy shit. Are you really talking to her?"

"She's mostly talking to me at the moment."

"So ask her questions. Hey, Macy, what's Shane's last name?"

"I already told you, Shane didn't kill me."

"Yes, but we're looking for him for another reason," I said. "That was why me and Beckett here came out to the alley in the first place."

"What other reason?"

"Well, actually, we're looking for Carlton Hines, but we heard Shane knows him."

"You're one of Carlton's customers? Because I heard he ripped off a whole bunch of people."

Was I the only person in the world oblivious to the fact that my significant other ran an apparently successful illegal enterprise?

"No, I was his girlfriend, and he stole some of my stuff."

"His girlfriend? Which one? The geek or the waitress?"

"The g— *What*? Carlton had more than one girlfriend?"

Beckett snorted out a laugh, and if I'd been carrying anything other than Lulu's purse, I'd have hurled it at his head. But if her Michael Kors landed in a fetid pile of—actually, in truth, I didn't want to think about it—I'd be joining Macy in the afterlife.

"You didn't know?" she asked.

"Clearly not."

"If it helps, I think the thing with the waitress was only casual. Until two months ago, he was seeing Becca from the coffee place on Hancock, but she dumped his ass after he poisoned her cat."

"He what?"

"From what I heard, it was an accident, but she was really *pissed*."

"Was Carlton doing the dirty on you?" Beckett asked.

"Shut up."

"I'll take that as a yes."

Macy started laughing too. "This is better than a soap opera."

"It's not funny. Not even a little bit."

Now Beckett joined in again. "It kind of is."

"You know, if Macy were still alive, you two would make the perfect couple."

"Too damn right we would. That man is *fine*." Macy glanced down at Beckett's boots. "What shoe size are you?" she asked him. "A twelve? Because you know what they say about the size of a man's feet."

"I keep telling you—he can't hear a word you're saying."

"Perhaps you could interpret?" Beckett suggested.

"Okay, sure. Macy was just making a derogatory comment about your feet."

"Weren't nothing derogatory about my comment. I was paying him a compliment."

"Just. Be. Quiet. Both of you!" How the hell did I get into this situation? Was it some sort of cosmic revenge for not doing my designated job properly? *Deep breaths, Nicole.* "Macy, I'm going to ask you a few questions. Please make an effort to answer them without getting sidetracked by my love life or Beckett's reproductive organs." I turned to idiot number two. "And you... Unless you have something constructive to say, zip it."

"I love it when a woman takes control."

"If you don't stop talking, I'm gonna buy you a gag."

"I'd probably like that."

For the first time in my life, I was tempted to kill somebody on purpose. Why me? What cruel twist of fate gave me the horrible ability to talk to both the dead and the living? Right now, I wasn't sure which was worse.

"Macy, can you start from the beginning? What happened the evening before last when you visited Jive?"

I wished I could record what she said because knowing me, I'd forget half of it. In the lab, I jotted endless notes and faithfully scanned everything into the cloud at the end of each day. An other-worldly dictation app would be a neat invention.

"I wasn't gonna go at all, but then I was speaking to my friend Karen, and she said—"

"How about we start from when you went outside?"

Because I didn't have an extra hour to spare.

"Oh, okay. So, I scrounged a smoke off this guy on the dance floor, and he was supposed to meet me out here when he'd been to the john, but he didn't, and I have no idea—"

"Is this relevant?"

She crinkled her nose. "I guess not. Anyhow, I went outside, and I was sort of crouched behind the dumpster in case Karen came out because like I said before, we had this pact that we'd both quit smoking and I didn't want her to think I had no willpower, and then Shane appeared."

"Did you speak to him?"

"I didn't get a chance to. The asshole with the scar materialised out of, like, nowhere, and Shane gave him a package."

"What kind of a package?"

"One of those padded envelopes. About this big." She demonstrated with her hands, and it looked to be roughly A5-sized. "And he said that Carlton was sorry he wasn't there to hand it over personally, but he'd gotten sick."

"Sick. Right. He was on the run with half of my stuff."

"Yeah, well, the scarred dude didn't seem to believe that story either."

"What did he do?"

"Shoved Shane up against the wall and said if he didn't tell him where Carlton was, he'd cut his fingers off one at a time."

Wow. Seemed I'd gotten off lightly with the bruises. "And did he tell him?"

"No, because something crawled across my foot, and I made a sound."

"A sound?"

"Fine, I screamed. And the scarred dude ran over and shot me before I even got my cell phone out of my purse."

"What did Shane do?"

"Who knows? I was too busy dying to check. I guess he ran off, the coward, because the next time I looked, he wasn't there."

A coward indeed. I could understand him wanting to get out of danger, but he hadn't come back to check on Macy or even given a statement afterwards.

"We need to try and find him because he's the only link we have to Carlton just now. Do you know Shane's surname? Or can you tell me more about what he looked like?"

"Never heard anyone use his surname. Uh, white guy, brown hair, medium height. Not too skinny, not too fat."

"Eye colour?"

Macy shrugged. "Never noticed. I'm no good with faces. When I was fifteen, my friend Tonya asked me to pass a note to this guy she liked, except I got him confused with someone else and she ended up going for milkshakes with a total weirdo."

"Can we focus here? I need to find Shane."

"No, lady, you need to find that son of a bitch with the scar. I can't believe he shot me. Like, he didn't even hesitate."

Which made an excellent reason to stay as far away from him as possible, but I couldn't tell Macy that if I wanted her to cooperate.

"At the moment, Shane's our best lead to the man who killed you. Perhaps Shane knows who he is? Can you try to remember if Shane had any distinctive features? Please?"

"Wouldn't it be easier if I just tell you where he lives?"

She knew his address? All that, and she knew his damn address?

"Yes! Beckett, I need a pen. And paper."

"Who uses those anymore?"

"If you want to know where Shane lives, you'll find me something to write with."

"You're shitting me?"

"Just get me a freaking pen."

He dug his phone out of his pocket. "Here, use this."

Finally, we were getting somewhere. For the first time in three days, I dared to hope. If Shane could lead us to Carlton-slash-Corey, I could retrieve my necklace, and better still, Beckett and his attitude could screw off all the way back to Sacramento.

I mustered up a smile for Macy. "Okay, I'm ready. Where do we find Shane?"

CHAPTER 14 - NICOLE

"READ OUT THE address again?" Beckett said.

Because this was Macy's doing, our instructions weren't as simple as a street number and a zip code. Oh, no.

"Past the apartment building with the crooked tree outside, then turn left." Riding around in Beckett's truck made a nice change from public transport. He did have his uses, even if I hated to admit it. "Then go down the hill until you get to the house with the bush that looks like a giant..." Macy had used the term "cock," but I wasn't going there with Beckett. I pointed instead. "That one."

"And then where?"

"The ugly brown house with the red mailboxes. It's been converted to apartments, and Shane lives on the top floor."

Beckett carried on along the street until we found a parking spot, which was half a freaking mile away, so I hoped we didn't have to make a quick getaway. Especially since the trip back would be uphill and I hadn't been to the gym since Lulu dragged me there on a guest pass the January before last. How did Beckett do this for a living? My legs were shaking so much I could hardly walk. Visiting drug dealers wasn't something I'd ever made a habit of.

"Do you think he'll be angry when we show up at his door? What if he's armed?"

"If he's armed, we duck."

"Be serious."

"I am. Do you want to get shot in the face?"

"I don't want to get shot at all!"

"Look, we know from Macy that Shane's not a murderer, and nothing we've heard suggests he's dangerous. I'm more concerned that he won't be there."

We know from Macy...

Beckett believed in ghosts. He believed in *me*. When my mom died, the fear that I'd have to live out the rest of my days without sharing my secret had given me sleepless nights. I mean, think about it... The biggest, most significant thing in my life, my whole reason for existing, and I couldn't tell a soul without them referring me to a psychiatrist.

When I confided in the professor, that burden had eased just a tad, and now with Beckett, the load had lightened again. He may have annoyed me in more ways than I could mention, but that plus point meant I couldn't entirely hate his company.

"Or what if he's there and he won't tell us anything?" I asked.

"If he's there, he'll talk."

"How do you know?"

Beckett shrugged. "Experience?"

"What, you just ask people questions and they spill their guts?"

"Something like that."

"You're not gonna hurt him, are you?"

"If I did, on a scale of one to ten, how upset would you be?"

"Uh, eleven. What if Shane's an innocent bystander in all of this?"

"He was friends with Carlton."

"And I was *dating* Carlton."

"Yeah, but you're..."

"I'm what? Stupid?"

Beckett's expression said he wished we'd never started this conversation. "Not stupid. More..."

"Desperate? Gullible?"

"I was going to say innocent."

"Isn't that just a polite way of saying I'm naïve?"

"Sprite, I know I'll never win this one, so I'm gonna fold."

"Sprite?"

"That's what you remind me of. A water sprite. Small, cute, and mostly harmless unless someone threatens you."

Cute? Beckett Sinclair thought I was cute, albeit in a weird sort of way? I didn't know whether to be flattered or kick him in the nuts for that comment.

"You... You..." What did I want to say? "You didn't answer my question properly."

"Which one?"

"About hurting Shane."

"I need to find Harmon, and you want to find your necklace. If that means applying a little pressure because someone's holding back, then yes, I'll do it. But don't worry; I won't leave any permanent marks."

"Hey. Hey! You can't—"

But then we were at Shane's place, and Beckett rang the buzzer for apartment number eight before I could stop him.

"Just be careful," I muttered, since making a scene

would draw unwanted attention.

"Always am."

Nobody answered, and Beckett stepped back to take a better look at the old building. Three floors, plus two tiny apartments squashed into the basement. The wooden window frames showed signs of rot, and several panes of glass had cracks in them. The place was one sagging door away from being condemned, and it made our tired house look like a palace.

"I don't think he's there," I said to Beckett. No lights were on, which was to be expected during the day, but it also felt still. No noise, no movement. "Unless he's sleeping."

"Or dead."

Whoa. "Wait a minute. You don't think...?"

"Scarface already killed one witness and then came after you."

"Should we call the— What are those?"

Beckett had taken two slim metal objects out of his wallet.

"Lock picks."

"You're gonna break in?"

"I'm concerned for his welfare."

Beckett's tone suggested otherwise, but what if Shane really was lying upstairs, injured? Or worse? I stood back as Beckett fiddled with the lock, and he got the exterior door open in under a minute. Impressive. Or extremely concerning, depending on which way I chose to look at it.

"Where did you learn to pick locks?"

"I got bored as a teenager."

As a teenager, I'd joined the science society at school and spent every spare moment researching

DNA. Even as a child, my goal had been to cure myself of my supernatural affliction. Mom had been so proud of my ambitions, and sometimes, I wondered if any relatives on my father's side had been scientists. Would I ever know for sure? Unlikely, since I avoided speaking to him wherever possible. My father had never been a talkative man unless it was to argue, and secretly, I suspected Mom was relieved when he ran out on us. I'd been eight years old when he left, and he'd been shirking his responsibilities ever since. No child support, no birthday cards, no flying visits or phone calls.

When I was seventeen, Mom had confessed I was the horrifying result of a drunken tryst, a tryst that went terribly wrong. Horrifying because although she loved me with every bit of her heart and soul, she'd never wanted to burden a child of hers with the extraordinary ability she'd hated her whole life. She knew she'd pass it on to me as my grandmother had passed it to her. The transfer wasn't sudden, more a fading of her powers and a strengthening of mine that began soon after my eighth birthday. By the time I was fourteen, she was supposed to have trained me to do my duty, but most of the time, she'd refused to even speak of it.

No, she'd wanted to erase the curse that possessed us just as much as me.

"Want to stay here? Or in the truck?" Beckett asked.

On my own? No, thanks. "I'm coming with you."

Despite Beckett's size, he moved through the house silently, pausing every so often to listen or to glare at me for breathing too loudly. On the third floor, he knocked at a door that wouldn't have withstood the girliest of kicks. Nothing.

"We're going in?" I whispered as he got his lock picks out again.

"I didn't come all the way over here to go home empty-handed."

"What are we looking for?"

"I'll know it when I see it," was his incredibly helpful answer.

Less than two minutes later, we stood in Shane's living room. And his bedroom, and his kitchen, because they were all the same room. A flimsy door separated off the minuscule bathroom, and I glanced inside.

"Shane's not here," Beckett said, stating the obvious.

No, but somebody else was. When I tiptoed into the bathroom, I found the spirit of a skinny man slumped in the shower stall with blood running from both wrists. Oh, shit. What were my chances of getting out of there without him seeing me?

"Hey! Are you one of those elected people?"

Not good, it seemed.

"It's Electi," I whispered.

He scrambled to his feet as if being taller than me would make a difference. "You're hella late. Eight damn years, I've been waiting. It was my ex-girlfriend. She drugged me and made it look like a suicide."

Aaaaand...this was why I rarely ventured out of the lab.

"I'm not here in a professional capacity."

"Why else would you come to this shithole? Used to be nice before the jerk-off moved in."

"The jerk-off?"

"Shane Willans. He does the old five-knuckle

shuffle in here every morning. On my damn face, half of the time. D'ya know what it's like having a man come on your face?" He looked me up and down. "No, I don't suppose you do."

"What's that supposed to mean?"

"Well, you don't look like the type."

"What type? Adventurous?"

"No, the type to have a boyfriend."

"For someone who wants my help, you're sure not endearing yourself."

With impeccable timing, Beckett chose that moment to make an appearance behind me. "Who are you talking to? A ghost?"

He seemed a lot more excited by the prospect than I did.

"A *rude* ghost. He got murdered by his girlfriend, and I can understand why."

Shower guy scowled. "Now who's being rude?" Beckett's turn to get the slow perusal. "This knuckle-dragger's your boyfriend?"

"He's not a knuckle-dragger. Why are you so judgemental?"

"Now you sound like her. 'Greg, why do you get so grouchy?'" He put on a whiny voice. "'Greg, why are you such a sourpuss?'"

"What's he saying?" Beckett asked.

"He's just whining."

"Whining?" Greg glared at me. "Do you treat all your clients this way?"

"You're not my client. I'm only here because I'm looking for Shane."

"Well, if you helped me instead of being snarky, I might consider telling you where he is."

"You know where he is? How? I mean, you're stuck here."

Now Greg grew smug. "Got eyes and ears, don't I? If you get me out of this damn shower, I'll help you to find the prick."

"I can't get you out of the shower."

"But it's your job."

"Oh, please. This is the twenty-first century. The world doesn't work that way anymore."

"But some spirit thing told me—"

"They're hopelessly out of date."

They'd probably been reeling off the same spiel for five thousand years, because let's face it, they had the easier job. Show up, mutter a few words of pseudo-sympathy, tick another departed spirit off the list.

But Greg didn't see it that way. "Don't you bother to communicate?"

"World doesn't work what way anymore?" Beckett asked.

Honestly, this was impossible. At this hour on a Saturday morning, I should have been fighting with our second-hand coffee machine and listening to Lulu recap the latest happenings in the world of reality TV, not arguing with both the living and the dead.

"It doesn't matter."

"It clearly does since you brought it up."

"Why do you have to be so nosy?"

"Because we're supposed to be working together? Why do you have to be so closed off?"

"Working together doesn't entitle you to my life's history. And you'd be closed off too if you constantly feared getting ridiculed for saying the wrong thing."

"I'm not ridiculing you. But come on, Nicole, you

can see ghosts. How can you tell me that and expect me not to be curious?"

So maybe he did have a point. He'd been surprisingly understanding so far, and if I told him the full story, what did it matter? It wasn't as if he could arrest me for murder.

"Fine. I'll tell you the rest. But I'm not discussing it in here with Mr. Know-it-all listening."

Beckett took a mock bow and gestured for me to go through the door. "After you."

I expected him to head back to the truck, but he stopped in the living room.

"We're staying here? What if Shane comes back?"

"Then it's a win-win situation, wouldn't you say? I'd offer to make you a coffee, except even I wouldn't drink out of one of those mugs."

"How can you act so calm? Do you do this often?"

"What, break into people's houses? It's not the first time, put it that way. But enough about me. Let's talk about you. Tell me more about the ghosts."

"Okay, here goes..." I gave him a brief rundown of my so-called purpose, the Electi, and the reason I hated talking to ghosts so much, keeping my voice low because while I may have entered into an awkward alliance with Beckett, my secrets were no business of Greg's. "So you see, I get shouted at like an A-list celebrity wherever I go. They all want me to do something for them." Silence. "Now do you think I'm crazy?"

He blew out a long breath. "Yes and no."

"Yes and no? What the hell is that supposed to mean?"

"It means I believe in you. The Electi." Beckett's

voice dropped to a whisper. "Because that's who Sergeant Dawkins told me would set us free. Holy fuck. All this time, I still doubted myself, but it's true. Everything's true. I wasn't hallucinating."

"But you still said yes and no?"

"Because you're saying that if I'd died in that hospital, *you* were the one who was meant to travel to Afghanistan and hunt down the jihadi that shot me? Sprite, you wouldn't even make it out of Kabul Airport without getting into trouble."

Kind of insulting, but absolutely true. "Exactly."

"How does it work? The whole freeing-souls thing? I can't imagine you with a gun."

"That makes two of us. I've never even held one."

"Then it could just be a story some prankster made up a couple of centuries ago?"

"It's not."

Beckett raised one thick eyebrow. "How do you know? Don't tell me...?"

"No! Not on purpose, anyway. There was an accident." Eight years ago now, but I still felt sick to my stomach every time I thought about it. "Back when I lived in Vermont, I was driving home late one evening and this guy... He just came out of nowhere in a dark-coloured car, blew through a red light, and rammed straight into me."

"He died?"

"Lesson number one—if you're running from the cops, it's important to wear a seat belt."

"But how does that fit in with the whole 'murdered souls are trapped on earth' thing? Wasn't it classed as an accident?"

"Because it turned out that he'd only gotten into the

chase after the cops found his wife shot to death in their kitchen. So, following the rules, her ghost should have been hanging out by the refrigerator, but when I checked later on, she wasn't there. Because technically, I killed the man, even if I didn't mean to."

"You *checked*?" Beckett's lips quirked up at the sides. "You did a little breaking and entering of your own?"

"Of course not. I called the real estate agent when the house went on the market and had her show me around." Which Beckett found funny. "Stop laughing. We don't all carry a set of freaking lock picks in our wallet."

"Okay, I'm sorry. And I'm sorry you had the accident. Did you get injured?"

"A cut arm and a concussion."

"Shit. Thank fuck it wasn't worse." Sympathy with swearing—typical Beckett. "So what about the asshole in the shower? He wants you to kill someone? Is that what you were discussing?"

"His ex-girlfriend. He says if I do, he'll tell us where Shane is."

"But surely if you killed her—which I'm not suggesting you do, by the way—he'd disappear?"

"Yep. He hasn't thought it through at all, but ghosts get desperate. I'm used to it."

"How does he even know where Shane is?"

"He didn't say. Maybe he overheard him on the phone or something?"

"Maybe." Beckett paused, pondering. "Or..."

"Yes?"

He put a finger to his lips. "Shh."

"Why?"

"Humour me."

Cars purred past on the road outside. A man shouted on the sidewalk. An odd humming noise came from somewhere downstairs, and then I heard quiet scratching above us. Ick.

"Is that a rat?"

"I'm wondering if it might be a really, really big rat."

Like a squirrel? Or a raccoon? The gleam in Beckett's eyes suggested something more interesting, and my heart thumped against my ribcage as his suspicions slowly dawned.

"Oh my gosh, you think—"

He clapped a hand over my mouth. "Tell the whole world, why don't you?"

I lowered my voice to the softest whisper. "Sorry." Had we truly found Shane? "How did he get up there?"

Beckett headed into the bathroom again, eyes fixed on the ceiling, and in amongst the mould and water stains above the toilet, I saw the faint outline of a loft hatch. And if that wasn't enough to convince me, Greg's groan from behind me clinched it.

We'd found Shane!

But with the discovery came a bigger problem. "How do we get him down from there?"

"That, Nicole, is the fifty-thousand-dollar question. If the man's scared enough to move into his damn attic, the chances are he's armed as well."

Which made sense. If I were a shady character hiding out, waiting for Scarface, I'd fire at anything that appeared through the freaking hatch. As long as my inner coward didn't drop the gun, obviously.

"So what do you suggest?"

"He's got to come down to take a leak sometime."

"We just wait? In here?"

"In the living room, and we pretend to leave first."

That could take hours. And there wasn't even anywhere to sit. Well, there was the bed, and a stained armchair, but the chances were I'd get bitten by bedbugs if I perched my behind on either of those. And every hour we were delayed allowed Carlton to get farther and farther away with my necklace.

I turned back to the shower.

"Greg, if you help us out here, I might consider writing to the cops and suggesting they take another look at your suicide," I said very, very quietly.

"And how will that help me? I'll still be stuck here, won't I?"

"Yes, but your girlfriend might go to prison, and that's got to be better than her taking a vacation to Las Vegas or Florida or LA."

Nothing.

"You won't get a better offer than that, because I'm not killing anybody."

Now he folded his arms like a petulant toddler.

"Greg?"

"I suppose."

Thank goodness. The breath I didn't realise I'd been holding leaked out of me. "When did Shane go into the attic?"

"Three nights ago."

"Wednesday night?"

"Who knows? I don't have a calendar in here."

"But it's gotten dark three times?"

"Just said that, didn't I?"

So that was right after Macy got killed. "What did

he take with him?"

"Bags and bags of food. Blankets. Bottles of water and toilet paper. A flashlight."

"Did he take a weapon with him?"

"Saw a gun. Piece-of-shit revolver."

Great. "And he hasn't come down since?"

"Once, on..." Greg counted on his fingers. "On Thursday. For his pillow."

Seemed as though Shane had moved up there for good, and the thought of hanging around for days on end made my stomach sink.

"What's up? What's he saying?" Beckett's voice sounded close to my ear, and I shivered as his breath puffed against my cheek. Stupid, because it really wasn't cold at all.

I relayed the message, and Beckett rivalled Greg in the happiness stakes. At least I wasn't the only person who didn't want to sit in this dump for ages.

"I'm on a deadline, remember? Two weeks and three days. Neither of us has time to wait around for Shane to show himself."

"What other option do we have? He's got a pistol, and I don't want to risk getting my head blown off."

Beckett sighed. "You won't, sprite. That's my job."

CHAPTER 15 - BECKETT

HOLY SHIT.

FOUR years of looking, four years of combing the dark depths of the internet and braving the tinfoil-hat brigade, and I'd stumbled across one of the Electi by accident. *Nicole?* All this time, I'd assumed I'd be looking for the real-life equivalent of Wonder Woman, not a waif who didn't know which end of a gun was which.

And that meant I had a bigger problem. If Nicole was the person chosen to set Anna free, we'd be waiting a long fucking time.

I should probably start at the beginning, shouldn't I? But to do that, I had to step back a decade, to that time at Fort Belvoir, Virginia, when I'd been plain ol' Private Sinclair and more interested in drinking beer with my buddies than kicking ass in fitness tests and spending hours on the shooting range.

I'd met Sarah in a bar off-base one night, and man, was she beautiful. The body of a Playboy centrefold, the face of an angel, and the mind of a psychopath.

Of course, I hadn't realised that third point right away. At that age, I'd thought with my dick, interested in little more than a night with a pretty girl and sometimes dinner if I didn't have anything better to do.

We'd been on four dates when the alarm bells

began to ring. The little gifts she delivered to me at the base, the hourly calls and text messages burning up my phone, the way she changed her Facebook status to "in a relationship" when in reality we'd only been out for dinner and fucked a few times.

I told her we should see other people.

She told me she was pregnant.

Looking back, I'm not sure whether she truly was, but at the time, as a panicked twenty-year-old, I'd tried to do the right thing. Supported her. Given her money and offered to come to the doctor's appointments.

Then she told my friends we were getting married and bought her own damn ring. My army buddies thought it was hilarious. I remember Joel cackling into his beer one night, but he soon stopped laughing when she slashed his tyres to prevent us from going on a rock-climbing weekend.

I didn't celebrate when she told me she'd miscarried, but I did feel an extraordinary relief. We weren't tied together anymore, and I thought I could finally get on with my life. But I'd thought wrong. Everywhere I went, she was there, spreading lies as she convinced more people to buy into her delusions that we were a couple.

In an effort to get away from her, I threw myself into my training and qualified for Ranger School, only for her to show up working as a waitress in a bar near Fort Benning—a far cry from the modelling she'd done when we first met. Guess all the bookers realised how difficult she was to deal with. At that time, I'd started seeing a local girl, but she ditched me after Sarah told her I had syphilis.

When I got reassigned to the 2nd Battalion in Fort

Lewis, Washington, Sarah turned into my fucking shadow, and I was the only person in the regiment actually happy about being sent to the Middle East. Honestly, I was surprised she hadn't appeared in Syria or Afghanistan wearing a bejewelled burka and professing her undying love. Or rather, her obsession.

Think I was overreacting? Imagine coming home from a trip to some godforsaken sandbox, aching for a hot shower and a cold beer, a few hours of peace in the tiny apartment you rented off-base because you valued your own space, only to find a naked psycho in your bed. My flight had gotten delayed, so she'd been there for five fucking days, and during that time, she'd managed to open my mail, redecorate my bedroom, and throw away my favourite T-shirts because they didn't fit with the image she had in her whacked-out little head.

That was when I moved back into barracks and got the restraining order. The judge smirked even as he granted it—I guess he'd looked at me, then looked at Miss Unhinged USA and wondered how much harm she could possibly do.

The answer? A devastating amount.

For a while, though, that piece of paper lulled me into a false sense of security, and I started dating Anna back home in Abbot's Creek. Nothing serious, but by then, I'd grown up enough to appreciate good conversation and a woman's company, and Anna was sweet but with enough grit to teach a class of fifteen-year-olds at the local high school. Always smiling. Being with her was easy. Comfortable.

Until Sarah showed up and burned Anna's fucking house down while she slept.

Sure, she went to prison after that, but the damage was done. A woman had lost her life because I'd been too stupid to recognise the warning signs, and worse, if what Sergeant Dawkins and now Nicole told me was correct, Anna was stuck on earth until one of the Electi dispatched Sarah to hell where she belonged.

From what I'd seen so far, no way was Nicole up to that task, and we still had the immediate problem of Shane hiding above our heads. *Focus, Sinclair. Deal with that asshole first.*

Back when I was fresh out of Ranger School, I didn't mind playing the hero. Enjoyed it, if I was honest. Top-notch training, a great team of buddies, and all the toys I could dream of meant I didn't hesitate to wade into the fray. But as I got older, I didn't bounce so well anymore. Then I came face to face with my own mortality and the heat that once burned through my veins like rocket fuel had fizzled to a tepid trickle.

That was the main reason I chose to work as a nightclub doorman most of the time rather than hunting down fugitives. Sure, I'd been discharged on medical grounds and that made a good excuse for taking it easy, but I'd made a pretty good recovery from my injuries now, physically at least. Mentally, I struggled more than I cared to admit. And it was far better to tangle with drunken assholes who couldn't swing a straight punch than criminals hell-bent on keeping their freedom. No, I didn't have the desire to fight anymore, and that included trying to get Shane Willans out of his bolthole.

But time was running out for Mrs. Harmon, and with every hour that passed, the likelihood of getting Nicole's necklace back grew slimmer. What if Corey had already sold it to fund his escape?

Funny how Nicole was growing on me. Sure, she had a sharp tongue and a personality like sandpaper, but the ghost thing was intriguing. I had a hundred questions, a thousand, but they'd have to wait until a time when we didn't have an armed asshole crouching over our heads. The biggest positive right now was that she didn't look at me like I was a freak when I spoke about what I'd seen, and I'd come across precious few believers in the years since the accident. And never one who saw the dead while she was alive.

It was my job to keep her that way while I caught us a conspirator.

"I need you to help me," I told Nicole.

"How?"

I shoved a pile of junk off a rickety wooden chair and put some weight on the seat. Yeah, it was strong enough to hold her. Now we needed something heavy. A golf club or a hammer would have been perfect, but the best I could come up with was an old umbrella.

"Climb on here. When I give you the signal, hit the umbrella on the ceiling as hard as you can, then run straight out the door."

"Why?"

"I need enough of a distraction that I can climb through that hatch without getting shot."

"But he'll hear you. You'll only have a second or two."

"That's enough."

At least, it would have been once. Years ago, I'd spent hours upon hours training for jobs like this one, but I wasn't in the same sort of shape anymore. Variables swam through my head, forming equations I couldn't solve without action. Muscle memory + desperation + adrenaline - strength - practice = ? Would my experience counteract Shane's fear?

Only one way to find out.

"Why do I have to run out the door?" Nicole asked.

"So if Shane shoots through the floor, you don't get a bullet through your pretty little head."

Nicole lost a few shades of colour and swallowed hard, but she didn't back away from the challenge. Another reason I liked her, even though I knew damn well I shouldn't. She had spunk.

"How will you get him down?"

Unconscious if necessary. "Let's cross that bridge when we come to it. Ready?"

A quick nod, and she climbed onto the chair. I passed her the umbrella, and once she'd wrapped her hands around the handle, I retrieved my own weapon from underneath my shirt. A Glock 19, ugly but tough and tenacious, which, oddly enough, was exactly how my former commanding officer used to describe me.

Nicole's eyes widened, and she scrambled off the chair to face me, hands on hips, which put her eyes about level with my chest.

"I didn't know you had a gun!" she said in a furious whisper.

"Don't worry; I also have a permit."

"Tell me you're not gonna shoot him?"

"No, I'm gonna scare him."

"But... But..."

She didn't move, and because I liked seeing the fire flash in her eyes, I lifted her back onto the chair. Yeah, that earned me an angry glare. Cute.

"I hate blood," she muttered. "Even in the lab, it's

icky."

"Well, I'll do my best to avoid making a mess."

In the bathroom, I climbed onto the toilet, careful to keep my weight to the edges of the plastic lid because falling through it into the bowl wouldn't be a good start. A smart guy would have weighed the hatch down, but when I pressed lightly on it, the wood moved a fraction of an inch. Seemed Shane wasn't the sharpest knife in the drawer. Good. I tucked the gun into the front of my waistband and bent my knees slightly. Ready.

I reached an arm behind me and held up three fingers to Nicole, hoping she hadn't quietly run out on me while I got into position.

Three...

Two...

One...

For a tiny woman, she sure gave the ceiling a hard *thwack*. And another. And another.

Get out of the fucking room, Nicole.

I didn't have time to remind her to run as I flung the hatch back and hoisted myself through in one smooth movement, just as I'd been taught. *Crouch, move, evaluate.* Shane already had an advantage because his eyes were accustomed to the gloom, and when I spotted him on the far side of the low-ceilinged space with a gun in his hands, aimed at the floor, I acted on instinct rather than following any rational thought.

Shane wasn't a big guy, and when I hit him, full force, his breath rushed out with a satisfying *oof*. Even better, the gun skittered away into a dark corner. All good so far? Not quite. When Shane toppled with my weight on top of him, he landed on the collection of plastic bottles and baggies he'd been using as a latrine, and fuck me, the stench was disgusting. Something slimy seeped through the knee of my jeans. Then it got worse. A creak, a crack, the floor gave way, and we both landed on the stained carpet in the living room below.

Fuck.

Bolts of pain shot through my wrists and knees as I hit the deck, red-hot ribbons that rippled through me and converged in my spine at the bottom of my ribcage. Suddenly, I was back in that room. A dusty house in Afghanistan, lying in the remains of a shattered ceiling, unable to move as a fucker with a scarf wrapped around his face unloaded three rounds into me. It would have been more, but the gun jammed. Lucky. The doctors, the guys in my unit, my family—they all said I'd been lucky, but it sure didn't feel that way to me.

Dainty sneaker-clad feet came into view just as my vision went white, and hands fumbled at my waist. I tried to speak, but no sound came out. Then the room, the scumbag underneath me, and Nicole faded away. Everything but the pain...faded away.

Chapter 16 - Beckett

"BECKETT?"

SOMEBODY PUSHED at my hip, and the jolt of agony that shot through my back made my eyes pop open. A groan came from underneath me, and Shane seemed to be in similar shape except flatter.

Movement from the left caught my eye, and I twisted to see my Glock in Nicole's trembling hands. No ghosts this time, but an actual, living person. Thank fuck.

"Keep your fingers away from the trigger, sprite."

A strangled sob burst from her throat. What was that? Fear? Relief? Regret that the asshole who'd waded into her life was still alive?

"Stop calling me that. Are you...? Should I call an ambulance?"

Slowly, I tested each limb. Apart from a bunch of bruises, nothing seemed too badly damaged. The pain in my back was a problem I'd learned to live with. Most of the time, it simmered along in the background, and only when I did something really fucking stupid did it become unbearable. Like now. But I'd have to deal with it because I still had Corey's friend to interrogate.

Block it out, block it out, block it out.

"No ambulance. Guess this answers your question about how we get him down, huh?"

My joints cracked as I lumbered to my feet, abused kneecaps clicking back into place and battered elbows protesting. Nicole tried to help by pulling on an arm, which was totally ineffective but kind of sweet, even if she did wave my gun all over the fucking place while she did it. Once I had the Glock back in my hand, I breathed easier.

Unlike Shane. He was still winded, and I hauled him into the filthy armchair and waited until he could speak again.

"Where's Carlton Hines?"

Might as well cut to the chase. He didn't look like the sort of guy who'd appreciate small talk. But even though he must've known what a bad position he was in, he tried to play innocent.

"Who?"

Fuck this shit. I needed painkillers, a shower, and twelve hours of sleep. Shane vomited over the arm of the chair when I booted him in the shin, but the stink barely registered against the stench of sewage.

"Just tell me and we'll leave."

"You think I'm that..." Shane paused to cough up bile, and I took half a step back so it didn't splash on my boots. "You think I'm that stupid? Caracortada said exactly the same, then he turned around and shot a girl. Fired at me too."

"Buddy, if I wanted you dead, you'd be lying there twitching and I'd be halfway out of the state by now. Who's Caracortada?"

"You don't work for him? I figured he was your boss."

"He's the asshole with the scar?" My Spanish was rusty, but *cara* meant face, and *cortada* meant cut.

"Our paths crossed when I broke his jaw, but I don't know anything about him."

"You broke his jaw?" Shane started laughing. "Then you're a dead man. You just don't know it yet."

"Why? Who *is* Caracortada?"

"Rex's henchman."

"Who the fuck is Rex?"

More laughter, and I was tempted to crack another jaw.

"Rex is the bloodthirsty motherfucker fighting his way to the top of the San Francisco underworld. He goes through anyone and anything in his path. Why do you think I was hiding in my damn attic? Word on the street says Caracortada's looking for me, and I'm not stupid enough to be walking around outside like some people."

Fuck. Aunt Tammy was definitely on my shit list. And Eric. How could a simple job turn into such a monumental fuck-up? If Shane was right, Nicole and I both had bigger problems than a lost necklace and an FTA.

"Anything about me?"

"Not yet, but if you've made Caracortada angry..." Shane shrugged. "I wouldn't stick around."

That window of time I had to catch Harmon? It'd just gotten narrower because I needed to find him fast, then get the hell out of Dodge. At least if Harmon was in jail, Scarface would have no reason to go after Nicole.

"I'll take that under advisement. But in the meantime, my boss wants Hines to reschedule his court appearance, so I need to find him."

"Court appearance?"

"For a DUI charge."

"So you're... You're a bounty hunter?"

"I need to take your buddy back to Sacramento. Where is he?"

"Fuck you." Now Shane realised I wasn't there to kill him, his attitude made an appearance. "You just destroyed my damn apartment. And you broke in. Are you allowed to break in?"

Technically no, not unless the fugitive owned the property. "I knocked first."

"Where's Carlton?" Nicole asked. "We know you're friends."

Shane turned his head to face her and winced. Probably I shouldn't have been glad he was in pain, but as my back throbbed with the results of his stupidity, I had to admit I was.

"Who the hell are you?"

"Carlton's ex-girlfriend."

"No, you're not. I've met— Oh. The, uh..." Shane flicked his gaze in my direction, but I didn't offer any help. Another prick who knew Harmon had cheated? He deserved to squirm.

Nicole's fists clenched before she answered. "Yes, I'm the other one. The one whose stuff he stole. And I want it back."

"Look, lady, I'm sorry that happened, but take my advice and forget him. He's skipped town."

My foot itched to connect with his other shin. "Forgetting him isn't an option."

"Screw you. Who cares about a DUI?"

"The family of the lady he killed while he was drunk."

That made Shane pause. "I didn't know that part."

"Yeah. Figured he didn't broadcast the information. You see now why we won't let this go?"

A glob of something I didn't want to think about dripped from the ceiling and landed on my head. This job was the worst Aunt Tammy had ever foisted on me, that was for sure. These jeans would be going straight into the garbage. At least my favourite leather jacket had escaped the worst when Shane cushioned my fall.

"Well, I can't help you."

"Can't or won't?"

"Can't." The fight went out of Shane, and he turned sullen instead. "Carlton's a self-centred prick. He almost got me killed, so if I knew where he was, I'd tell you."

"You were in the alley because of him?"

"He asked me to deliver a package while he picked up a new kitten for...for..."

"For one of his other ex-girlfriends?" Nicole asked.

"Becca. You know about her?"

"I've found out a lot since he disappeared. And the same man who shot at you tried to strangle me." Nicole pulled her collar down to show the bruises. "Carlton's the key to all this, and we need to find him before anybody else gets hurt."

"I swear I don't know where he is. I tried to call him, but his phone's been disconnected."

"Did he mention going to visit anyone?" I asked. "Friends? Family? Not his mom, because she's looking for him too."

"He didn't have many friends. Becca dumped him, and Lillian had her suspicions he was cheating with her"—he waved towards Nicole—"so I don't reckon she'd have gone out of her way to help. And look at how he treated me! He never mentioned his mom, just a grandma. In Nevada, I think."

"A grandma? His grandma's dead."

On his mother's side, anyway, and as far as I knew, he didn't speak to his father's side of the family. Clyde Harmon had left Abbot's Creek when his son was a toddler, and when I asked her, Mrs. Harmon said she hadn't heard from him since. But what about Corey? Since Clyde hadn't been much more than a sperm donor, I'd never looked into any possible connection, but what if Corey had gotten curious about where his bad genes came from? Had he been in touch with his father?

Shane shrugged, a move he quickly regretted judging by his grimace. "Only telling you what I heard. Carlton never went out of his way to chat."

"How did you meet him?"

"At Jive. He passed clients my way, and I paid him commission."

"Clients?" Now Nicole sounded slightly pious. "For drugs?"

"Rush and G3. The new stuff. Those'll give you a high like no other, and they're practically legal."

"Practically?"

"Nobody's got around to banning them yet," I told her. They were just two of the many dubious substances that had flooded into California in the last year. "But since a dozen people have died from taking them in the last month alone, it's only a matter of time."

"They don't drink enough water," Shane said. "I always tell my clients to drink plenty of water."

Speaking of water, I needed to wash my hands

before I ventured anywhere near my truck. There wasn't much I could do about the rest of me without taking a shower, and I wasn't gonna do that at Shane's place, partly because I'd end up dirtier than when I started but mostly because there was a dead guy in there. Nicole's life must get damn awkward if she had to share it with a legion of ghosts twenty-four-seven.

"What're you doing?" Shane asked.

"What does it look like?"

"You're just gonna leave me with all this mess?"

"Technically, you made it."

And I didn't have much sympathy for a man who sold drugs without remorse, borderline legal or not. If he was scrubbing his apartment, he wouldn't be clogging up the emergency room with fresh casualties.

Except when I'd finished drying my hands on a wad of toilet paper, I turned to find Shane stuffing the clothes that were strewn across the bed and floor into a duffel bag.

"Going somewhere?"

"The landlord's an asshole, and I'm not gonna sit around and wait for Caracortada to finish the job. I should have left in the first place. It's not like I'll get my security deposit back."

In his position, I'd have done the same thing. "Why *didn't* you leave in the first place?"

"My customer base is here. Getting established doesn't happen overnight, you know."

Ah, yes. The drugs. "Did Carlton ever mention whereabouts in Nevada his grandmother lived?"

"Nope. Just that she liked to play slots on the weekend, so I'd guess at someplace near Vegas. But if you do track him down, do me a favour and give him a punch in the face from me. He deserves it."

A punch in the face? No. Corey Harmon deserved so much more than that.

Chapter 17 - Beckett

"BECKETT, ARE YOU okay?"

Nicole scurried along beside me as I strode up the hill to my truck. A woman coming the other way with one of those tiny rat-dogs wrinkled her nose and stepped into the street to avoid us, because yeah, I fuckin' stank.

"I'm fine."

"Really?" she asked. "Because you look sort of stiff. Do you need to go to the hospital?"

"Aw, you *do* care." She turned pink and spluttered a bit, but when I laughed, I wished I hadn't because that sent another twinge through the muscles either side of my spine. "But I don't need to go to the hospital. I've got problems with my back that no doctor can fix."

"Have you tried yoga? I don't do it myself, but Lulu goes twice a week and swears it helps with her posture."

"It's not my posture that's the problem. My spine's made from titanium."

Nicole stopped dead, but I didn't wait for her. I needed to get back to Joel's and bathe in Lysol. Anyhow, she soon jogged to catch up.

"Titanium. You...what? You broke it? In the accident you had?"

"Clever girl."

"Shouldn't you get it checked? I mean, you fell through the freaking ceiling."

"The pain's nothing new. It'll hurt like hell for a few days, then settle down."

"Do you need somewhere to stay? Carlton's old room's small, but the bed's comfortable." Nicole made a face. "I hate that I know that."

"I don't have time to sleep. I need to pack a bag and get to Nevada."

"Don't you mean *we* need to pack bags?"

That brought me to a standstill. Then Nicole bumped into me and sent another spike of pain through that fragile tangle of nerves that I'd come so close to losing.

"Fuck."

"Sorry. I'm sorry! But you said we were working as a team, and this is my necklace we're looking for. And I apologise for being so bitchy this morning. I just... I'm just... I can't believe this is happening."

Did I want Nicole by my side? *Did I?* Until that moment, I hadn't realised how easy that question would be to answer. Yeah, she was feisty as hell with a smart mouth to match, but she was also the only girl I'd met in a long time that I wanted to get to know better. Firstly, there was the ghost thing. That day in Afghanistan had changed my life, made me question everything I thought I knew and changed my plans for the future. Ruined them. And until now, I hadn't had anybody I could talk to openly about it. Was Nicole that person? I believed in fate now, and something I couldn't identify—something intangible—told me not to let her go.

Secondly, there was Caracortada. If Shane was

telling the truth, and I was inclined to believe he was, I couldn't leave her here in San Francisco alone. Either both of us went looking for Harmon in Nevada, or neither of us did. Was it fair to drag her across two states on what promised to be a tough, uncomfortable, and possibly dangerous journey?

"Don't you have work to do here?" I asked.

"The professor'll be fine with me taking some time off."

"We'll be stuck in a truck together for hours."

"As long as you promise to take a shower before we leave, I think my olfactory receptors can cope."

"What if we catch up with Harmon?"

"I'd appreciate if you'd turn your head while I kick him in the balls." See? Feisty. "And..." Uh-oh. Her bottom lip quivered. I hated when that happened. "And I don't want to stay here while Scarface is looking for me. I won't feel safe until the police put him in jail."

"And how will they do that? You can't exactly walk into a police station and announce you've found out who your attacker is, or they'll ask questions. A lot of questions."

"I'll do what I always do—find a payphone and call the SFPD tip line. Probably once we get to Nevada. If I tell them everything I know about Macy's murder, they can start looking into it while we hunt for Corey. If Scarface is as dangerous as Shane seems to think, he should be locked up for the rest of his life."

Jail was too good for that fucker.

"Good plan. I'll make the call if you like."

"Fine. Can we get going? If Scarface is nearby, hanging around in San Francisco's a bad idea."

"Sure you can put up with me for longer than

twenty-four hours? I'd hate to wake up and find my balls missing."

"Right now, the safest place for me is beside you, even if the idea of you shooting somebody makes me feel sick."

Good. That meant she still had her humanity, whereas I'd left mine scattered between the disputed oilfields of Iraq, the war-torn streets of Syria, and the dusty, half-hidden caves and high passes of eastern Afghanistan. As I fought through six months of basic training followed by four years as an Army Ranger and a year in a hush-hush unit under CIA control, my handlers had stripped me of empathy until I could put a bullet through a man's head with less emotion than a sport shooter picking off a cantaloupe in his backyard. It took dying to make me feel again.

And there was something about Nicole's messed-up combination of nerves and haughtiness and courage and compassion and sharp edges that made me want to spend more time with her. Like a moth to the fucking sun.

"I'll try to avoid making a mess."

"Then I can come?"

"Yeah, sprite. You can come."

CHAPTER 18 - NICOLE

"YOU'RE TAKING OFF with Thor?" Lulu asked as I shoved my clothes into a bag in much the same way as Shane had earlier. "Are you sure that's a good idea?"

Beckett had dropped me at home while he went to take a shower, and I'd scrubbed myself until the water ran cold. Just breathing the air in Shane's apartment had left me feeling filthy from the inside out, without landing in...ugh—I didn't even want to think about it.

The stink. The squelch. Ugh, no.

"What happened to you raving about Beckett's muscles?"

"I thought he'd be good as a temporary distraction, not...not..."

"Not what?"

"Gallivanting halfway across the country after an escaped felon might be dangerous."

"It's Carlton. He might have skipped bail, but I doubt he'll shoot me on sight. Besides, we're only going to Nevada. You won't forget to feed George and Tempi, will you?"

She waved the sheet of instructions I'd hastily written out. "Pellets and fresh water in the evening, plus raw fruit and veg."

"No grapes. And no citrus. Or onions."

"You put all that at the bottom. Nicole..."

"I'm going. I *have* to go."

Lulu turned away in a huff and twitched her nose at the boys, who were watching us between the bars of their cage. "We're gonna catch up on *Love Inferno* tonight. I've missed three episodes. They can have popcorn, right?"

So now she was going for denial. I knew she must be worried at the thought of her bestie departing on a questionable journey with a virtual stranger, and I was nervous at the prospect too, but I didn't have any choice in the matter if I wanted to find my necklace.

"Only if the popcorn doesn't have salt or butter."

"That's no fun, is it, little buddies?" She straightened up. "Carlton's probably a thousand miles away. What if you don't find him? Perhaps you could go to Vegas with Thor and stay in one of those swanky hotel suites instead?"

Vegas? No way. "It's not that sort of a trip. This is business."

"I get that, but you're allowed to have fun as well, you know. You deserve it after what Carlton did."

"Promise me you'll be careful while I'm gone," I said. "Don't go on any more blind dates with weirdos."

She followed me down the stairs.

"I'll be good, Scout's honour. Worry about finding your necklace and getting some with that hot bounty hunter, not about me, and don't forget to give Carlton or Corey or whatever his name is a kick in the teeth with my name on it if you track him down. Did you pick up a new cell phone?"

"I'll buy one on the way and text you the number."

"Ooh, here he is," she said as a honk sounded from outside. "That's one hot truck he drives." She tried to wink, but Lulu had never been able to manage that properly and it came out as a squinty-eyed blink instead. I didn't have the heart to tell her how weird it looked. "Enjoy your vacation."

"It's not a—" She pushed me out the door, bag and all, then closed it behind me. "Vacation."

Beckett's hair was still damp, the ends curling almost to his shoulders as he climbed out of the driver's side to take my bag. He'd lied about not being hurt, hadn't he? I saw the stiffness in his gait, the tension in his shoulders. What was it with men and acting macho? Did they take them aside in high school for special classes? Apart from the soccer players, obviously—one gentle tap and *they* writhed in agony.

"Ready to go?" Beckett asked.

Yes. No. What was I doing? A week ago, I'd have laughed hysterically if anyone had suggested I might take off cross-country with Duane Chapman's hotter cousin. Yet there I was.

"Let's get this over with."

As we drove through the city, it struck me just how much San Francisco had changed. *America* had changed. It wasn't only idiots like Carlton and Shane that were multiplying like rabbits. A dark heart beat through our country, malevolence flowing through the streets, sticky like blood. Beckett stopped for a light, and a skinny ghost bleeding from a stab wound in his chest started yelling at me, his shouts loud enough to be heard through the glass. Angry. Frustrated. Discomforting. Every day, new ghosts appeared, and at times, they outnumbered the humans.

"Do you have any idea where we're heading?" I asked Beckett. "Or are we just gonna go to Nevada and drive around?"

"My cousin's on his way to visit Corey's mom to find out what she knows. I doubt it's much since she hasn't been in touch with that side of the family for years, but all we need is a name. Then we can start searching online."

"Like on Google?"

"Eric's a licenced private investigator, which gives him access to shit you wouldn't believe. Harmon has been driving him crazy for months because he's the only person who's disappeared on us without a trace."

"Because he was busy lying to me. I think that's what hurts more than anything—that he lied and I didn't even realise until it was too late."

Beckett glanced towards me, just for a second because he was manoeuvring through traffic, but his actions said more than his words when he reached across and squeezed my hand.

"I'll probably act like an asshole—hell, I'll definitely act like an asshole—but I promise I'll never lie to you."

Wow. That was... Hmm... That was weirdly kind of sweet. If I wasn't careful, I might actually start to like Beckett Sinclair.

***

It was almost midnight when we rolled into the town of Humble's Corner, population 2,317 and a donkey who could count, according to the town's Wikipedia page. I'd checked the place out using my rudimentary search tools while Beckett drove along one barren road after another.

According to Mrs. Harmon, Corey's paternal

grandma had moved away when Corey was a baby to get away from her no-good, stinkin' husband and her no-good, stinkin' son. Eric's research showed Wilma Trim had lived in the same trailer park ever since, a motley collection of shabby units surrounded by the arid plains of the Mojave Desert.

The whole town was past its prime, only fifty miles north-west of Las Vegas but it might as well have been a world away. Humble's Corner was the hangover to Sin City's bachelorette party. While Vegas had its monstrous hotels and legions of selfie-taking tourists, Main Street in Humble's Corner was quiet as the grave. Although that didn't stop a whiskery old guy wearing chaps, a Stetson, and a mighty pissed-off expression from yelling at me when Beckett paused to let a stray dog cross the road. Probably something to do with the arrow sticking out of his chest. The old-timer's, not Beckett's.

"'Bout time you got here. Took your dodgasted time, lady. I bin waitin' over a hundred years."

My own fault for opening the window. I rolled it up, but even then, his Wild West curses still reached my ears.

"Y'all will go to Jericho! Bad cess to you, you pair of varmints."

"Asshole."

"What did I do?" Beckett asked. "Are you still pissed I ate the last peanut butter cup?"

"No. Well, yes, but that's not it."

"Sprite, you've got to learn to communicate better."

"I think some antique cowboy just insulted us."

Beckett glanced all around, which was cute. I might have giggled. "Where?"

"Back by the dog."

"Ah. A dead guy?"

"Dead and rude."

He gave his head a little shake. "You know, even after seeing what I saw, I'm still not sure I'll ever get used to you meeting ghosts on every corner."

"You mean you're having second thoughts?"

"About believing you? I never said that. But our whole life, we're taught to trust what we see with our own eyes, and yet when the two of us look at the same spot, we see something different. That's...that's like witchcraft."

"I'm not a witch. At least, I don't think so. Whoever created us was hazy on the details."

"No spells?"

"Not unless you count the time I got inspired by *Harry Potter* and tried to turn my mom into a pony."

"A pony?"

"Revenge for vetoing a second popsicle. Plus I'd always wanted a horse, so I figured I'd kill two birds with one stone."

"You like animals?"

"Better than I like most people. George and Tempi definitely trump Carlton."

"Who are George and Tempi?"

"My rats."

He did a double take. "Rats? You have rats? Like, pet rats?"

"No, they just ate their way through the drywall one day, and I decided to keep feeding them." Oh, his expression. "Of course they're pets. I got them from the shelter I volunteer at. Nobody else wanted them."

"I'd never really pictured you as a rat person."

"So what pet did you think I'd own?"

"Uh…"

"I'm waiting.

"A cat? Or maybe a chinchilla. Tiny and fluffy with a sharp bite."

Fluffy? Dammit, had my hair gone frizzy again? Usually, it was the damp that made it wild, not the heat. I smoothed a hand over the crown of my head and discovered Beckett was talking garbage again.

"I am *not* fluffy. Or tiny." Five feet one wasn't *that* small, right?

"Sprite, you don't even come up to my shoulder."

"And stop calling me sprite. I'm surprised you even know what a sprite is. I figured you were more of a comic-book guy, not a folklore fan."

"My sister used to make me read her bedtime stories every night when she was little." He gave a one-shouldered shrug. "Folklore and fairy tales were what she liked."

"You have a sister? How old?"

"Just turned seventeen."

And Beckett was, what, thirty? "She's a lot younger than you."

"After my dad died, my mom remarried and had Rosalie."

He'd lost his father? He spoke matter-of-factly, his voice flat, but I knew the pain of losing a parent, that there was no way to fix the cracks in your heart where the agony leached out. Sure, the flow of pain eased over time, but it never dried up completely.

"I'm so sorry about your dad."

"It was a long time ago."

"Even so, it still hurts."

"You sound like you're speaking from experience. You lost your father too?"

"My mother. My father's still alive and well and living in Atlantic City." I managed to refrain from adding "unfortunately" at the end of the sentence.

"You don't get along?"

Was it that obvious?

"He slept with at least four other women behind my mom's back, with me *in the freaking house*, and she had to work two jobs because he couldn't hold down one. Then, after he'd left both of us to move in with a cocktail waitress he met on an impromptu trip to gamble away the last of the housekeeping budget and ignored me for most of my life, he tried to swindle me out of the life insurance settlement that was meant to put me through college."

"Well, shit."

"Yup. Mom said the only reason she couldn't call him the biggest mistake of her life was because she ended up with me."

Beckett squeezed my shoulder in a kindly gesture. "I'm sorry about your mom. Was it sudden?"

"After breakfast, she asked if I wanted anything from the grocery store, kissed me goodbye, then dropped down dead in the produce aisle from a burst aneurysm. The doctors said she wouldn't have felt anything, but..."

"That doesn't make it any easier, does it?"

I shook my head, throat clogged with emotion. Tears welled up behind my eyelids and I blinked them back.

"How about your dad?"

"Sepsis. He cut himself harvesting potatoes, and

next thing we knew, his entire body shut down. At first, he insisted it was just flu, and by the time he saw a doctor, it was too late."

"I'm so sorry."

I reached across to return his shoulder squeeze, and it was like squishing a rock. Nothing yielded. But I did get a smile.

"Why don't we worry about the present rather than the past for a few minutes? Where's this motel you booked us into?"

Since neither of us wanted to knock on Wilma Trim's door so late in the evening and risk scaring her, we'd decided to stay overnight and visit after breakfast. A small delay was better than her refusing to speak to us. And if Corey happened to be there too, it would be easier to chase him in daylight if he ran.

Google had come to the rescue again, this time with the Cherry Tree Lodge, Humble's Corner's one and only place to stay, unless you counted the rooming house that got one-star ratings across the board. The Cherry Tree Lodge scored a solid three and a half, and the worst review had clearly been written by one of those internet whiners who didn't have a nice word to say about anybody.

I'd called ahead and snagged the last two rooms while Beckett drove us through the wilderness near Death Valley National Park. Not next to each other, the man on the phone had said apologetically, but I didn't mind that one bit. Being near Beckett unsettled me in ways I didn't entirely understand.

"Take the next left, and it should be half a mile along the street."

"Want to get food before or after?"

"After." Too much coffee meant I needed to use the bathroom first.

The Cherry Tree Lodge's website showed a long, low building, freshly painted in pale pink with white trim and red doors. A neatly mowed lawn lay to the left, complete with picnic tables and a handful of sun loungers for those with time on their hands and the urge to get skin cancer. Except when we drew up outside, it turned out the owners were far better at marketing than maintenance.

"This is it?" Beckett asked.

"I don't believe it. They even photoshopped the freaking cherry tree."

Instead of pretty pink blossoms beside the front door, there was a dead cactus. And the situation only got worse when we stepped inside.

"My name's Nicole Bordais. I called earlier and booked two rooms."

The grey-haired lady shoved her glasses up her nose and studied the old-fashioned paper ledger in front of her. "You did? There's nothing in the ledger."

"Definitely. I spoke to a gentleman."

"That'd be my Wilbur." She shook her head and tutted as she sifted through scraps of paper littering the desk. "He's terrible at writing things down."

"Perhaps he put it in the computer?" I suggested, nodding at the monitor sitting dark beside her.

"That thing? Our grandson set it up last time he came home from college, but Wilbur doesn't even know how to turn it on. Ah, here it is. Yes, two rooms, name of Bordais. Dang, I wish I'd spotted this earlier. I just rented one of the rooms to someone else."

"You what?" A chill started in my toes and spread

all the way to my fingertips, and it was nothing to do with the AC, which didn't seem to be working either. "But we *need* those rooms."

"It was a late booking, hun. A young couple and their baby broke down on their way through town. Bobby at the auto shop's gonna fix it, but he can't get the parts until Monday."

"Aren't there any other rooms at all?"

She leaned over the counter to pat my hand. "Abstinence before marriage is an admirable quality. Those trashy magazines and reality TV shows have corrupted the youth of today. But the room has two beds, and I'm sure your young man can keep his hands off you for one night."

"Oh, we're not—"

"We'll take it," Beckett interrupted. "Is cash okay?"

"I always like cash, hun. Never did trust those credit card companies. Or banks. There was a story on the news the other day about a poor girl from San Diego who went to buy groceries and found all her money had disappeared because someone pressed the wrong button."

Beckett dropped a hundred-dollar bill on the counter before the lady finished the sentence. "If we could get the key..."

"Just a few rules first. No loud music, no parties, no smoking in the rooms, no alcohol on the premises, and definitely no drugs. You don't have any pets, do you? Because there's an extra deposit payable for those."

"Not with us."

"Good, good. You need to park your vehicle nose-first so the exhaust fumes don't go into the rooms, and we don't allow bikinis on the sunbeds. Young ladies should dress modestly. Now, where did I put that key?"

By the time we got into room number three, I'd heard enough about the moral bankruptcy of everyone under the age of thirty-five that I was almost ready to sleep in the truck. Mrs. Wilbur—I hadn't dared to ask her actual name in case it somehow drew forth another lecture—seemed to blame my generation for everything from the rising crime rates to the high cost of healthcare.

"Fuck me," Beckett muttered as he dumped his duffel bag on the nearest bed. "If I ever end up that bitter, I hope someone puts me out of my misery before I inflict myself on the general public."

"I'm tempted to buy a bikini just to see what she says."

"Can't say I'd complain."

"Pig."

"What if I put on a pair of Speedos and joined you?"

A flash of heat zapped through me at the thought of Beckett in tiny swimming trunks. I'd glimpsed the bumps of a six-pack through his shirt, and ten bucks said his hips had the deep V of muscle that made my mouth go dry. Tight pectorals too, and maybe a dusting of hair disappearing down into— *Enough!* What was I thinking? This was *Beckett*, and I didn't even like him.

"That won't be necessary."

Plus Mrs. Wilbur would probably get her camera out. At least, she would if she knew how to work it.

"Your loss. Where d'you want to go for dinner? I saw a diner open as we passed through."

"Anywhere's fine. I'm so hungry I could eat a— Oh, freaking hell!"

"What?"

"This bathroom has no door."

I suppose I shouldn't have been surprised given the state of outside, but honestly... No door? And I definitely wasn't surprised when Beckett started laughing.

"It isn't funny. And why did you just agree to share a room without any complaint?"

"Because we both need sleep. Look on the bright side—I'm not gonna do a runner with half of your stuff in the middle of the night."

Gee, thanks. *Keep reminding me of my poor judgement, why don't you?*

"It wasn't my fault Carlton lied about everything. And he was really good at it too."

"Hurry up and shit, sprite. I'll wait in the truck."

CHAPTER **19** - NICOLE

THE SOUND OF the shower woke me up. Ordinarily, that wouldn't have been a problem, but we hadn't miraculously grown a bathroom door during the night, and of course, I looked. It was a reflex reaction, okay? Instinct. Not to mention the fact that my bed was right next to the doorway, so glancing in that direction was practically unavoidable.

The shower curtain might have been white with a hint of mould when it was dry, but when it was wet, it went a little bit see-through, and the light filtering through the grubby window above the sink gave me what could best be described as a life-size shadow-puppet show in more detail than I ever thought possible. Yes, Beckett did indeed have muscles upon muscles, and when he turned sideways to rinse his hair... *Dammit, Nicole!*

I rolled onto my other side and screwed my eyes shut. If I wasn't careful, I'd turn into Lulu, stuck in a constant cycle of rebounds where a mistake with one idiot led to an incomprehensible craving to make an even bigger mistake with the next dick to come along. No, what I had with Beckett was purely a business relationship, and one I'd more or less been forced into against my will by the actions of Carlton and Scarface.

The water shut off, and I heard Beckett moving

around in the bathroom. A squirt of deodorant. The *shh-shh* noise of a toothbrush. Then soft footsteps came closer...closer...

"You awake, sprite?"

"No."

"Nicole?" He gave my shoulder a shake. "Wake up. We need to get going."

"I'm awake, okay?"

"Really? Because you've been talking in your sleep all night."

I cracked an eye open and got rewarded with a faceful of abs as Beckett leaned over me in nothing but a towel. *Was* I awake? Because this would have been a pretty good dream.

Until I saw the scars. A jagged starburst on one shoulder. A raised line slicing through his left pectoral. A cluster of bumps above one hip as if he'd been caught in an explosion of some sort. Before I realised what I was doing, I'd reached out to trace a finger up the neatly healed incision on the edge of his ribcage.

"That one was from my first operation." He twisted so I could see a matching scar next to his spine. "They went in twice—once from the side, and once from the back."

"And the others?" I pointed at his shoulder. "Is that a bullet wound?"

"Yeah, but it passed straight through. Then this one..."—he touched his chest—"happened when I got too close to an asshole with a knife, and this collection came from the edge of an IED blast."

"That's... That's horrible."

He looked genuinely crestfallen, but only for a second, and I realised Beckett was more sensitive than

I'd thought. Then he forced a smile. "Well, it's me. All part of who I am. Shame you feel that way, because you said such nice things about my abs during the night."

"No, no, I meant what happened to you was horrible. Not that the scars are horrible. Wait. What did I say about your abs last night?"

Now the sparkle came back into his eyes. "Just that you wanted to lick them."

"I did not."

At least, I hoped not. Because it wouldn't have been the first time my subconscious got me into trouble as I slept. Carlton got all huffy when I accidentally called him a dimwit one night, and I had to pretend I was talking about a different Carlton I'd known in high school. With hindsight, perhaps I should have listened to my inner self at that point rather than writing it off as the mental ramblings of a girl under stress.

"If you're so sure you didn't say it, then why ask?"

I didn't have an answer to that question, so I changed the subject instead. "Like you said, we need to get going. Can you wait outside while I use the bathroom?"

"I need to get dressed. But I promise I won't look while you get into the shower."

"What about when I'm in it?"

"It's got a curtain."

"The curtain's see-through." Oops. I clapped a hand over my mouth. "Or so I'd imagine."

He turned away, but not before I glimpsed his grin. "I'm not looking. Get in the shower, Nicole."

I hadn't managed to tear my eyes away from his ass when he dropped the towel, and my gasp gave my ogling away. Beckett's chuckles followed me through to the bathroom, and never in my life had I wanted a door to slam more than at that moment.

***

At least once we'd picked up breakfast sandwiches to eat on the ride to Wilma Trim's, I could focus on my food and avoid any awkward discussions about this morning's shower antics. After a moment of indecision, I'd decided my hair was too nasty to go another day without a wash and leapt under the water. I don't think Beckett looked. When I walked back into the bedroom, he was lying on the bed—dressed, thankfully—looking at his phone.

And now he'd bought me breakfast. He'd insisted on paying for dinner last night too, which made a pleasant change from Carlton, who'd always added up what each of us ate on his phone then paid accordingly. Carlton had refused to tip as well, so I ended up leaving enough extra for both of us.

Beckett had left twenty percent and gotten the waitress's phone number in return.

"What are you gonna say to Carlton's grandma?" I asked. "Will you tell her who we are?"

"Depends."

"On what?"

"Whether I think full disclosure'll help or hinder our cause. I've had relatives lie to my face while the FTA was in the next room."

"What should I do?"

"Follow my lead."

***

"What's that good-for-nothing asshole done now?" Wilma Trim asked the moment she opened the door. She was even shorter than me, despite having added three inches by back-combing her hair and pinning it on top of her head, but her attitude made her seem bigger than Beckett. She drew herself up to her full height, hands on hips as she faced us down.

Beckett and I glanced at each other.

"I'm sorry?" he said.

"My grandson. What's he done? Don't you try to bullshit me—there's only one reason three strangers from out of town would turn up on my doorstep, and it's not to tell me I've won the lotto."

"Three strangers?"

"You two and the man yesterday."

"What man?"

"The one with the scar on his face. Wore a fancy suit in this heat, and he sounded like an extra from *Goodfellas*, if *Goodfellas* was set in Mexico."

Oh, shit. Scarface was on Carlton's tail too? Maybe I *should* have stayed behind in San Francisco after all. I moved closer to Beckett without thinking, then jumped when he squeezed my arm.

"Did he say why he was looking for Corey?" Beckett asked.

It still sounded weird hearing his real name. To me, he was still Carlton and probably always would be. Or "asshole." Wilma's choice worked too.

"Said Corey owes him money. No surprises there. Corey always owes people money, and he rarely pays up. The moment he arrived on my doorstep, I hid my purse and all the rest of my valuables. That boy only shows his face when he wants something. Why are *you* looking for him?"

Beckett stuck to the truth. "Nicole here used to date him, and he stole some of her belongings."

"A TV? He had a flat-screen in the back of his car. Told me he won it in a poker game."

"Yeah, the TV was hers, but it's a necklace she really wants back. It belonged to her late mother."

Wilma gave me a look that was half sympathetic, half what-the-hell-were-you-thinking. "Why'd you get involved with him, sweetie?"

Something I'd asked myself over and over again without coming to a satisfactory answer. "I guess... I guess it was convenient."

"Convenient? Take my advice—never date a man because it's easy. I made that mistake with Corey's grandfather and look where that got me—left penniless with a difficult son and a grandkid who's worse. But after that layabout, I met my Verne. We might have fought like cat and dog every other day, but we had twelve good years together, and I loved that man until the day he passed. Still do."

Wilma wiped away a tear, and I didn't know what to say. Providing emotional support had never been my strongest suit, which was perhaps why I felt so at home in the lab. Petri dishes and test tubes didn't ask difficult questions or need reassurance every five minutes. The socially awkward scientist—that was me.

Beckett fished around in his pocket and came up with a tissue. "I'm sorry for your loss."

"Verne always said I should cut Corey off, but he's still family. We fought about that too."

"When did Corey leave?"

"The night before last, along with the gas he siphoned out of Lester Quaid's station wagon. I should feel bad for Lester, but at least Corey's gone now. I thought he was gonna stick around for weeks like he did the last time he got into trouble."

"What changed his mind?"

"Who knows? Corey never was one for sharing. One minute, he was watching the news—some story about a murder in an alley behind a bar in San Francisco—and the next, he hightailed it out of here."

A murder in an alley? Macy's murder? Could that have triggered Carlton to run again?

"Did he say where he was going?"

Wilma tugged the faded lapels of her dressing gown tighter around herself. She hadn't invited us in, and I guess I couldn't blame her for that. Who wanted to rehash a family member's misdeeds over coffee and cookies? The drapes twitched in the trailer next door, and Wilma gave the curious face that appeared a dirty glare.

"That's Lester. Always got his nose in everybody else's business. Perhaps gettin' his gas stolen was karma. Do you believe in karma?"

She asked me rather than Beckett, and I wasn't prepared for the question because my breakfast sandwich was busy threatening to make a reappearance if I didn't quell my rising sense of panic. My necklace was on the move again, and this time with a crime lord's enforcer in hot pursuit.

"Uh, I believe the choices we make can have an impact later on."

"Did Corey say where he was going, Ms. Trim?" Beckett asked again.

"*Mrs.* Trim. My Verne may have passed, but we'll always be together in spirit. As for Corey's grandfather, I divorced that lazy bum two decades ago. The whole male side of the family took after my ex-husband." She shook her head, but her tight curls didn't move. "Bad genes."

"Mrs. Trim—my apologies."

Wilma patted Beckett on the arm and smiled for the first time. "That's something the Harmon men never knew how to do—apologise." She addressed me again. "You hang onto this one, sweetie. He's a keeper."

"We're not—"

Beckett slipped an arm around my waist and tugged me into his side. When I opened my mouth to ask what the hell he thought he was doing, he shot me a look that quickly made me shut it again. Ah, yes. *Follow his lead*, even if that lead meant having his hand dangerously close to my freaking ass.

"Did Corey mention where he was heading?" he asked. Third time lucky?

"He *told* me he was going to Tucson. Said he might visit Mexico for a vacation while he was down there."

Mexico? The only thing worse than going to another state with Beckett would be visiting a whole other country. If it weren't for my necklace, I'd suggest leaving Carlton to Scarface and going home now that San Francisco seemed a tiny bit safer.

"But you don't believe that?" Beckett asked.

"Corey lies more often than he tells the truth. If he said he was going to Mexico, he's most probably gone someplace else."

"Any idea where?"

Wilma nodded, looking smug. "You look like a

strong young man. How about you give me a hand watering the plants while we talk? That man yesterday had no manners whatsoever. When I asked for a hand moving my rocking chair onto the porch, he said he didn't have time for that shit. So I told him Corey went to Portland."

"And he didn't?"

"Not in a million years. He had a few legal problems there a while back."

She'd sent Scarface on a wild goose chase? I choked back a laugh, and judging by Beckett's clamped lips, he'd just done the same. But we still weren't out of the woods. Once Scarface realised he'd been duped, he'd come back, and worse, he'd be pissed. The fact that he'd gotten to Wilma before we did meant he had good sources of information, so time was of the essence.

"Sure, we'll water the plants, won't we, Nicole?" Beckett said. "And I'll move your chair too. Where's your spigot?"

CHAPTER 20 - BECKETT

THAT OLD LADY sure knew how to bargain. Hard labour in exchange for information. There was no garden hose, only a pair of watering cans and a fucking jungle of potted plants behind her trailer. Everything from roses to peach trees to...

"Is this marijuana?"

Wilma folded her arms. "It's for medicinal use."

I should've borrowed some for Nicole. It might have mellowed her out a bit. Although it *was* fun teasing her, especially now, after she'd accidentally confessed to watching me in the shower. Not that I minded her doing that. I'd have invited her to join me if I thought it wouldn't earn me a swift kick in the nuts.

Right then, she looked as if she wanted to kill somebody, and I wasn't sure whether that was me, Wilma Trim, Corey, Scarface, or all of the above. I figured I should probably avoid putting my hand on her ass again.

"So, where's Corey?" I asked Wilma. "We don't want to miss him again."

"That lemon tree needs more water. Did you add the fertiliser before you filled the can?"

"Just like you showed me."

Maybe when I finally got off this case, I should start up a gardening service. That had to be easier than hunting FTAs and safer than being a nightclub bouncer too. My back still hurt from falling through the ceiling at Shane's, and every time I picked up a full can, hot twinges of pain shot up my spine.

Wilma remained tight-lipped until Nicole helped me to move the rocking chair onto the porch. Me? I couldn't hold back the string of curses when Nicole tripped over a loose board and slammed into my side. A fresh wave of agony knocked me for six, and this time, it was Nicole who wrapped her arm around *my* waist.

"I'm so sorry. That hurt, didn't it?"

"I'm fine."

"Does 'fine' mean the same for a man as for a woman?"

I managed to nod as I waited for the pain to subside. The doctors said my bone structure was sound, but all those damaged nerve endings took longer to settle. Eventually, I should be able to live a normal life again, but to heal fully would take years rather than months.

"Mrs. Trim," Nicole said. "We've done everything you asked. Can you please tell us where Corey went? Because if we don't follow him right away, I'll never get my necklace back."

Wilma settled into the rocking chair and surveyed her empire of plastic pots and garish statues. I'd always wondered who bought those ugly gnomes, but now I knew.

"The day before he split, I overheard him on the phone to Kenneth Corwin."

A spark of recognition lit in Nicole's eyes. "I've heard that name before. They went to school together, didn't they?"

"Elementary school. Corey used to tell me stories about their antics over dinner, on the rare occasions he behaved like a good grandson. But the Corwin family moved to Colorado before the kids started high school."

"And you think he's gone to see Kenneth?"

She nodded, and her hair stayed solid as a rock. "He doesn't have many friends left, and like I said before, he only gets in contact if he wants something."

***

"Where to?" I asked Nicole once we were back in the truck. "Colorado or Arizona? You know Harmon better than I do."

"Right now, I feel like I barely know him at all. Can somebody you work with help to track down Kenneth Corwin?"

Unfortunately, Wilma didn't have an address for him.

"Probably. But there's gonna be more than one person with that name, and narrowing it down'll take time."

"What if we get all the way there and find out we're wrong? How long will it take to get to Colorado, anyway?"

"To the state line? About nine hours non-stop. But if he's in Denver or somewhere, we're talking another three."

"And Tucson?"

"Eight hours in the other direction."

"How can we narrow it down?"

A good question. Harmon undoubtedly had the documents to cross the border into Mexico, but he hadn't done that the last time he ran. No, he'd played it safe and stayed in the good old US of A.

"Did Harmon ever travel abroad that you know of?"

"No, never. I got offered a bargain vacation for two to Cancun once, and he said he couldn't get the time off work. When I offered to beg his boss, he told me we'd both end up with food poisoning and the climate disagreed with him." Nicole bit her lip again, and I resisted the urge to free it from her teeth. "So I guess maybe Mexico wouldn't be his first choice of destinations if he was on the run."

"Colorado, then?"

She nodded. "Colorado."

***

We had a plan. If Harmon was driving to Colorado, he'd most likely take I-15 to Saint George at least. After that, he'd have the choice of taking US-160 if he was headed to the south of the state or carrying on along I-15 for the north. By then, I hoped Eric and Aunt Tammy would've come up with a lead on Kenneth Corwin.

And to check we were on the right track, I planned to stop at each gas station along the route and see if anyone recalled seeing Harmon. I'd take the live witnesses while Nicole questioned the dead. She had a whole bunch of pictures of him saved in her cloud account, photos taken in better times, and my heart lurched when I saw her grinning properly for the first time. Now if she smiled at all, it was a small, hesitant flicker that vanished as soon as it appeared, and I hated Harmon for stealing her happiness.

Yes, stopping to ask questions would slow us down, but with Scarface on his way to Oregon, we had enough time to spare, and better to confirm we were on track sooner rather than later. If we got to Saint George with no sign of him, we could re-evaluate our plan.

"I've found a list of gas stations," Nicole announced. "And I think we can eliminate anything branded as a 7-Eleven. Carlton had an argument with the manager of our local store back in San Francisco and refused to ever give them another cent of his money."

"An argument over what?"

"The coffee machine served the wrong coffee, and the guy wouldn't refund him."

"Couldn't he just have asked for the right coffee?"

"He'd already drunk it by that point. Freaking hell, why did I put up with him for so long? Watching you drag him off in handcuffs is gonna be the high point of my year. You do have handcuffs, don't you?"

"Yeah, I've got handcuffs."

We'd hit nine gas stations by the time I found a cashier who remembered Corey. Apparently, he'd been up to his old tricks the previous day, dispensing a macchiato then claiming it should have been a cappuccino.

"Who drinks half then asks for a refund?" the girl asked. "And he definitely did order a macchiato. I checked the machine afterwards. He's not a friend of yours, is he?"

"No, he's a thief." I jerked my head towards Nicole, who'd stayed in the truck this time. Apparently, there was a group of dead people right next to the store's entrance, and she wanted to avoid them if possible. She'd only planned to get out if my questions drew a blank. "He stole some belongings from a friend of mine."

"I knew there was something shifty about him."

"Did you give him a refund?"

"I had to. He threatened to tell my boss, and I didn't need that hassle."

Asshole. "Did he mention where he was heading?"

"Sorry, he didn't. Here, take a coffee out to your friend, on the house. If she got mixed up with that douchebag, she deserves it."

Back in the truck, Nicole stared at the mocha when I dropped it into the cupholder.

"I said I didn't want another coffee. I've already drunk six today, and my hands are shaking."

"It was free. A gesture of sympathy from the latest member of the 'Corey Harmon is a dick' club."

As though a switch had been flicked, Nicole's peeved expression morphed into hope. "She saw him?"

"He passed through yesterday morning."

"Woohoo!" Nicole flung her arms around my neck, then dropped them just as fast, quickly retreating back into the shell where she hid her true feelings. "Sorry. I shouldn't... I mean... There's not much good news at the moment, so I couldn't help it."

"You're allowed to celebrate the small victories, sprite." I was starting to understand her better now. Nicole never liked to draw attention to herself, and although she talked and socialised, she also threw up invisible barriers to keep anyone from getting too close. Was that why she'd dated a man she hadn't really been into? Because subconsciously, she wanted the illusion of companionship but without true commitment? "And speaking of celebrating, we should get some dinner.

Where do you want to stay tonight?"

"I've drunk so much coffee, I'm not sure I'll ever sleep again. Can't we just keep going?"

Once again, my body was letting me down. "I've got to stretch my back out for a few hours at least. Sorry, Nicole."

"No, I'm the one who's sorry. Are you in a lot of pain?"

Not as much as I could have been since I'd given in and taken Vicodin—just a low dose that I knew from experience wouldn't make me too drowsy, or I wouldn't have risked getting behind the wheel at all. But I needed another pill and a rest.

"I'll survive. Why don't we stop for food, then carry on driving for another hour and find somewhere to sleep?"

"Okay."

"You can pick both places."

"You trust me to find a hotel after the last time?"

"When you call, just check they have doors."

CHAPTER 21 - BECKETT

A BOWLING ALLEY. Of all the places we could have eaten, we ended up in a bowling alley because the specials board outside advertised steak with peanut sauce and that was what Nicole wanted to eat.

"We've got our two-plus-two Sunday offer on tonight," the hostess told us. "Any two meals plus two games of ten-pin bowling for only forty bucks."

"Sure, let's go for that."

"And do you want your steak with the peanut sauce as well, sir?"

Hell, no. "I'll have mine with the pepper sauce."

"I'll give you lane six. You can collect your shoes right over there." She waved us towards the kiosk in the corner and beamed at the couple behind us. "Hi, Wayne. Are you here for the two-plus-two?"

"We don't have time for this," Nicole hissed as we waited in line for shoes. "What happened to finding Carlton?"

"It'll take them at least twenty minutes to bring our food, and we can't come to a bowling alley without bowling."

"What about your back?"

The Vicodin had me nicely mellow now. "I'll manage. Come on, Nicole—don't be a party pooper."

Now she turned pink and stood on tiptoe to whisper

in my ear. "I don't know how to bowl, okay?"

She what? "How can you have gotten through twenty-something years on this earth without learning how to bowl?"

"Twenty-six years, and I just haven't. I've always been the girl who stayed home and studied. Lulu was the only person who ever made me go out, and she never goes bowling because she sprained a finger doing it once, and she doesn't want to risk another injury interfering with her dental studies."

"Then it looks as if I'm teaching you to bowl tonight. I take you on all the best dates, sprite."

Just as I thought, that got her nicely riled up. "This is *not* a date."

"Dinner for two, a private bowling lane, you whispering sweet talk in my ear. I'd say this is exactly like a date."

"You're... You're..." Nothing, it would seem, because she ran out of words and we reached the counter.

"What size, hun?"

"A four, please."

"And you?" The woman looked me up and down. Twice.

"A twelve."

One of the girls in the group who'd just picked up their shoes sidled up to Nicole and leaned in close, but not close enough because I still heard every word.

"Is it true what they say? About dick size being proportional to shoe size?"

Nicole went from pink to red, and I figured she'd tell the girl to get lost, but no.

"That's none of your business."

Hmm. Seemed as if she'd gotten a better look at me

in the shower than I thought.

***

"What's the secret? How do you get the ball to go straight?"

Five frames in, and Nicole still hadn't gotten a single ball to stay in the lane all the way to the end. She'd gone from embarrassed to annoyed to disheartened and even tried drawing herself a diagram on a napkin with fancy equations all over it, but the balls still rolled into the gutter.

Don't laugh, Beck.

"The key is to aim well. Just look straight at the pins and swing your arm towards the centre one."

Annnnd she missed again.

"It's impossible."

"Want me to get you a ball ramp?"

"Isn't that what kids use?"

"Uh, sometimes."

"Then no, I don't want one. How can people do this for fun? It's so frustrating."

"Here, take one of my balls."

There, that was a sentence I never thought would leave my lips. I waited until she had a good grip, then wrapped my arm around her, gently clasping her wrist to give her some guidance. She stiffened as I leaned into her, and I figured it was fifty-fifty whether I got a kick in the shin.

"I'm only trying to help. Once you've got the hang of it, you can try it on your own again."

Just like that, she relaxed, and her body pressing against mine felt far better than it had a right to. A buzz ran through me, or perhaps that was just the Vicodin talking.

She released the ball too late, but it went more-or-less straight and took four of the pins down. And I got happy Nicole, who twisted to hug me in a repeat of the truck scene earlier, except this time she didn't let go. No, it was me who broke the hold because those rare moments when she let her guard down and acted sweet made my dick swell, and I didn't want to risk scaring her off. That was when it struck me like a runaway bowling ball—I *did* want this to be a date.

Fuck.

At first, I'd tried to kid myself that my interest in her was purely because she could lead me to Harmon. Then because she had the ability to talk to ghosts, something that unsettled me and fascinated me in equal measure. But now? I had to admit to liking her in the most dangerous way a man can like a woman. The way that was liable to leave me with a broken heart if she didn't feel the same.

"Beckett? Are you okay? You look all spaced out."

"Call me Beck."

"Huh?"

"Only my mom calls me Beckett, and that's when I'm in her bad books. My friends call me Beck."

"And we're friends now?"

"You were staring at my ass this morning. I'd say that gives you some sort of privileges."

She gave me a hard shove to the chest, which did absolutely nothing. "You're a swine, Beck Sinclair." Then, "Can you help me with another ball?"

"Yeah, I can help you with another ball."

***

"Oh, thank goodness. This is nice, isn't it?"

Tonight's accommodation, the Double Nugget—which sounded more like a casino than a motel, but there you go—was thankfully in better condition than the Cherry Tree Lodge. No weeds in the blacktop, no peeling paint, plenty of doors, and a brightly lit reception area welcoming us in. And a good thing too, because I needed sleep in a hurry. We'd lost time bowling, but once Nicole started hitting the pins, she didn't want to stop, and I hated to spoil her fun. She could catch up on sleep in the truck tomorrow, but I needed to drive.

The guy behind the reception desk—Simon, according to his badge—knew how to use the computer, and he had the keys ready for us, which was another improvement on the last place.

"So that's two rooms? Are you here on business?"

His gaze lingered a little too long on Nicole, and I didn't like that one bit. "Business. Yeah."

"Well, you've come to the right place. We've got free Wi-Fi in every room, and if you need to use the fax or the copier, just holler." Fax? Who had a fax machine nowadays? "And there's a vending machine right over there if you want any snacks. Do either of you need an iron and ironing board?"

My philosophy when it came to pressing clothes was simple—if it needed ironing, I didn't buy it. "Nicole?"

She shook her head, stifling a yawn.

"Just the room keys, buddy."

Our rooms weren't next to each other, but I checked

an exhausted Nicole was safely locked inside before heading to mine at the end of the row. This time, I had a king-sized bed, which I always appreciated because then I could sleep diagonally without my feet hanging off the end. Back home, I had a custom-made bed with a memory-foam mattress—one of the few indulgences I'd spent my hazardous-duty pay on. Once upon a time, with my regular army pay plus all the imminent-danger pay and hardship-duty pay I'd accumulated over the years, I'd had a nice amount stashed in the bank. Even though I'd spent most of it cleaning up after Sarah, I still sometimes questioned my sanity for letting Aunt Tammy push me into doing her dirty work.

Although if she hadn't, I'd never have met Nicole.

Fuck, what was I gonna do about her?

I needed sleep, but it didn't come easy. When my head hit the pillow, all I could think of was her and how she'd felt in my arms tonight. If only we'd met under different circumstances… Oh, who was I kidding? Our paths would never have crossed, and we had nothing in common. A scientist and an Army Ranger-turned-nightclub bouncer?

A soft knock at the door dragged me out of my thoughts, which was probably a good thing, but who the hell was there at this time of night? I picked up my gun and chambered a round before I stood to the side of the door, out of the way in case some asshole decided to fire through it.

"Who's there?"

"It's me."

Nicole? Why was she still awake? And more to the point, why did she have her suitcase, a pillow, and her quilt?

"What's up?"

"There's a ghost in my room."

Well, life with Nicole would never be boring. "Why don't you check my room? If I don't have a ghost, we can swap."

"Can I just sleep in here?"

"There's only one bed."

"Then I'll sleep on the floor."

This was more than just a ghost. Now that I'd turned the light on, Nicole was pale as fuck, and worse, she was shaking.

"What the hell happened?"

"She's in the bath."

"Who's in the bath?"

"Charlotte. This is why I mostly avoid talking to them. They tell me things I don't want to hear. Except since you came along, I've begun to think that maybe I should do more to help, like with Macy in the alley because I know who killed her and...and..."

I wiped Nicole's tears away with my thumbs and sat her on the bed. "You're not making a whole lot of sense, sprite. It's admirable that you want to help, but that doesn't explain why you want to sleep on the floor."

"Because the guy who checked us in was the one who killed Charlotte! He must have had a key, because he climbed on top of her in the middle of the night and raped her, then strangled her in the bath. And he's still here!"

"Are you certain of this?"

"She recognised him, and she said his name was Simon and he works here, and that sometimes he slips into the room in the early hours and watches women while they're sleeping. I don't want to stay on my own."

Aw, fuck. I put my gun down on the nightstand before I got tempted to use it. What was I supposed to do in this situation? I wasn't a cop. I couldn't arrest the guy on the word of a dead woman. But one thing was for sure—Nicole wasn't going back to her room, nor was she sleeping on the floor.

"Take the bed. Let's get some sleep, and we can work out what to do about Simon in the morning."

"I'm not taking your bed, especially when your back's bad."

"I spent years sleeping in far worse places than this. One night won't hurt, and we'll be far away from here tomorrow."

"I'm sleeping on the floor."

Nicole threw her quilt and pillow down and burrowed into the pile like a gopher. What could I do but play her at her own game? I stretched out beside her and pulled my own quilt over me, and damn, it was uncomfortable. Whoever furnished the motel had picked out a carpet with the texture of steel wool, and up close, it smelled faintly of urine.

"You can't stay on the floor," she said.

"Watch me."

If I picked her up and put her on the bed, she was stubborn enough to get off it again, and I both loved and hated that about her. If she believed in something, she was tenacious enough to see it through, but she sure did leave me exasperated on occasion.

"Then why don't we both sleep in the bed? It'll be just like sleeping next to each other on the floor except without the backache."

Silence.

"Nicole? I won't take advantage of you in your

sleep, if that's what you're worried about."

"This carpet smells nasty."

"Does that mean you'll sleep in the bed?"

"You promise you won't touch me?"

I wouldn't fucking dare. "Cross my heart."

CHAPTER 22 - NICOLE

WHY WAS I so warm? And why was this mattress so lumpy?

Uh-oh.

The events of last night came rushing back... The dead girl floating in my bathtub with bruises around her neck, her wet hair dangling. My panicked escape to Beck's room when I realised her killer was the slimeball behind the desk who'd been leering at me earlier. The argument over floor versus bed. The promise I'd elicited from Beck that he wouldn't touch me.

And now look what had happened—I'd draped myself all over him like an amorous cat. *Way to go, Nicole.* Carlton had always hated when I gravitated to him like that. He said it made him hot and gave him pins and needles.

Thank goodness Beck was still asleep. I untangled my legs and rolled away to the cold part of the bed, well away from the sexy bounty hunter with a sweet side that threatened to be my undoing if I didn't keep my guard up.

After Carlton had shown me just how impaired my judgement was, I swore to myself I wouldn't get involved with a man again, but no matter how much I tried not to think about Beck, he refused to get out of my headspace. When we first left San Francisco, I'd dreaded spending days riding in a truck with him. Now? I was worried I wouldn't want to stop.

A shrill beeping made me jump, and Beck's phone vibrated across the bedside table until it hit his gun. *The gun.* I'd never liked those things, but I felt safe when Beck was around. Nobody was going to get near me if they had to go through him first.

Beck's arm snaked out, reaching across me until he found the phone and shut the noise off, and I tugged the quilt around me, suddenly embarrassed by my DNA pyjamas. The professor had bought them for me last Christmas on Darlene's instruction after she saw them on the shopping channel. Not much of a surprise since I'd relayed the message, but a kind gesture nonetheless.

Beck wore a faded T-shirt that looked like a relic from his army days, plus a pair of boxers that proved that girl from the bowling alley absolutely right. I almost wished he was the complete asshole I'd initially thought he was, because that would make pushing him away so much easier.

"Sleep okay, sprite?"

Even the stupid nickname was growing on me now. "Better than I thought."

"Same. Do you want the first turn in the bathroom? Don't worry; it's got a door this time."

That was a shame. "Please. Oh, dammit. I left my toiletry bag in the other room."

"I'll get it. Where's your key?"

See? Too freaking sweet. What the hell was I supposed to do about Beck Sinclair?

***

"If you keep this up, they'll have to give you your own hotline."

Oh, how little did Beck know. "One of the TV channels suggested it after I turned in six murderers in a month. After that, I started putting on different voices. Thanks for taking a turn."

For years, I'd been anonymously passing on information given to me by ghosts. I'd called the SFPD tip line so many times I knew the number by heart. At first, it had been exciting—I'd whisper my message, then watch the news to see what happened, kind of like my own reality show. In the beginning, the arrests had come quickly, snippets on the local network about the capture of killers following tips from some secret source. But now? The cops rarely seemed to act anymore. Two months ago, I'd told them the name and address of a man who killed his wife then blamed it on a hit-and-run, and they'd done absolutely nothing. I'd given up wrestling the remote control from Lulu in the evenings to check. It was just too depressing.

Would they bother to act on this latest information? It was the second day running we'd called in an anonymous tip on a murder. First Macy, and now Charlotte. Beck used the payphone at the gas station to point the local police in Simon's direction while I picked up two coffees and all the nut products I could eat. Hey, I might as well make the best of my time away from Lulu.

"You're the one doing most of the work, sprite." He took a sip of his drink. "This coffee isn't as good as the ampm yesterday."

"How sad is it that we're becoming connoisseurs of roadside coffee?"

"Fuckin' tragic. Did you get food?"

"Cinnamon danish for you, maple pecan for me."

Cinnamon was his favourite. He took his coffee black and strong, he favoured mint shower gel, and country music was his guilty pleasure. All these little things I'd learned about Beck in only two days, and when I thought back, I had no idea what Carlton liked to listen to.

"Eric called while you were inside. The good news is that he's found seven possibles for Kenneth Corwin in Colorado."

"What's the bad news?"

"They're all over the damn state."

"So what do we do? Where do we go?"

"My vote is that we start off in Alamosa and work our way upwards. We might get lucky and find him at the bottom end."

In the absence of a better idea, what could I do but agree? "How long will it take to get there?"

"I reckon about four hours."

"Then let's go."

We had drinks, we had snacks, and we had Beck's phone linked into the truck's speakers via Bluetooth. He had reasonable taste in music, which was just as well since I hadn't gotten around to downloading anything onto my new phone yet. But there was nothing wrong with its ringer. Lulu called just as we pulled back onto US-160.

"Where are you? Have you found that stinking pig yet?"

"Not yet. We're in Arizona, heading for Colorado. Is everything okay?"

"I think so. Some guy from your lab came by

looking for you. Said he had a question about the project you're working on."

"The professor?" Why hadn't he called? I'd given him my new number.

"No, not him. Danny? I'm sure that was it."

"Damien?"

"Oh, probably."

Why hadn't he just asked the professor? I'd emailed him notes on everything. Unless the professor had gone to a last-minute meeting. Or gotten stuck at home for some reason. What if he'd tripped and had a fall?

"I'll call him." Damien could check on the professor in my absence. "How are George and Tempi?"

"Busy eating blueberries and watching a rerun of *Celebs and their Dogs*."

"Thanks for taking care of them."

"Any time, chica. Is that big stud taking care of you yet?"

"I'm going to hang up now."

She was still laughing when I pressed the button. Thank goodness she hadn't been on speaker, or I'd have been forced to jump out of the truck and roll in front of oncoming traffic.

"Are the rats okay?" Beck asked.

"Yes, but I miss them."

"I guess I can understand that. I miss my dog. Eric's taking care of him while I do his dirty work."

Beck had a dog? "What kind of dog do you have?"

"Promise you won't laugh?"

"I won't."

"So, I went to the shelter to get a cool dog to ride around in the truck with me. Like a pit bull or a Doberman or a German shepherd. But then Gibby was there, and he just looked so sad."

"And? What breed is he?"

"A Yorkshire terrier. With three legs. Hey, you said you wouldn't laugh."

"You..." I couldn't stop giggling even though Gibby pushed Beck up a notch or two in my estimation, because who didn't love a cute dog? "You have a Yorkie?"

"He has to sit on a cushion to see out the window, but the ladies love him. Don't you have another call to make?"

Yes, but there was no answer from Damien, so I tapped out a text instead.

Me: Is everything okay? Lulu said you came over?

The professor didn't pick up either, which wasn't necessarily a cause for concern since he had a habit of turning his phone onto silent and forgetting all about it when he got engrossed in research. But the lack of communication still left me antsy.

"You all right?" Beck asked.

"I'm not sure." I explained the conversation with Lulu. "If only one of them would answer."

"Does Damien visit often?"

"Not really. Once or twice, maybe, usually to drop off papers."

"Does he live nearby?"

"A fifteen-minute walk."

"So it's not as if he went significantly out of his way to swing by. Perhaps he was on his way home and didn't realise you had a new phone?"

"I guess."

"Is there anyone else you can call at the university?"

"There's the lady who runs the departmental office.

She might know if there's a problem."

"Then what are you waiting for?"

Lynn picked up almost immediately, the same as she always did, and I explained the situation.

"I haven't seen Damien today," she said. "But Professor Fairchild's upstairs. He seemed quite animated this morning."

Which was how he acted whenever he got to an interesting part of his research. Probably everything was okay.

"If you do see Damien, can you ask him to call me?" I rattled off my temporary number.

"Of course. Enjoy your vacation."

Vacation. Right. Although as Beck's truck ate up the miles, I couldn't complain too much about the trip. I'd barely travelled outside of California and Vermont before, and now I got to see a bit more of the great country I lived in, from the scrubby plains of Arizona to the forests of southern Colorado.

I was grateful I didn't have to drive either. Yes, I'd gotten back behind the wheel after my accident, but every turn, every junction left me nervous, and I hadn't owned a car since I moved to San Francisco. Being a passenger was much better, and the company wasn't too bad either.

"Do you need to stop?" Beck asked as we approached another rest area.

"What, you didn't take me to enough gas stations yesterday? Boy, you really know how to show a girl a good time."

"I'm just thinking of all that coffee you drank earlier. Plus I'm about to eat your last peanut butter cup."

I tried to grab it off him, but he was too fast. "Asshole. I was saving that."

"What for? I'll buy you another package."

"Fine, we'll go to the gas station. And make it two packages because I bet you'll eat all of those too."

Little did I know that Beck's candy addiction was about to change my life.

CHAPTER 23 - NICOLE

BECK PUMPED THE gas, and I may have focused a little harder than I should have on the back view as he walked to the kiosk to pay. And get more coffee. Probably he was right about using the bathroom. He'd been right about most things if I cared to admit it.

Where was the ladies'? I spotted a tiny arrow pointing around the side of the building and hopped out of the truck, then stifled a groan when I rounded the corner and saw a young blonde woman squashed against the side of the cinderblock building. And I mean squashed. The bottom half of her was all flattened and misshapen.

"Hey. Hey!" She waved her arms, eyes wide in surprise. "Are you one of those Electi? You are, aren't you?"

Here we go again.

I quickly checked that nobody was watching. "I'm not killing anybody for you. No way. The best I can offer is to report the details to the police if you tell me who did this to you."

"Oh, I don't need none of that, hun. My two-year-old was the one who took off the parking brake and let the car roll down the slope. I just want someone to talk to. Do you know how long it's been since anyone spoke to me?"

"Uh, no?"

"Neither do I, exactly. Four years? Five years? My little boy must be at school now. Can you find out how he's doing?"

I didn't want to keep Beck waiting, but the poor girl was only my age. And she wasn't asking for much, was she? Not when her whole life had been snatched away from her.

"I'm not sure where to start. Facebook?"

The girl beamed at me. "My mom has a page. She used to post everything. Like, *ev-ery-thing*. I bet she has pictures, and she always set them to public by accident, no matter how many times I explained the privacy settings to her."

I pulled out my phone. "What's her name?"

"Debi Frederick. That's Debi with one B and an I at the end. And I'm Shelley."

A minute later, my small screen filled with pictures of a young boy and his obviously proud grandma—playing in the garden, carrying his school backpack, riding a pony. Shelley sniffed and swiped at her cheeks even though ghosts couldn't cry.

"He looks as if he's doing okay, huh?"

"He does. The last time I saw him, he was screaming and screaming because I wouldn't wake up, then the EMTs took him away and I worried I'd never find out how he was. The spirit guide thing said one of you Electi people might come, but between you and me, she said you were a bunch of slackers."

At first, I bristled at the insult, but how could I argue when it was true? Perhaps I should make the effort to do more. Seeing how happy I'd made Shelley made me want to help, albeit in a slightly different capacity to my original purpose. What if I tried a combination of dialogue and stepping up the anonymous reporting? That could bring some comfort to the dead, which was better than nothing.

"I should try harder, I guess. It's just that there are so many dead people stuck here on earth, and it's overwhelming."

"At least you stopped to talk. The other two just ignored me completely."

"It's something I could try—" Uh, *what*? "I'm sorry? What other two?"

"Your colleagues. The white one and the pink one. They just walked right past into the bathroom even when I begged them to stop. I get that you're busy right now with so many murders happening everywhere, but that was plain rude."

"Hold on. Back up. *Back up*. You saw two other Electi? Together?"

"Well, yes. Which was why I got kinda surprised to see another one so soon. I mean, shouldn't you be dividing the work so you cover different areas?"

"I don't know who they are. I never have. None of us have been in touch for years." Over a century, if the tales passed down from my grandma and my great grandma were anything to go by. "At least, I thought we hadn't until now."

Two of them had found each other? Or had they been in contact all along? Did they work together? If they'd ignored Shelley, it seemed they weren't doing a thorough job of completing their duties, but were they doing more than me?

"Really? I figured you were all hooked up."

"I don't even know their names. When were they

here?"

Shelley stared at the sky for a moment, thinking. Grey clouds had gathered overhead, but warmth spread through me as I realised how close I'd been to finding my kindred spirits.

"The day before yesterday."

That recently? My heart sped up. "Do you know which direction they headed?"

"Las Vegas."

"Are you sure?"

"I think they were on vacation. When they went into the bathroom, I overheard them talking, and the blonde one said something about visiting a casino, then the brunette said she'd rather skip the gambling and go to the art gallery at the Bellagio."

Holy hell. My initial shock turned to a fizzing excitement with the knowledge that they were so near.

"Did they say how long they were staying?"

Shelley shook her head. "Nuh-uh. But if I had to guess, I'd say they were on a road trip. They sure did have nice cars."

"What cars?"

"The brunette was in an old red convertible with white stripes down the side, and the blonde climbed into a real smart SUV. A black one. I think it was a Porsche."

"Were they on their own?"

Another shake of the head. "It was a man driving the convertible. And the blonde got into the passenger side of the SUV, but I couldn't see who was behind the wheel."

"Do you remember anything else? Did you see the licence plates?"

Too late, I realised Shelley had focused on something behind me, and I turned slowly to find two middle-aged women staring at me as if I'd grown another head.

"You okay, miss?" the one in the flowery kaftan asked.

"Oh, I'm fine."

"Are you sure? It's just that you were talking to thin air. Should we call somebody?"

An arm sliding around my waist made me jump, but it was only Beck. I was still at a loss for words, but at least I had some support in my moment of total mortification.

"You okay, sprite?" He lowered his voice to a conspiratorial whisper as he turned to the women. "Her mom's sick in the hospital. She's been praying every spare moment, but it's not looking good."

Now the other women smiled. Kaftan-lady's glasses slipped down her nose, but she pushed them back into place in a smooth gesture that spoke of habit.

"The good Lord works in mysterious ways." She grasped my hands in hers. "We should pray for her recovery together. Four voices are louder than one."

We all closed our eyes, and I tuned out her soft words as I thought over what she'd just said. I'd seen too much of the afterlife to believe in a traditional god, but something strange had happened to put me on the same path as half of the Electi. Mysterious ways indeed. The only question was, what should I do about it? They were so close, but we had Carlton to catch and my necklace to find. I hadn't come to a decision when Beck gently steered me back towards the truck alongside our two new friends.

"The brunette wasn't American," Shelley called after me. "I think she might have been from England, but she had a strange accent mixed with something else. Middle Eastern, maybe? I hope you find them."

I turned to offer one last smile before I moved out of her sight, then settled against Beck and let him take over as my mind churned. Now what? Should I stick with the plan or try to find my two so-called colleagues?

Chapter 24 - Beckett

"WHAT THE HELL happened back there, Nicole?"

Even though her eyes were open, she'd zoned out completely. I didn't get a single snarky comment as I lifted her into the truck and fastened her seat belt.

"Was there a ghost?"

A nod.

"And? What did they say?"

"I don't know what to do."

"The ghost doesn't know what to do?"

"Two of the others were here."

"Others? What others? You're speaking in riddles."

"The Electi. Another two of the Electi were here the day before yesterday. The ghost by the bathroom saw them and they ignored her."

Whatever I'd been expecting Nicole to say, it sure wasn't that. Four Electi on earth, needles in the proverbial haystack, and we'd missed them by two days? Gutting. I could only imagine what it was like to go through life with a strange ability you could hardly share with anybody, and the people who'd understand most had been so close before vanishing back into a crowd of seven billion people. No wonder she looked shocked.

"Were they sharing a car? Perhaps I could ask if there's any security camera footage? They might be from around here."

I scanned the area, but the single camera I saw hanging skewed on its pole didn't fill me with hope.

"They've gone to Las Vegas. At least, that's what Shelley said."

"Shelley?"

"The ghost. One of them wanted to visit the art gallery at the Bellagio. She thinks they were on vacation. A road trip in a red convertible and a black Porsche."

Ah, shit. On any other day, I'd have jumped into the driver's seat, turned towards Sin City, and put my foot down. Nicole needed to find her people, and the prospect of two other Electi being so close by lit a small spark of hope in my chest.

But we had Corey Harmon to catch, and the clock was ticking on his mom's home. One week and six days left. Could I sacrifice the future of the living for the freedom of the dead?

When I got back from Afghanistan with my new-found knowledge of the afterlife, the guilt had kicked in, and I'd done everything I could to make things better for Anna while I searched for a permanent solution. I'd spent most of my savings on her ruined house, razed the burned remains to the ground, and turned it into a garden. She'd always loved flowers. Now, she spent her days surrounded by lavender and rose bushes and bougainvillea. But was it enough?

"Sprite, can ghosts smell things?"

"No, but what's that got to do with anything?"

Fuck. "Nothing."

What if we could go to Las Vegas, find the other two Electi, then get back to the search for Harmon? Seven possible locations for Kenneth Corwin, and we had to allow at least a day for each, plus one day left over to transport him back to Sacramento. Add two more days to drive to Las Vegas and get back to Colorado. Ten days, and we had thirteen.

Maybe, just maybe, one of the other Electi could help with the Sarah problem. And even if they couldn't, there was still a chance they'd be able to give Nicole the support she needed. Support I wouldn't be able to provide, no matter how much I wanted to. Six days, I'd known her, but for a tiny sprite, she'd made a big impression and it felt like much longer. I wanted to wake up next to her *every* morning. The thought of her choosing another man because of my fucked-up past drove white-hot needles of anger through my veins.

But dealing with Sarah would have to wait because time was fast running out to solve the two other problems—Harmon and the missing Electi. I jogged to the other side of the car, climbed behind the wheel, and started the engine.

"What are you doing?" Nicole asked.

The road was clear, and I turned back the way we'd come.

"Wait! Where are you going? Didn't we come from this direction?"

"We're going to Las Vegas."

"But we need to find Carlton."

"You can't pass up this chance."

"He's got my necklace, and I need to get it back. It's important!"

"I know it belonged to your mom, but if she was anything like you, she'd understand."

"It's not just that. It's important to the Electi."

"In what way?"

"I don't know the details," Nicole admitted. "Only that one day, we're supposed to save the world and my gold talisman is a key part of that."

No pressure, then. Why didn't she tell me this before? I'd never met such a frustrating woman, nor one who fascinated me quite so much.

"Maybe the others know what the necklace does? I'd hazard a guess that whatever you're supposed to do with it, you're not meant to do it alone. What if this is fate leading you to them?"

"Fate? You believe in fate?"

"I'm starting to."

And I didn't want to tell her there was a good chance that a thieving little fucker like Harmon had sold her necklace on already. A gold piece like that? It was easy money. But we'd have to cross that bridge when we came to it. Our chances of finding two women in one city were better than if we had to scour the entire world, and if they *were* on a road trip as the ghost seemed to think, they probably wouldn't stay in Vegas for more than a few days.

"So, Vegas then?" I asked.

"Where would we even start looking when we got there?"

"At the Bellagio. If one of them's driving a Porsche, they've got money, and if they're heading to Vegas for a brief stop, fifty bucks says they're staying on the Strip."

"But there must be at least twenty hotels there. And how many thousand rooms?"

"From what you've said, you're the supernatural equivalent of a movie star. There's gonna be a hell of a lot of excited ghosts, and they'll tell you where to go."

CHAPTER 25 - NICOLE

WELCOME TO FABULOUS Las Vegas.

I'd always shied away from visiting. The city was too busy for me. Too loud. Too bright. But when we passed the famous sign, it seemed I couldn't avoid the place my whole life.

At eight o'clock in the evening, the sun was setting, its rays gradually replaced by the twinkling lights of the Strip blinking on and off in every colour of the rainbow. Glowing billboards advertised singers, magicians, and shows I'd never get to see. Everything was so big, so garish. A city on steroids.

"Have you been to Vegas before?" I asked Beck.

"Eric had his bachelor party here, although truthfully, I don't remember much of it. My biggest achievement that weekend was making it home without getting arrested."

"I can't imagine you being wild like that."

He just laughed. "I'm on my best behaviour around you."

We'd start at the Bellagio, Beck had said. He made it sound so simple, although I was secretly glad he'd taken over because otherwise, we'd still be sitting at a gas station in rural Colorado while I freaked out. I held up a hand in front of me, and sure enough, it was shaking.

"You okay, sprite?"

"No."

He gave a funny little smile as he slowed for a traffic light.

"Why are you happy about me not being okay?"

"I'm happy because you're being honest. Sometimes, it's hard to fathom you out, but if you straight-up tell what you're thinking, I can work with that."

Oh. I guess that was good. Learning a whole new person was strange, and when I reflected, I'd only done that a handful of times in my life. My parents. The professor. Lulu. Carlton? I hadn't so much gotten to know him as avoided him in the difficult times, but I couldn't avoid Beck because there wasn't anywhere to hide in the truck.

Nor did I really want to.

I took a long look at him the next time the traffic slowed. He'd been driving for over twelve hours today, but he hadn't complained, not once. How many people would do that for someone they barely knew? Beck talked about fate leading me to the other Electi, but what had led me to him? The more time I spent in his company, the less I wanted to say goodbye.

But right now, he looked tired. Dark circles smudged the skin underneath his eyes, and I'd caught him yawning more than once in the last half hour. No amount of coffee was a replacement for sleep. I snuck another glance. What were the chances of a hotel in Vegas having only one room left?

"Where are we gonna stay tonight?" I asked.

Normally, I'd have made a plan already, but I'd spent the entire drive shell-shocked. Now the hustle and bustle outside spurred me into action because I didn't want to try finding a hotel room at midnight.

"Try one of the quieter hotels?" Beck suggested. "I'm not on the breadline, but I can't run to a high-roller suite."

"I'll pay half."

"No, you won't."

Talk about stubborn... "Then I'll sleep in your room again."

"If by in my room, you mean in my bed, then fine."

Wow. That was easy. "Fine."

While Beck found us a parking spot at the Bellagio, I booked us a room at the Tropicana on my phone, guts churning. Last week, I'd fallen out of my life and landed in a strange, parallel universe. One that looked like earth and sounded like earth but where none of the principles I'd lived by my whole life applied anymore.

Focus on finding a cure for my affliction.

Avoid talking to ghosts whenever possible.

Protect my heart.

I hadn't done a great job of any of those tasks this week, but breaking the rules didn't feel as bad as I thought it would.

"Ready to go?" Beck asked, holding out a hand as he opened my door.

Not really, but I put my hand into his anyway. Time to go ghost-hunting.

Finding our first victim turned out to be easy. We passed him in the parking garage, sitting cross-legged in the middle of the lane wearing a sullen expression as cars drove straight through him. The sitting was an illusion—unlike humans, ghosts didn't get tired, so his position was more of a protest than anything else.

In some ways, ghosts didn't have a bad deal—they didn't feel pain, or heat or cold either. If it weren't for the fact that they were stuck in one place forever, I might actually have been envious.

"Hi."

The man looked up at me, and I realised he was younger than I'd first thought. Late teens or early twenties, with dark skin and hair braided into cornrows.

"Took your damn time, woman. The motherfucker that ran me down was in a white SUV. You can get the licence number from the police report."

"Uh, if the police have already looked into this, there's not much I can do."

He rose to his feet and stared down, trying to intimidate me. It half worked. Even though I knew he couldn't touch me, I still stepped back until I was squashed against Beck.

"Do I have to explain your own damn job to you?"

"No, but—"

"Just shoot her. It's not difficult. I'd even give you a gun if I was still alive."

"This is the twenty-first century. I can't go around shooting people or I'd end up in jail."

"Then how do I get out of this shithole?"

"Uh, I don't think you can."

He tried taking a step towards me, but while his legs moved, he didn't go anywhere. The action reminded me of old-school hip-hop. The running man, except without the music.

"I didn't stick around for six years for some lazy-ass bitch to make excuses."

"Beck? I think we're done here."

"He was difficult?" Beck asked as we walked away. "You've gone pale."

"This is like landing a job I didn't apply for, and somehow, I have to be a diplomat, a detective, and a guidance counsellor all in one."

"If only you could put that list on your résumé."

A snort of laughter escaped. Trust him to make me feel better in the throes of this nightmare.

"Shall we start at the art gallery and work our way out to the street?"

The gallery was closed when we got there, and for a moment, I felt a pang of disappointment because the current exhibition was a study of Japanese art I'd have loved to see. Then I realised we had no time anyway.

"Is there another ghost?" Beck asked.

"Not here."

"It's just that you look sadder than usual."

"I always look sad?"

He shrugged. "Mostly."

How long had it been since I had fun? Apart from bowling with Beck, I couldn't remember. My days were spent in the lab, and even when I did have free time, I rarely left the house unless it was to buy food. Carlton had simply oozed into that lifestyle, and I'd lain back and let him.

"I guess I should get out more. If nothing else, this experience has shown me that the world's passing me by."

"Get this over with, and I'll take you out somewhere afterwards."

My spine stiffened all of its own accord. "Like a date?"

"Like two friends doing something fun to forget a

really shitty month."

Not a date, then. That pang of disappointment? It turned into more of a chasm, but I still nodded because Beck had gotten under my skin and no matter how much I scratched, I couldn't get rid of him.

"Deal. Hey, there's another one."

A group ahead of us parted to reveal a lonely figure waving at me. A petite blonde wearing a colourful wrap dress and a pair of sunglasses. On the surface, she looked undamaged, but appearances could be deceptive.

"Where?" Beck asked.

"Standing in the most awkward place possible. Right in the middle of the hallway. How am I supposed to talk to her? There are people everywhere."

"I'll be your cover story. Just pretend you're talking to me."

Beck wrapped one arm around me and steered me towards the spot I'd indicated. If that was the result of seeing ghosts, I should do it more often. I didn't even care that his hand was a bit low.

"Tell me when to stop," he murmured.

"You don't have to stop. I like it."

"I meant location-wise."

"Oh. Right." I felt my cheeks heat. "Here's good."

Up close, the girl's gaudy outfit didn't quite counteract the miserable set to her mouth, and unless I was mistaken, the darkness at the edge of her sunglasses was a bruise, not a shadow. A victim of domestic violence? I'd seen that a time or two before, and of all the dead people I came across, those were the ones that affected me the most.

"Hey," I whispered, angling our bodies so she

formed a tight triangle with Beck and me. "I'm Nicole."

"Do they teach you to do that?"

"Do what?"

"Stand like that. The others did it too."

A long breath of relief leached out of me. All day, I'd secretly been worried that we'd made the wrong decision to come to Las Vegas, to blow off the hunt for Corey and my necklace in search of my own holy grail. But they were here. The two girls were here.

"The other two Electi?" I asked, just to make sure.

She nodded. "I understand you can't do anything to help me, but it's nice to have someone to listen, you know?"

"Sure. Do you want to talk? I'm not sure how long I can stay here, but..."

"I still can't believe I died right here, in the freaking Bellagio. But I guess it could've been worse—like if I'd collapsed at home, I'd have been stuck with that monster for the rest of my life." She clapped a hand over her mouth and hiccuped out a sob. "What am I even saying? I'm not alive anymore."

"Your soul's still alive."

"But I kind of wish it wasn't. Reincarnation would be cool. Do they take past lives into account? Like, if you got murdered once, do you get to avoid it the second time around?"

"Honestly? I have no idea. I'm not sure it's predetermined that way. And I think everything gets wiped clean, so you don't remember anyway."

"You think? Don't they tell you this stuff?"

"Nope. You probably know as much as I do."

"Really? Wow. When the guide told me about you people, I figured you were, like, cosmic gurus."

"Yes, really. In fact, you might even know more. The other girls you spoke to? I heard they were here, but I've never met them before."

Her forehead crinkled in surprise. "No way?"

This girl was adorably sweet, and a tight bud of anger formed in the pit of my stomach. Who had killed her? Presumably the monster she'd referred to earlier. Who was he? Was he in jail? I hated that someone had stolen her life like that, and if he'd gotten away with his crime... I wasn't sure I wanted to find out, because if he was still free, I couldn't do anything about it.

I must have tensed up because Beck started rubbing little circles on my back with his thumb in a soothing motion. Mmmm... I might have sighed.

"We got split up years ago, and I don't even know their names."

"Kimberly and Rania. They told me."

Now it was my turn to sob. At that moment, my emotions were so close to the surface that any news, good or bad, made them bubble over.

"You okay?" Beck asked. He had a habit of doing that. Caring, I mean.

"I have their names," I whispered back. "Kimberly and Rania."

His arm tightened as he nodded to himself. "That's good news."

"Did they say where they were staying?" I asked the girl.

"Sorry, they didn't. It was me who did most of the talking. I'd been blaming myself for so long, and they helped me to see that none of what happened was my fault. I know I'm stuck here, but at least I can live with myself now."

"If you see them again, could you tell them I'm looking for them? My name's Nicole Bordais, and I live in San Francisco. I study at the Institute for Human Genetics there."

"Nicole Bordais. San Francisco. Genetics. Got it."

Now what was I supposed to do? I could hardly wish her a happy eternity. "Thanks for your help."

"I really hope you find them, Nicole." Her sad smile returned. "And if you're ever in Las Vegas again, I'd love to chat with you."

Nine ghosts later, we knew that Kimberly and Rania had watched the pirate show at Treasure Island, the two guys with them were hot, and Kimberly was a stupid whore because she'd refused to ensure a nasty death for a lady who accidentally tripped and pushed a teenager into the path of an oncoming vehicle.

"Ugh. What an asshole. I'd have pushed him myself given the opportunity," I told Beck. "We know they came this way, though. Shall we—" He caught me as I tripped and almost fell into the road myself. "Shall we try the Venetian next?"

"No, we'll get some sleep next. It's three a.m., and you can barely stay upright."

"But—"

"They'll be asleep too. Come on—it's a mile back to our hotel."

He was right. I knew he was right, but I still didn't like it. "Can we get up early?"

"Early as you want."

When I left San Francisco on Saturday, not for one minute did I think I'd be walking down the Las Vegas Strip with Beck Sinclair's arm around my shoulders at crazy o'clock in the morning. But I couldn't say I hated it. Just for a moment, I let myself forget the circumstances and pretend I was on vacation, that we were two more tourists ambling along the sidewalk after a night at the blackjack tables. Of course with my luck, I'd have lost all my money, so perhaps it was a good thing I hadn't tried gambling. But there were definitely worse places I could be.

"Thank you for being here," I mumbled.

Beck gave me a squeeze. "Nowhere else I'd rather be right now."

I liked sweet Beck. Sweet Beck made my heartbeat go all skippy, but in a good way, and I so nearly wrapped my arm around his waist. I wanted to.

But at the Tropicana, I got incredulous Beck.

"You only booked one room?"

One room with a king-sized bed. "I said that was what I was doing."

"I didn't think you were serious."

Dammit, I'd misinterpreted everything, hadn't I? Stupid me had mistaken kindness for interest and Beck keeping an exhausted freak on her feet for something more.

"I... I... I don't know what I was thinking, okay? I'm sorry."

The receptionist's gaze swung between us like a spectator's at a tennis match. "We have more rooms available. Do you want another room?"

Beck took a deep breath and closed his eyes for a moment. What was he thinking? If only I could read minds. It sure would be a more useful skill than talking to dead people. I'd spent most of my life avoiding superfluous interactions, and now I'd met a man I really wanted to like me, I didn't know how to deal with it. Lab specimens were more my thing.

Slowly, slowly, Beck reached out and slid the plastic key card off the counter.

"No, we're good."

We were? "Are you sure about this?"

"Yeah, but if you drape yourself all over me again, I'm not responsible for where my hands end up."

CHAPTER 26 - NICOLE

OOPS. I DID it again.

But this time, instead of disentangling myself straight away, I allowed myself two minutes of king-sized bliss. Two more minutes wrapped up in Beck before I rejoined the real world. He'd warned me about his hands, but I quite liked them exactly where they were—one on my ass and the other splayed across my back while I used his good shoulder as a pillow.

The downside was the heat. Sleeping on Beck was like roasting myself on a furnace, but then again, we were both fully clothed. If I shed a few layers...

No, Nicole. Just turn the AC up like a normal person.

Except what was normal about this? Regular people didn't take off across the country with men they barely knew but who drove them crazy, then end up sharing a bed with them. I'd clearly lost my damn mind. But just for a moment, I had no desire to find it.

Beck moved his right hand, running a finger along that sensitive seam where my ass cheek met the top of my thigh, and I squirmed tighter against him. Closer. Snugger. Only for my fingertips to bump into... Hell, that wasn't morning wood, that was a freaking sapling. The girl in the bowling alley had been one hundred percent right. I'd always thought that comparison was an old wives' tale, an urban legend, but as a scientist, I believed in hard evidence and it was right there in front of me. Underneath me. Whatever.

His eyes fluttered open. "Hey."

Caught with my hand in the proverbial cookie jar. Dammit. "Hey."

"I'd apologise for my wandering hands, but I'm not sorry." His lips curved up into a cheeky grin, and he squeezed. "You've got a nice ass."

"Did you take romance lessons in high school? Because I think they brought down your GPA."

"Says the woman who was fondling my dick."

Now I scrambled away. Denial was so much easier than admitting how I felt. "My hand slipped."

"Sure, that's what they all say."

"It's true! I've got no interest in your anatomy whatsoever."

He just chuckled as he sat up himself. "Sorry to disappoint you, honey, but we've got a bathroom door again."

Good. That meant I could slam it.

Inside, I sank down onto the toilet seat and put my head in my hands. Why did every important conversation with Beck go so wrong? I'd insulted him yet again when what I'd really wanted to do was stick my tongue in his mouth. Things hadn't been this difficult with Carlton. He'd just kissed me on the sofa one night after we watched the latest superhero movie and that was that. Simple. Straightforward. Forgettable. Beck had me all twisted up inside, and I was so scared of getting something wrong that I got *everything* wrong.

Usually, I did my best thinking in the shower, but

even after I accidentally shampooed my hair twice, I hadn't come up with any brainwaves. *I* was the one who needed to take lessons in this stuff. How come I could decode chunks of the human genome but I couldn't tell a guy that I kind of liked him?

"Nicole? Are you okay in there?"

"Why wouldn't I be?"

"Uh, the door's been closed for forty minutes, and I thought you were in a hurry?"

Sugar-honey-iced-tea.

***

As we headed for the Strip, the chasm of awkwardness opened up further when Beck let me go first through the door but didn't take my hand the way he had yesterday. I'd messed up—I knew I had—and I didn't know how to fix it.

"Not that way," he said, turning me in the other direction along the sidewalk. "That's where all those people got shot at a music festival, and you'll get mobbed. I bet the others have avoided the area for the same reason. Let's go back to the Flamingo. If we don't have any luck with the ghosts, perhaps we could start asking the staff at the hotels now that we have names?"

"I doubt they'll give out that information."

"If I go in alone and ask a female receptionist, they probably will."

Of course they would. They'd probably curtsy at his feet and offer to bear his children too.

"So what am I supposed to do? Just wait outside while you flirt?"

"It's work, Nicole. This is how I do my job."

"Look, there's another ghost." I spotted the grey-haired lady standing ahead by the edge of the road, bleeding from a head wound. A mugging victim? Or had a vehicle jumped the kerb and ploughed into her? "Maybe she saw Kimberly and Rania."

"Sprite, don't be like this."

But I was gone, striding towards a ghost that a week ago, I'd have made every effort to avoid. I was starting to realise they were just people, really—some were nice, some were assholes, and there was a whole range in between. I should start a rating scale. One to ten. Unbearable to somewhat pleasant.

The lady put her hands on her hips as I approached, squaring up, and I rated her a three on initial impressions.

"I suppose you're going to tell me you're on vacation too."

Or maybe a two.

"What do you mean?"

"Your friends are shirking their duty. I've been standing here for three darn years, and they're going to a casino? They don't have time for that, and you should tell them so."

"Excellent idea. Where are they?"

She extended one clawed digit. "Over there in Planet Hollywood. You need to go and get them back out here to deal with my problem."

They were in the hotel? Right now? I ran. How many rooms did Planet Hollywood have? I'd have to apologise to Beck and get him to do his flirting thing and— "Sorry!" I called out to a man whose foot I tripped over.

"Nicole? Where are you going?"

"They're in here somewhere. We need to…"

I trailed off because suddenly, it didn't matter anymore.

Was I seeing what the ghosts saw? Two magical, ethereal beings that flowed and shimmered as they moved?

Their heads snapped around, and they looked at me the way I imagined I was looking at them. Mouths open, eyes wide and full of shock. The blonde clutched at the brunette's arm.

"Is that…?" Beck asked.

I managed to nod.

The two men standing behind them looked adorably confused. And hot—the ghosts had been absolutely right on that. The one on the right was almost as big as Beck, but he hovered over the blonde with a protectiveness that made my heart seize.

The others moved first. I couldn't—my feet had frozen to the spot.

Then they hugged me, and I was home. In a busy hotel in Las Vegas that I'd never stepped into before, I'd finally found my place in life.

"Nia, what's going on?" the smaller guy asked. "Who's this?"

"One of us."

Her words meant they knew. The other men knew who we were, and they were there for my sisters. My *sisters*. That's who they were. I felt it—a strange wave of energy flowing through my veins, fizzing and buzzing, giving me new strength.

Tears cooled on my cheeks, and I tried to blink them back but they kept coming. The blonde was sniffing too, and the brunette cursed under her breath as she freed a hand to wipe her eyes.

"Bloody hell. Am I dreaming this?"

"I've been looking for you," I blurted.

They glanced at each other.

"I don't understand," the blonde said.

"We were in Colorado yesterday, and a ghost at a gas station told me you were on your way to Vegas, so we dropped everything and followed. I know that might sound crazy, but I've spent my whole life wondering who you were, and I couldn't not come. Have you always known each other?"

The blonde sucked in a breath. "Where do we start? I'm Kimberly, and this is Rania."

"I'm Nicole. And this is Beck."

The smaller of the men stepped forward. "I'm Will, and this is Reed. I realise we need to talk, but can I suggest we go somewhere more private?"

A small crowd had gathered, watching three overly emotional women with undisguised curiosity. Yes, Will was right. And also English. He sounded as if he'd stepped off the set of *Sherlock*.

"Our hotel room?" Kimberly suggested. "I don't care about going to the spa anymore."

Room? It was a suite. A fancy one at the top of the Mandarin Oriental. Kimberly called down for drinks while I squashed next to Beck on a sofa. We'd found them. We'd really found them, but I'd been so focused on the chase I hadn't given one tiny thought as to what we did next.

Thankfully, Will didn't seem so off balance.

"This wasn't quite what I expected when we came to the US on holiday, but it's certainly an interesting development. Do you live around here?"

"San Francisco. And Beck's from Sacramento."

"You're on vacation too?"

"Uh, not exactly. We're... We're..."

Beck took over. "We're hunting down Nicole's ex-boyfriend."

"Why?" Kim asked. "Sometimes, it's best to just burn their stuff and move on."

"He's in violation of his bail bond."

Her mouth formed a perfect little O that reminded me of Lulu. Kim was one of those perfectly put-together women who always made me feel inadequate—neatly styled hair, airbrushed make-up, accessories and shoes that matched her oh-so-fashionable outfit. Today, she'd worn cream pants with a crease down the front, a pale-pink silk camisole, and shiny hot-pink pumps. Dammit, she even managed to coordinate with her aura.

"You dated a criminal?"

"I didn't know he was a criminal at the time. He lied about everything."

"I guess I can understand that. I accidentally went on a date with a psycho-nuts murderer once. He seemed nice until he tried to kidnap me."

"A murderer? Carlton killed a lady, but he ran her over when he was drunk, so I think it was an accident."

"It's a really long story. But it turned out good in the end because that was how I met Reed. He was the private investigator I hired to help me find the lunatic."

"And did he? Find him, I mean."

"It was a team effort." Kimberly shuddered even though it wasn't cold. "And he's gone now."

"Gone as in...prison?"

"I shot him," Rania said softly. "To free one of the spirits."

Holy shit. "You mean you actually do your job?"

"Not often. Not anymore. But when I lived in Syria, I didn't have a choice."

Beck seemed less shocked than me by Rania's revelation, and I gripped his hand for support. There was so much to process, and as Kimberly had said, where did we start?

"You're Syrian?" I asked, desperately trying to keep my voice level. Was that where Rania's strange, underlying accent was from?

"Yes, but I live in England now. With Will. He's also a private investigator."

"How did you meet?"

"At work. My boss's daughter got killed, and Will was hired to solve the case, and then one murder turned into two..."

"And did he solve it?"

"Yes, thank goodness. Her spirit was driving me insane."

"And what happened to the culprit?"

Rania shifted in her seat. "One's in prison, and the other... Honestly, I'm not some bloodthirsty killer. It was more of an accident."

"Stay calm," Beck whispered in my ear. "Can we start at the beginning here? Because I for one only walked into the middle of this last week, and I've got a lot of catching up to do."

Reed nodded. "Kinda crazy, isn't it? Suddenly being asked to believe in ghosts?"

"I already believed in ghosts. It was being asked to believe that Nicole here wa a supernatural assassin that I struggled with." He glanced sideways at Rania. "You, I don't need so much convincing about. You've got an edge. I see it in your eyes."

"Why did you believe?" Rania asked, not bothering to deny his assessment of her. "Few people are so open-minded."

"I died once. In Afghanistan. Just for a few minutes, I saw what you see."

Cue a virtual interrogation from Will and Reed. It seemed that asking questions came naturally to them. Beck took it with good grace, and when he said he'd been an Army Ranger, that was met with a low whistle from Reed.

"Nothing but respect for you guys. I'm a vet too, but regular infantry. Will was a cop in a previous life."

"What's an Army Ranger?" I asked. "Is it anything like a park ranger?"

All three men burst out laughing, which wasn't really fair because how was I supposed to know anything about military matters? If they'd asked me to name the twenty amino acids that appeared in the genetic code, I could have done it in a heartbeat.

"Special forces, babe," Reed told me. "Your man's a badass."

"Oh, he's not my man."

Reed looked pointedly at our joined hands. "Really?"

I let go in a hurry. "I'm not totally sure what's going on."

More laughter. I was so out of my depth here.

A room-service cart arrived with enough food to feed half of San Francisco, and this time, we *did* start at the beginning. Rania told tales of her upbringing in Syria, the war that followed, and the death of Helene, her former colleague in England, and how she'd been cajoled and blackmailed into solving her murder and that of another ghost who'd inhabited the same building. Helene was still stuck there, apparently.

Then came Kimberly's story, starting with her childhood as the daughter of a political lobbyist who'd had her mom committed when she admitted she saw ghosts. No wonder Kimberly kept her abilities quiet. Then she moved on to her job as a wedding planner and finally her abduction, which had apparently made the news all over the United States, except I'd missed it on account of Lulu finding the real world too depressing to watch.

My turn arrived, and I started with the basics. My early years in Vermont had been tough with little money, but there'd been no shortage of love from my mom. Talking about her death, even remembering it made me choke up, but Kimberly and Rania were there with hugs, and I realised that while I'd lost my first family, I'd gained a new one that day in Las Vegas. Talking about my studies was easier, but then I had to rehash my mistakes with Carlton for an audience. I half expected them to look down on me for being so stupid, but all I got was sympathy.

"When you say he stole your necklace, do you mean your gold piece?" Rania asked.

I nodded miserably. "He took it from around my neck while I slept."

She fumbled around her collar and drew out her own talisman, hanging securely on a leather cord. Kimberly did the same, except she wore hers on a gold chain. Two abstract shapes, each with a hole in the middle and the same ancient markings that had become so familiar to me.

"Mine fits in here." I ran a finger along one edge of Kimberly's. "I recognise the outline."

"Then we've got to find it," Rania said. "My mother told me these charms were important to us, but I don't know why and neither does Kim. Do you?"

I shook my head. "My mom told me the same. But what do you mean *we've* got to find it? You're on vacation."

"Not anymore. This is far more important. And without wanting to sound rude, we've probably had more practice at this than you."

"My pet rats have had more practice at this than me."

Kimberly's mouth dropped open. "You keep rats as pets?"

"They're cute, honestly. Tempi's quite timid, but George gets curious about everything."

"Rania, do you like rats?"

"I used to eat them in Syria when the food ran out. They taste okay."

Beck burst out laughing, and I elbowed him in the side, only for him to grunt in pain.

"Sorry! I'm so sorry."

"Buddy, are you okay?" Reed asked.

"I have some back problems."

"Like arthritis?"

"Like my spine's made of metal."

"Fuck."

"I'm learning to live with it. Don't worry about me—Corey Harmon is the bigger problem. Corey Harmon, also known as Carlton Hines. Are you serious about lending a hand?"

"Will and Rania have a flexible schedule and so do

I. Kim needs to be back in Maryland for her next wedding, which is two weeks from Saturday. We're all yours until then. To tell you the truth, I'm sick of watching Kim lose money in the casino, anyway."

"I won three hundred dollars last night!"

"But you spent five hundred to do it, sweetheart."

Kim picked up her drink, a garish cocktail despite the early hour, and sipped through the straw with no further argument. Clearly Reed was right, and I stifled a giggle. I liked these people. The camaraderie, the banter, the way they had each other's backs. And by some strange genetic quirk, I'd ended up as one of them. I only hoped I could live up to their expectations as well as my own.

CHAPTER 27 - BECKETT

"GOOD NEWS, BUDDY." Eric sounded abnormally upbeat. As if his good mood was forced, almost. "I've eliminated one of our seven possibles. The Kenneth Corwin in Castle Rock grew up in New York City. He's an Elvis impersonator, and I found a newspaper article about him."

That *was* good news, but it didn't explain Eric's demeanour.

"How's the baby? Shown any signs of arriving yet?"

"Lucy thought she was going into labour yesterday, but it turned out to be gas."

A simple "no" would have been plenty. "And how are things in Abbot's Creek?"

Silence. So that was where the problem was.

"What aren't you telling me?"

"It might be nothing."

"How about you let me make that decision?"

Eric took a deep breath. Paused. Shit. He normally delivered gossip with the enthusiasm of a cable news anchor, so this was bad.

"Bethy Fincher thinks she saw Sarah yesterday."

Yeah, now I understood why he didn't want to tell me.

"Is she sure? How old is she now? Ninety?"

"Eighty-six according to Aunt Tammy, but you

know how nosy Bethy is, and she never forgets a face. She swears Sarah was in the diner on Spruce Street, only now she's got brown hair. I guess that could be a wig."

Bethy and her friends attended public court hearings like other people went to the theatre. After a particularly good trial, they held a potluck supper and dissected the happenings over iced tea and ginger beer on the back porch of Bethy's ranch house. I knew she'd attended Sarah's trial because I'd been there too, so if anybody was gonna recognise the bitch, it was old Mrs. Fincher.

Fuck. Perhaps that was why my attorney had emailed me? That message I'd carefully filed in the "later" folder.

"And Lucy says Gibby kept barking at the window yesterday evening," Eric continued. "But when she went outside, there was nobody there."

"Stay close to Lucy. If Sarah's off her meds again, who knows what she'll do."

"I will."

"And if you see the bitch, do me a favour and tell her I'm dead."

"She'd probably set up camp on your grave, buddy."

I was careful to keep my face neutral when Eric delivered the news because Nicole was sitting across the room, sneaking glances at me every so often, as was her habit. She thought I didn't notice, but I saw them. Fucking treasured every one because it meant I was gradually reeling in my nervous little sprite.

Nicole threw off more mixed signals than a corrupt politician, but after last night, when she muttered in her sleep about all the filthy things she wanted me to do to her, I realised she was fighting a battle with herself. Head versus heart, fear against want. I'd planned to bide my time and wait for her head to catch up with her subconscious, but if Sarah was back? That changed everything.

I couldn't have a future with Nicole if Sarah was in it too.

"There's always cremation," I told Eric.

"What're you gonna do about her?"

"Who the hell knows? Right now, I need to focus on finding Harmon and getting him back into court."

And work out what to tell Nicole. She wasn't the kind of girl a man slept with then abandoned by the kerb like yesterday's trash, and if I didn't keep my dick under control, that was where we were headed.

"Good luck." Eric's voice said I'd need it. "I'll call if I find out anything else."

Two hours later, we had a plan. Each pair would take two Kenneths to split the load, and we'd have help with background checks from a hacker buddy of Will's plus a cop Reed knew. Neither form of assistance was particularly legal, but as long as we didn't get caught, I didn't care. I'd bent the law enough times in the past and gotten away with it.

I wasn't entirely convinced of Kimberly's competence, but Reed seemed to know what he was doing, and if he wanted his girlfriend with him, I had to respect that. As for Will and Rania, their biggest problem was that they were both from overseas and couldn't blend in, but if they posed as tourists, they'd most likely get away with the subterfuge. And I didn't worry about their abilities. In fact, I had the opposite concern in Rania's case. She had that hardness in her eyes, a haunted yet steely resolve I'd seen in my former colleagues as well as my reflection in the mirror every morning. She'd seen tough times, and no matter how much Will tried to shelter her from the past, she was a killer.

Yes, Rania *could* free Anna, but from what she'd said, I knew she wouldn't want to. And how the fuck did I even broach the subject? I'd held back the truth from Nicole, and I'd known Rania for less than a day.

"Do you guys want to stay here tonight?" Kimberly asked. "I can have them find another room."

"I've already got a room at the Tropicana." I could eat the sixty bucks a night, but after today's revelations, I needed space to think. "But if Nicole wants to stay here..."

She didn't bite. "I'll come with you."

I didn't want to be that man—the one who led a girl on then let her down—but the asshole in me wouldn't say no to sharing a bed with Nicole again. Nothing would happen. I'd keep my hands off and be a pillow, no more.

And if the past was any indication, I'd spend the whole night wondering what the hell to do about the Sarah situation.

***

Fuck my damn life.

Nicole let out a quiet whimper as she rubbed her pussy against my thigh, and I watched in guilty fascination as her hand crept between her legs. She may masquerade as a strait-laced scientist during the day, but at night when she slept, she turned into a dirty little succubus. My cock was hard enough to hammer nails, and if she so much as twitched wrong, it'd explode.

My hands clenched into fists as slender fingers moved underneath those ridiculous pyjama shorts, circling and stroking as her subconscious sought relief. If that crazy bitch wasn't waiting for me back in Abbot's Creek, I'd have told my willpower to take a hike and finished the job for Nicole myself.

What was she thinking about? More importantly, *who* was she thinking about? I wanted to be that man, but at the same time, I feared it.

"Beck," she gasped as every muscle went rigid.

Guess that answered that question.

I couldn't resist holding her closer as she relaxed, and when she didn't wake, I pressed a kiss to her hair. The shampoo she used smelled like a strawberry milkshake. Did she know that was my favourite flavour? Probably not, because we'd spent too much of our time together worrying about shit like Corey Harmon and not enough time on the normal stuff. Nicole was the kind of girl I wanted to take on a weekend date to a secluded cabin so we could spend the whole time talking and I wouldn't have to share her with anyone else. And yes, I do mean talking. I liked to know every inch of a girl's mind as well as her body.

Unless that girl was Sarah. Her, I'd willingly leave to the men in white coats.

Should I try moving house again? Tempting, but she'd track me down. She'd already proven herself proficient at finding me, and much as I used my natural charm to get ahead in the game, so did she. As a human Barbie doll, she only had to stick out her cleavage and smile and men handed over information that was supposed to stay private. Aunt Tammy would have given her a job if she hadn't been a raving lunatic.

No, moving was the last resort. I was sick of starting my life over, anyway.

My best bet was to get her locked up again, but how? And who decided to let her out in the first place? She should have gotten life for first-degree murder, but her attorney convinced the jury she didn't mean to do it and argued it down to voluntary manslaughter instead. Six years, and she'd gotten out in three. Was this another result of the increase in crime rates? Prisons were full—the crowded conditions had been splashed all over the news recently—but rather than overhaul the system, the state had rewritten the parole laws instead.

Why worry about building new prisons when they could just let the prisoners out?

I fired off a quick message to Eric: *Did Sarah get released or did she escape?* If it was the latter, I'd personally hog-tie her and dump her back in her padded cell.

I'd resorted to breathing exercises by the time the sun crawled over the horizon. In on three, out on six, the kind of meditation that had helped me to concentrate on long surveillance stints. Except that day, as my mind replayed Nicole pleasuring herself over and over, I struggled to focus. When the alarm went off, I'd barely slept at all.

Nicole stirred in my arms, and fuck, I could still smell her arousal. If I touched her, I bet she'd be dripping. *If I touched her, we wouldn't leave this hotel room for a week.*

"You awake, sprite?"

"Not really."

"Sweet dreams?"

Fuck, why did I ask that? She raised her head to look at me, and I brushed the waterfall of hair away from her face.

"I don't really remember."

Oh, she did. Otherwise she wouldn't have turned scarlet.

"Ready for a trip to Colorado?"

"Did yesterday actually happen? I still can't believe it happened. Will you pinch me?"

I squeezed her butt instead, which was a dick move for so many reasons, but instead of sprinting into the bathroom like she did yesterday, she curled tighter against me. Shit. This was the romantic equivalent of a slow-motion car crash. Nicole's mess colliding with my screwed-up past.

"How's your back feeling now?" she asked.

"Better."

Today, I'd go without the Vicodin because I needed all my wits about me. An edge of pain would only sharpen my senses. We'd drawn western Colorado, where Kenneth Corwin number one lived with his girlfriend in a third-floor apartment in Montrose and Kenneth Corwin number two owned a ramshackle house on a small lot forty miles outside of town. The first option seemed unlikely, because what girlfriend would put up with an idiot like Harmon sleeping on the couch? But it still needed to be checked.

And it needed to be checked quickly because I couldn't deal with Nicole in my bed for much longer.

CHAPTER 28 - BECKETT

"IT'S NOT HIM."

Easiest elimination of a suspect ever. Nicole talked to the ghost outside Kenneth Corwin number two's home, a ghost who'd been standing in the same spot for the past seventy years and watched as young Kenneth moved there with his parents from Texas sixteen years ago. They'd arrived with Texas licence plates, Texas accents, and constant complaints about the weather in Colorado that continued to this day. No, this family of Corwins hadn't come from Sacramento.

Which left us with the apartment to check.

Rania called while we were en route to say Corwin number three was a bust as well. She'd searched his home—or shack, as she described it—while he went to work at the local feed store, and a helpful spirit who'd died back in the days of Christopher Columbus told her he hadn't had any visitors for over a year.

Nicole had been quiet on the trip to Colorado. Thinking. In all honesty, I'd rather she kept talking because I couldn't begin to guess what was going on in that complicated mind of hers. Halfway, Eric sent me a text to say Sandra Cummins swore she'd seen Sarah at the pharmacy near my house, and ever since, I'd been checking the remote-monitoring app for my security system with an obsession that bordered on Sarah's. Set one foot over the threshold, bitch...

"Are you okay, Beck?"

"Why do you ask?"

"You seem distracted."

"Just thinking through the logistics of this job."

I almost wished I was back in Afghanistan. Sure, the likelihood of death was higher, but at least over there, the rules were simple for my unit. Get in, eliminate the bad guys, and get out again, preferably without being seen.

"I've been thinking too." Uh-oh. "Is it strange that I'm happy? I know we're right in the middle of a nightmare with Carlton and Scarface and my missing necklace, but I've found Kimberly and Rania." She did that sideways glance thing again. "And you."

Ah, shit. *Tell her. Just tell her.*

"Which is really strange because you're not the kind of guy I'd normally talk to at all. I guess it goes to show that we shouldn't judge on appearances, huh? And the bed-sharing thing's weird, but I sleep better with you there, which is odd because with Carlton I used to lie awake for hours wishing he'd quit with his annoying little snuffle-snorts... You didn't need to know that, did you? This is why I'm awful with men. I never know what to say, so I end up rambling on about random stuff and... I'm doing it again. Uh, I like you. That's it."

What the hell was I supposed to say to that? She was offering me a piece of her damn heart, and I had to crush it.

"Beck?"

"I like you too, sprite."

You fucking coward, Sinclair.

***

Two miles outside of Montrose, and we'd stopped to stretch our legs at one of our favourite places—another gas station—when Nicole's phone buzzed.

"Huh, that's odd."

"What's odd?"

"Damien says he didn't come to my place the other day. His boyfriend took him on a surprise minibreak. So why did Lulu say he did?"

"I don't know. Maybe she got the name wrong? Why don't you ask her?"

But as Nicole pressed the phone to her ear, a sliver of doubt needled at me. Someone had visited, and if it wasn't Damien, who else could it have been? The obvious answer was a scout, someone posing as him to get information on Nicole's whereabouts—probably one of Rex's crew—which meant they knew her address. How could I let her go home unprotected once we found Carlton? Men like Rex didn't appreciate being crossed, and revenge came high on their list of priorities.

I should've introduced him to Sarah. They'd have made a great couple.

"Lulu isn't answering. She normally goes to yoga on a Wednesday evening, and the teacher gets really snippy if phones ring in class. I'll have to try again later."

"Let's do a drive-by of this apartment. You can check for ghosts while I get an idea of the security. Then we should find a place to stay tonight."

"I'll look for a hotel while you drive." Nicole held up her phone, and it vibrated in her hand. "Ohmigosh!

They found him! Reed and Kimberly found Carlton. We need to go to Colorado Springs."

She flung her arms around my neck and kissed me, just a quick peck, but as she stood on tiptoes with the length of her body pressed against mine, I saw what she wanted. Those blue eyes were filled with hope and expectation, expectation I'd put there with all the wrong signals I'd been giving her.

This couldn't carry on. It wasn't fair. Nicole had to know the truth, and I had to face the consequences of my actions.

CHAPTER 29 - NICOLE

WHAT WAS WRONG? The only time I'd ever made the first move on a guy, and Beck was just staring at me like I'd lost my mind. Had I? I mean, we'd been sharing the same bed for days, so a kiss didn't seem entirely unreasonable. And he'd said he liked me. I'd assumed that meant he *liked* me, but what if he just meant he was fond of me in the same way that I was fond of Reese's Pieces?

Had I miscalculated yet again?

"Beck?"

"Nicole, I can't do this."

"Do what?"

He gently unpeeled my arms from around his neck and stepped back a pace. "This. Us."

Oh, hell. I *had* messed everything up. Stupid, *stupid* Nicole. This was why I should never have left the lab. I was far better at understanding people when they were just base pairs in a Petri dish. Actual walking, talking humans? Forget it.

A peal of hysterical laughter burst from my lips. "So sorry. I just got overexcited again." I opened up the distance between us to a metre. "You can probably tell I don't get out much."

"We need to talk."

"Talk? No, we don't. We need to get to Colorado

Springs. Kimberly said Reed'll call with an update in a few minutes, and I guess we'll need to capture Carlton as soon as possible, so we should head off right away."

I didn't look back as I scrambled into the truck and fastened my seat belt. If they *had* Carlton, this whole nightmare could be over in just a few days. Maybe even one if we got lucky. One more day. *One more day.* One more day until I could go back to my regular life among electron microscopes and centrifuges and ridiculously long grant-proposal forms. One more day until I could go home.

The cab felt much smaller when Beck climbed behind the wheel. Before, I'd relished the closeness, but now I wanted to ride in the back seat.

Focus on the future, Nicole. Don't get distracted by the hot bounty hunter. If I could get DNA samples from Kimberly and Rania, I'd be able to map the similarities between us. Would they agree? I'd keep the results confidential, of course, and—

"Nicole, it's not what you think."

"It doesn't matter. I totally get it. I'm not your type, and you were just being nice earlier. You belong with a statuesque blonde supermodel, not a lab rat who gets so engrossed in research she forgets to eat."

"I do not belong with a blonde model." His vehemence surprised me. "And if the circumstances were different, I'd have been eating your fucking tonsils back then."

"Circumstances? What circumstances? If it's about the ghost thing, once Carlton's in jail where he belongs, I'll just go back to pretending I can't see them like I always have."

"The ghosts aren't the problem. Well, they are, but

not in the way you think."

"What do you mean?"

"It's a long story."

"We've got all the way to Colorado Springs, so feel free to start." I folded my arms. "Anytime soon."

I was back to being bitchy, I knew that, but I didn't care. It was the only way I could protect the fragile jumble of emotions threatening to burst out through the cracks in my defences.

"Ten years ago, I made the worst mistake of my life. She was called Sarah, and she makes Corey Harmon look like a saint. She lied about me, she stalked me, and then she killed my girlfriend."

Beck's tale of Sarah's depravity was so wild, so crazy, I had to google it on my phone to see if it was true. But there it was, in black and white on the Sacramento Bee's website. Three years ago, Sarah Renwick had killed Anna Quinn in a fit of jealous rage over an unnamed man.

"It wasn't until I died in Afghanistan that I realised the extent of the problem," Beck continued. "That Anna must still be trapped in Abbot's Creek at the spot where she died, and she'd never be free unless one of the Electi killed Sarah."

Ah. *Now* I understood. And you know what? That was actually worse.

I'd been a tool for Beck; that was all. A means to an end.

Yesterday, I'd been happy. Today, I felt as if my heart had been gouged out with a melon baller.

"And that's why you kept helping me, wasn't it?" I said. "Because you want me to kill Sarah and free Anna."

"No! I'll admit the thought crossed my mind, and that was why I'd originally hoped to find one of the Electi, but the moment I met you, I knew you wouldn't. *Couldn't.* That's not who you are, and I'd never ask you to change."

"What about Kimberly and Rania? You were the one who pushed to go to Las Vegas."

He didn't answer, which was an answer in itself. My eyes began prickling. Dammit, why did this keep happening? Every time I met a guy I vaguely liked, they just used me then threw me away when they were done.

Never again. I was never going through this again. I'd rather stay celibate for the rest of my life than open myself up to more pain.

"Just find Corey, okay? Make him say what he did with my necklace, then get the hell away from me."

At least at the end of this, I'd still have Kimberly and Rania, and much as I hated to admit it, I had to thank Beck for that. They didn't have any ulterior motives for talking to me, of that I was certain. We were connected, and we always would be now that we'd found each other. And Lulu and Damien and the professor would be waiting for me back in San Francisco. I wouldn't be alone.

"Sprite..."

"Don't start with the nickname, okay? I'm Nicole. You lost the right to call me anything else when you lied to me."

"I never lied."

"All right—when you left out great chunks of the truth."

And to think I'd wanted a relationship with this man. What would it have been based on? A shaky foundation of shadows and whispers and snippets of information doled out as Beck saw fit? That was worse than Carlton's flat-out dishonesty.

"I'll do everything in my power to get your necklace back. I promise."

Arms folded, I twisted in my seat so I didn't have to look at him anymore. What a mess. As the truck ate up the miles, I pulled *Pride and Prejudice* out of my purse in an attempt to distract myself, but reading about Mr. Darcy only made me sniffle, and when Beck offered me a tissue, the sniffles turned to proper tears. What an absolute shambles my world had become.

***

"Nicole?" Kimberly murmured as she hugged me tightly. "What happened?"

"What happened with what?"

"With you and Beckett? You look as if you're about to cry, and he's staring at you like a lost puppy."

"Some new information came to light on the way here, and I realised he misrepresented his intentions."

"What new information?" Rania asked from over my shoulder. "It must have been something serious."

"He used me. He wanted to use all of us."

"Reed, can you take Nicole's bag?" Kimberly asked.

"I've got it," Beck told her, and she gave him such a glare he backed away three steps.

"Reed, the bag? Darn it, I only booked three rooms. I'll organise another."

We'd arrived at the Fleur-de-lis Hotel in the middle of the night after an uncomfortable journey across the state. Apart from one time I needed to stop to use the bathroom, I hadn't said a single word to Beck, and he hadn't tried to talk to me either. Now we were standing in the parking lot, and the others had come out to meet us. It should have been a joyful reunion, but the atmosphere was so strained I thought my last nerve would snap like an overstretched elastic band.

"What do you mean, he wanted to use us?" Rania asked.

"Can we talk inside?"

Kimberly looped her arm through mine. "I'll order wine. And some fizzy water for Rania on account of she doesn't drink."

Inside, we regrouped. Kimberly sure knew how to organise things—I had my own room within minutes, and the room-service cart arrived before I even got my bag open. Wine, more wine, and a selection of desserts, which wasn't what I usually ate at two a.m. but I went with it.

Kimberly and Rania clearly had money, and since they'd chosen our accommodation for tonight, it was fancier than any place I'd ever stayed. A four-poster bed, velvet drapes, and a marble bathroom with two sinks and a whole basket of luxury toiletries. Paying for it would bankrupt me, but I didn't dare to complain in case I looked ungrateful.

"You look like you need chocolate," Kimberly said. "And a glass of Cave des Vignerons de Chablis. My ex-husband introduced me to it, which, looking back, was the high point of my marriage."

"You were married?"

She pulled a face. "Everyone makes mistakes."

With that, I told the tale of my latest. "I can't believe he wanted one of us to commit murder. I mean, who goes around killing people in this day and age?"

"Beck does," Rania said. "Or at least, he did."

"Huh?"

"I see it in his eyes as he saw it in mine. He was in the army, yes?"

"You really think he killed people?"

"War isn't all about soldiers handing out candy to the local kids while someone in a control room thousands of miles away launches smart bombs at the hospital. There are men on the ground doing the real dirty work. Fighting to the death for the greed of a few in the name of a god they don't truly understand. Or sometimes they're fighting for politicians who think they're gods, which is just as bad."

"Whose side were you on in Syria?"

"My own side."

"You must have seen some atrocities. The news..." I trailed off. Rania probably didn't want to talk about it.

"Yes. But it means I can understand why Beck thought some of the things he did. After a while, you become numb to death. It's just one more move in pursuit of an endgame."

"You're saying you condone the way he treated me? Treated us?"

"I'm saying I understand it. And he's given to you as well as taken."

"What if he asked you to kill Sarah? Would you be upset?"

"We all get asked to kill people every day. The only difference is that this time, it's by the living rather than the dead."

Kimberly waved a half-full glass in her direction, and the wine came dangerously close to slopping over the edges. "You sound as if you're on Beckett's side."

"I also see why both of you would assume the worst about men. You've been hurt by them, and for you, Nicole, those wounds are still so raw they're bleeding."

Rania was right. Dammit, she was absolutely right. Why did she have to be so perceptive?

"Another betrayal feels like a twist of the knife," I whispered. "Why didn't he just tell me about Anna and Sarah at the beginning?"

"I can't answer that."

"Maybe he dug himself into a hole he didn't know how to get out of?" Kimberly suggested. "I saw the way he looked at you yesterday. He cares, and you can't fake that. Believe me, I've seen men try. Every time I watch a couple walk down the aisle, I ask myself whether they'll still be together in two years, and so far, my guesses have been eighty-seven percent correct. I'm good at recognising true love."

"Wait. You're saying Beck loves me?"

She picked up a dessert fork and took a dainty mouthful of chocolate cake before she answered, chewing thoughtfully. I felt too sick to eat, so I guess she didn't want it to go to waste.

"Yes, I think he does."

Chapter 30 - Beckett

I'D FUCKED UP. Badly, maybe even irreparably.

Why hadn't I come clean about Sarah sooner? Fear? Dread? Denial? Denial—that was a good word. For a few blissful days, I'd pretended the crazy bitch didn't exist.

Except now she was back, and even if Nicole didn't hate the very air I breathed right now, taking things any further between us was out of the question. I wouldn't make the same fatal gamble with her life as I had with Anna's.

But I still liked Nicole. More than I should. That girl would leave a mark on my heart when we parted ways, although at the moment, it felt more like I'd been shanked with no hope of making it to the emergency room in time.

How could I patch things up? Perhaps I never would, but if I could get her necklace back, that might at least get her to smile again. Which meant working with Will and Reed, who were currently standing on the other side of Will's hotel room, looking slightly uncomfortable with the whole situation. Something I identified with.

"So…" Will started. "Harmon?"

"One of us should be watching the house."

In fact, I didn't understand why neither of them

was. What if Harmon decided to move on overnight?

Reed chuckled. "Enid's watching the house."

"Who's Enid? Another ghost?"

"Nope, although she does have white hair. Kim met her earlier when we were scouting out the neighbourhood, and she's one smart old lady. Once Kim told her we were hunting for an escaped fugitive, she wanted to know if we could deputise her..." Reed's lips quirked as he tried to keep a straight face. "And her cat."

"Her cat?"

"Binky. A purebred Siamese, apparently."

"Are you kidding?"

Will cut in. "That's exactly what I said, but she's for real. Apparently, between her meds and her bladder, she's up all night anyway, so she offered to take the late surveillance shift. Kimberly went to the store earlier and bought her a box of candied fruits and a new coffee machine."

"She's also the reason we know Harmon is at Corwin's house," Reed said. "She spends most of her time 'keeping an eye' on her neighbours, and she doesn't like Kenneth Corwin much so she pays particular attention to his place."

"Why doesn't she like him?"

"Kenneth fixes up old cars in his spare time, which means his yard's full of rusting eyesores and he's revving engines at seven o'clock in the morning. Since Enid's a night owl, that's not something she appreciates. She likes to write everything down for her monthly report to the sheriff, and that's why she noticed Harmon arriving three days ago. He talked to Kenneth outside for a minute or two before they went into the house."

"She's sure it was him? How far away is her window?"

"About two hundred yards, but she has binoculars."

Binoculars? I wasn't sure whether to be thrilled or appalled. Enid must've been real popular with her neighbours.

"Has she seen him since? How do we know he's still there?"

"She hasn't seen him leave, and just in case, she promised to go over the footage from her security cameras while she's snacking on her candied fruit tonight. We thought we might also take a look in the old barn out back—that's where he parked his car."

Finally, something practical to do. I'd spent so long cooped up in the truck, a little breaking and entering would provide a welcome respite.

"I can do that."

"And once we've confirmed his vehicle's still there, we need to decide how to get him out of the house. The bad news is that Enid says Kenneth's in the habit of carrying a gun."

"Is there any good news?"

"Last time he tried to shoot somebody, he missed."

Me and Reed, we had very different ideas of good. But no matter—I'd faced men with guns enough times in my life that I felt resigned rather than nervous. After all, death came to everybody someday, and right at that moment, I didn't feel as if I had a hell of a lot to live for anyway.

"Corwin's home too?"

"He was earlier. I saw him in the yard. Big guy. Walks with a limp, but it doesn't slow him down."

Great. "What time do you want to leave to check out this barn?"

"Whenever you're ready."

"No time like the present."

Will and Reed glanced at each other.

"Sure you don't want a break for an hour?" Will asked. "I mean, you just got here, and things seemed kind of...fraught?"

I couldn't hide the falling-out with Nicole. One minute with their girls, and Will and Reed would know more about the situation than I did. Before, I'd been happy Nicole had two new friends to talk to, to lean on, but now? Not so much. I gave the two men a summary of my fuck-up, keeping it brief.

"So let me get this straight," Will said. "You've got a psycho ex who enjoys hurting your girlfriends, one of whom is now dead and stuck in a burned-out building in your hometown, and you didn't think it would be a good idea to mention that to Nicole at the start? Schoolboy error, mate."

"At the start, I didn't know I was going to fall in love with her."

Fuck.

Because that was what I'd gone and done. It'd crept up on me like the fog rolling into San Francisco.

Will's eyes saucered. "It's that serious?"

"For me it is. I'm not sure how Nicole felt. She flips between being sweet and chewing me out ten times a day."

Reed snorted a laugh. "What are you, a masochist?"

"Something like that. Can we just get this job finished?"

So I could crawl back to Abbot's Creek and lick my

wounds. And possibly pack up my belongings and move to Alaska. Somewhere, anywhere, that Sarah couldn't find me. My earlier determination to stay put in my house had evaporated. I'd rather live in an igloo and hunt seals to survive than tangle with that woman again.

"Sure, let's go. Uh, how are you with dogs?"

Oh, this got better and better.

"Kenneth has a dog?"

"Some mangy thing that barks constantly. Looks like a pit bull."

With God and two private investigators as my witnesses, I was never working for Aunt Tammy again. I didn't care how guilty she made me feel.

"In that case, we need to go via the grocery store."

***

An hour and a half later, I stood at the edge of Kenneth Corwin's property armed with my Glock 19, a bag of doggy treats, and three large steaks. Will and Reed crouched behind me, listening to the growling coming from the other side of the fence. Kimberly had warned Enid we'd be prowling around, and she'd promised to call the cops if anyone shot at us. Comforting.

The girls had stayed behind at the hotel with Nicole, who was apparently feeling somewhat fragile. Kimberly's frostiness came through loud and clear when my name was mentioned over the speaker on Reed's SUV. I was definitely still in the proverbial doghouse.

"Are you sure this is a good idea?" Will asked. "I'm not sure my travel insurance covers dog bites."

"We don't have a choice. Corey Harmon isn't gonna walk out the front gate if we buzz on the intercom. We'll have to go onto the property, and at least this way, we stand a chance of not becoming dinner."

"Dogs hate me. Back before I met Rania, I got a ton of lost-dog cases, and the little bastards always nipped." He held up an arm, not that I could see much in the gloom. "Bichon Frise. Seven stitches and a tetanus shot."

"I'll go first, okay?"

I'd always been fond of dogs. After I got Gibby, I'd even run a half marathon to raise money for the sanctuary that saved him. A wet nose appeared through a gap in the fence, and I shoved a treat underneath, hastily withdrawing my fingers as teeth snapped too close for comfort.

"Hey, puppy. Do you like that?" Crunching sounded from the other side of the boards, not more than two feet away. "Want another one?"

Another treat, and another snap, although that one didn't seem quite so close. More crunching. Luckily, I'd bought the economy-sized pack. A dozen treats later, and we'd progressed to snuffling. This was good.

"Can you guys give me a boost so I can see over the fence?" I asked.

They took a leg each and lifted. Will huffed a bit, but ten seconds later, I was looking down onto a canine welfare case. I could count every rib, but that didn't stop the mutt from unleashing a volley of barks. I tossed a steak in his direction, and for once in my life, I was happy to see a skinny animal because he attacked it like a thing possessed.

What now? Should I risk going over the fence? Or

would I get the same treatment as the rib-eye?

Ah, fuck it. What was life without taking a few risks? I hoisted myself, swung my legs over the top, and dropped down on the other side. The dog growled. Took a step towards me. Looked back at the steak.

I turned into a statue. *C'mon, buddy. You know you're hungry…*

A nerve-racking hour passed. At least, it felt like an hour. In reality, it was probably only thirty seconds. Thirty seconds of my heart pounding against my ribs like a cocaine-addled cage fighter. Then the steak won the battle, and I let out the breath I'd been holding. The dog watched me carefully with wary eyes that glinted in the moonlight as he finished wolfing down his prize.

"Hey, boy, you want another treat?"

He did, and this time, he licked my hand. Half a dozen Smokehouse Jerky Rolls later, he rolled over and waved his legs in the air, and I realised he was actually a she.

"Guys, I think it's safe to come over now."

Will didn't sound convinced. "Are you sure?"

"She's more bark than bite, and the chances are, it'll take all three of us to get Harmon out of his spider hole."

Reed came first, vaulting over the fence as I gave our new friend another steak. I moved to scratch her ears, but she yelped as my fingers caught a sore patch. She was holding up one back leg too. Usually, I tried not to cause too much damage when I apprehended FTAs, but I'd make a special exception when I finally met Harmon and his pal Kenneth. The damn dog needed to see a veterinarian.

Will landed beside me, and the dog gave him a

cursory sniff before going back to the food. What do you know? Starving an animal to keep it hungry and mean didn't work too well when it came to home security.

"Do you two want to wait here with Muttley while I check out this shed?"

Because "barn" was too grand a word for it. The building was outlined in black against the full moon, around the size of a three-car garage, and the state of disrepair was evident by the sagging roof and jagged siding.

Skulking around in the dark came naturally to me. Years of teenage rebellion had been shaped and honed in the army until I could move swiftly, silently, like a shadow in the night. Nothing stirred as I crossed the yard and let myself into the shed through a side door. Yes, it was padlocked, but I'd spent enough time with my lock picks that it barely slowed me down.

And there it was. Corey Harmon's old Ford, dented and dusty in the beam from my flashlight. Sure, he could've left in another vehicle or taken the bus, but it was unlikely. From what Nicole said, he wasn't made of money despite his criminal enterprises. And why go to all the trouble of coming to Corwin's only to leave again right away?

Fifty bucks said he was inside. We just had to get him out.

Back at the fence, Will and Reed were petting the dog in the dappled shadows of an old sycamore tree. Food was definitely the way to that girl's heart. If only something so simple would work with Nicole.

"Well?" Will asked.

"Car's there."

"Which means Harmon most likely is too. The question is, how do we get him out?"

"Way I see it, we've got two options. The first is to sneak into the house and hunt him down, but that carries the risk of being spotted and some asshole's bound to call the cops."

"And the second?"

"He thinks I'm working alone, and he's a runner. I bet if I hop over the gate and knock on the front door, he'll go straight out the back."

Reed nodded to himself. "And even if he doesn't, we've still got option one, although we'd lose the element of surprise."

"Are you allowed to go into the house after him?" Will asked. "I bet that'd flush him out."

"That area of the law's hazy. I'm allowed into *his* residence—I don't even have to knock—but other people's houses? Different courts say different things."

"We're not in court."

No, we weren't. As long as I had a reasonable suspicion that Harmon was in the house, I'd probably get away with forcing my way inside. And thanks to the vehicle parked out back and Enid's obsession with spying on her neighbours, I had grounds for my beliefs.

"I'll go inside."

Reed grinned, moonlight glinting off his teeth, while shadows darkened the furrows in Will's brow.

"I'm not sure—"

"When do you want to do this?" Reed asked.

"Early. Let's grab a couple of hours' sleep and more doggy treats, then make a move. Kimberly might want to distract Enid."

"I'll get her to take a package of decaf over."

CHAPTER 31 - BECKETT

"KENNETH CORWIN? MY name's Beckett Sinclair, and I'm working on behalf of—"

The front door bounced off my boot when Kenneth tried to slam it. Guess that answered one of my questions. Corwin wasn't merely an innocent bystander in this mess—he knew exactly why Harmon was hanging out in his house, and he'd aided and abetted a fugitive.

Which was why I didn't feel too guilty when I shoved Corwin inside and pinned him against the wall. His head bounced off the sheetrock with a satisfying *crack*, and for a moment, his eyes wobbled.

"Where's Corey Harmon?"

"He didn't do nothing."

"That wasn't what I asked."

"Fuck you."

"I'll have to pass on that."

Weight-wise, Corwin and I were pretty evenly matched, but he was six inches shorter and most of his bulk was fat. He squirmed in my grip, and I knew what he was trying to reach—the gun stuffed into his waistband. He lost his balance as I spun him around, and five seconds later, he was on the floor, the semi-automatic was in my hand, the magazine was in my pocket, and I'd ejected the round from the chamber.

The jackass hadn't even put the safety on. Ten bucks said he got that limp by shooting himself in the foot.

"You're harbouring a felon."

"Bullshit. You're the felon. You broke into my fuckin' house."

"Technically, you opened the door."

Corwin tried to get to his feet, but since he moved with the grace of a stranded walrus, it was easy to flip him onto his stomach. He teetered like a Weeble as I secured his hands behind his back with a pair of flex cuffs.

Where was Harmon? I hadn't heard any movement from the house, and if he'd run out the back, Will or Reed would've shouted.

"How do you want to play this?" I asked Corwin. "I know Corey's here, so unless you want me to tear the place apart looking for him, tell me where he's hiding."

"You can't do this!"

The asshole wouldn't stop writhing around, so I cuffed his ankles too, just in case.

"Get your goldarn filthy hands off me, you motherfuckin' piece of shit! I'm gonna hunt you down like a dog and rip your guts out, one damn organ at a time, then I'll string you up out back and use you for target practice, you cocksuckin' pig."

I think I preferred the writhing.

For good measure, I hog-tied Corwin and wedged him behind the front door so Harmon couldn't get out of it, but his yells still followed me as I headed into the living room. Next time, I'd make sure to bring duct tape. Hold on... What the fuck was I talking about? There wouldn't be a next time. I'd gift the duct tape to

Eric for Christmas.

Ironic that Corwin had called me a pig when he was the one who lived in a sty. Dirty takeout containers littered every surface, and there was half an engine sitting on the coffee table. If I were Harmon, I'd have picked jail. One of the girls would have hand sanitiser, right?

To make sure Harmon didn't slip past me, I cleared one room at a time, working my way towards the back of the house and keeping an eye on the stairs. Nothing stirred as I snooped around, moving silently as though I was creeping through enemy territory overseas.

Hmm, what was this? A cupboard in the kitchen held baggies filled with little coloured pills, and I hazarded a guess that they weren't entirely legal. No wonder Corwin's shouts had grown more frantic when I moved in that direction. At least that meant he was unlikely to call the cops after we left, because no amateur drug dealer wanted law enforcement sniffing around his stash.

I spied Reed outside, and he held his hands out in a *well?* gesture. Nothing so far. I shook my head.

Time to head upstairs, but the damn things creaked as I climbed. Fuck, this whole house was jerry-built.

Then I heard a creak that wasn't mine.

Harmon.

When I ran into the world's untidiest bedroom, he was halfway out of a window, sitting on the sill with his legs dangling outside.

"Hey, asshole."

He looked around, and I was kind of disappointed when he jumped. I'd secretly been hoping for a fight because nothing would've given me greater pleasure than breaking his nose.

But I didn't get the chance. A howl of pain came from outside, followed by shouts as Will and Reed pounced. When I looked out the window, Harmon was rocking on his back, clutching one ankle as Reed tried to prise his hands away for cuffing.

We had our man.

"Will went to get the SUV," Reed said when I got outside. "We can cuff our new friend to the tie-down points in the back."

I stared down at Harmon. I'd expected him to struggle like Corwin did, but he seemed more afraid than anything else, curled up into a foetal position with his chin tucked against his chest. But when my shadow fell over him, he looked up.

"You're here to take me to jail, aren't you?"

"Give the man a gold star."

"You know I'll die there, don't you? My blood'll be on your hands."

That fucker. "You mean the way Alicia Thomas's blood is on your hands?"

Silence. He turned his head away.

"Jail has rules. It's not total anarchy in there. If you behave yourself and keep out of trouble, you'll walk out in three or four years."

"You think? They'll carry me out in a casket. Rex has men everywhere, even in the police force. You know who Rex is, don't you? Everybody knows who Rex is."

"That's why you ran? Because of Rex?"

"If you were in my position, you'd have gotten the hell out of there too. Once he found out I was wanted by the cops, I became a liability."

"Why? Weren't you just selling phoney IDs?"

Now he focused on me again, this time with an *Are you stupid?* look.

"IDs for *Rex's men*."

"And...?"

"They're *criminals*, and I'm probably the only person outside of his organisation who knows their new identities."

Ah, now I began to understand. "And he thinks you'll trade that information for a lighter sentence?"

"Guess you deserve a gold star too." He closed his eyes for a moment. "I didn't realise how deep into the shit I was until it reached my neck. At first, I thought it was just the usual—documents for immigrants who wanted to work and drive in the US. By the time I realised they were all hardened criminals, I couldn't quit."

"How did you find out?"

"I fell asleep on the sofa one evening. Lulu's show finished, and when I woke up, it was late, and there was some program playing about gang wars in Honduras. They showed a bunch of mugshots, and I recognised my customers." Harmon turned a funny shade of green. "One of them raped a ten-year-old girl and left her for dead. Then there were the two brothers who lined up all the men from a village and shot them. Another guy who removed a boy's eyeballs when he saw something he shouldn't. You want me to carry on?"

"That's enough."

"They're monsters, every single one of them. The military clamped down in Honduras, so now Rex wants to take over San Francisco instead."

For a moment, I almost felt sorry for the guy

because Scarface was one mean motherfucker, and if Rex and the rest of the gang were anywhere near as bad —and it sounded like they were—Harmon was screwed. I *almost* felt sorry for him, but not quite. Because his story didn't entirely add up.

"Wait. You went on the run from Abbot's Creek six months ago, way before you got tangled up with Rex in San Francisco."

"Yeah, but that was only supposed to be temporary. I needed to earn some cash to pay for a decent attorney. Did you ever meet the idiot they assigned to me from the public defender's office? He spelled his own name wrong in my first bunch of court papers. He'd probably have pled my DUI down to first-degree murder. Although now I kind of wish I'd just gone to jail because even picking up soap in the shower would've been better than this."

"That's karma at work."

"Karma. Right." Harmon's voice quieted. "Look, I changed, okay? I quit drinking, and then I met my girlfriend."

Fire raced through my veins again, and my fingers inched towards my gun in an unconscious gesture before I stilled my hand. *Unclench your teeth, Sinclair.* I didn't have dental insurance.

"Met her? You *stole* from Nicole."

"You know Nicole?"

"Of course I know her. She's been helping me to look for your sorry ass. She wants her damn necklace back."

"Huh?" Now, that was a look I hadn't been expecting from Harmon. Confusion. "Her gold necklace? I didn't take any necklace. No way. That thing belonged to her mom."

"You expect me to believe that? You cleaned her out, and your other roommate too."

"No, it was more of a loan. I've got a couple of deals in the pipeline, and then I can pay them back. Nicole knows that, man."

"How does she know that? She hasn't spoken to you since you left."

"Because I said so in my note. Yeah, I felt shitty about taking her laptop, but she's got backups of everything. I even asked her that the day before I left to make sure. And Lulu watches way too much TV. She should get out more."

Note? What note? Nicole hadn't mentioned any note. Why did I always feel two steps behind in this investigation?

"Nobody found a note."

More puzzlement. "I left it on the table downstairs. I mean, I knew Nicole would be pissed, and Lulu probably wants my balls, but I was desperate, okay? My attorney refused to do anything else until I paid his last bill. Can't you give me another week? I was gonna come back, I swear."

"No, I'm not giving you another week. You killed a woman, you asshole."

"Not on purpose."

Because that made it so much better.

I glanced at Reed, and he shrugged. Seemed Harmon wasn't quite what he'd expected either. Back in Abbot's Creek, I'd crossed paths with Corey once or twice, and I remembered him as a mouthy little guy who always had a beer in his hand. Aunt Tammy said he'd cried in court, and Nicole had made her feelings about him clear. But right here, right now? The cockroach at my feet might have been sullen and self-centred, but strangely, he didn't come across as a liar.

And neither did Nicole. If she'd been faking her panic over her necklace disappearing, or her initial reluctance about having to hunt for Harmon with me to get it back, she deserved an Oscar.

"If you didn't take the necklace, then who did?"

"How should I know? Maybe Nicole lost it?"

Could it be in her bedroom somewhere? She said she woke up and it was missing, right? Had she checked under her pillow? Under the bed?

"This other housemate..." Reed said. "How well do you know her?"

Lulu? Seriously?

Harmon tried to shrug, but seeing as he was trussed up like a dungeon mistress's plaything, his shoulders didn't move much.

"I guess she could've done it."

"But why?" I asked.

"Money trouble? A few weeks before I left, I overheard her on the phone to someone, asking for more time to make repayments."

An engine rumbled close by, quickly followed by Will pulling up beside us in Reed and Kimberly's SUV. We'd have to finish this discussion later.

"Can't I sit in the back seat?" Harmon asked when we moved to stuff him into the trunk. "I'll get a cricked neck in here."

No, he damn well couldn't. Not only did I suspect he'd run at the first set of lights, but he didn't deserve that dignity after what he'd done to Alicia Thomas and Nicole.

"Should've thought of that before you jumped bail, shouldn't you?"

Before we drove off, I went back inside and tossed a nail file I'd found upstairs to Corwin. If he shut up for a moment, he could use it to free himself, but it would take enough time for him to saw through the flex cuffs that we'd make a clean escape. Not that I seriously thought Corwin would come to Harmon's aid. No honour among thieves and all that.

Reed climbed into the front of the SUV with Will, and I took the back seat so I could keep an eye on Harmon. We'd gotten halfway down the driveway when I glanced behind me, and I couldn't help groaning.

"Ah, fuck."

"What is it?" Will asked.

It was the dog. The damn dog, running on three legs, chasing after her meal ticket with her ears flapping in the wind, wheezing like an asthmatic.

"Corwin's mutt's following us."

"It'll turn around."

I already had a dog. I didn't need another one. But I couldn't leave her behind with a man who treated her like shit. He'd be furious when he got free, and what if he took his anger out on the first thing to hand?

"Stop the car."

Will's turn to groan. "You can't be serious?"

"She needs to see a veterinarian, and Corwin won't take her."

Will shook his head, but the car slowed, and I leaned across to open the other door. The dog leapt in and sprawled on the seat, exhausted from her wild run. Laughter came from behind me.

"You're stealing Kenneth's dog?"

"Why? Are you gonna tell him?"

"Not me, man. He never feeds her properly. I figured I'd drop her off at the shelter when I left."

Harmon was an asshole, no doubt about that. But maybe, just maybe, he wasn't quite as much of an asshole as I'd first assumed.

CHAPTER 32 - NICOLE

"THEY'VE GOT HIM."

Kimberly hung up the phone, but she didn't look particularly pleased by the news. More...uncertain. Why? What was wrong?

"But that's good, right?"

"Uh, yes. Of course it is." She smiled, but it seemed forced. "They're on their way here, and apparently, we need to pack up ready to go and also buy some dog food."

"Dog food?"

"Reed told me it was better not to ask."

"Did he say anything about my necklace?"

"Only that Harmon didn't have it. I'm so sorry, Nicole."

She gave me a hug while Rania smiled sympathetically. Which was nice, but all the hugs in the world couldn't replace the necklace I'd lost.

"Is that all Reed said?"

She hesitated.

"What aren't you telling me?"

"He just mentioned Corey Harmon wasn't quite what he expected, and that's it, I swear. I don't really know what it means either. But they'll be back in twenty minutes, and then we can ask them."

More like half an hour. While we waited for the

SUV to pull into the parking lot, we'd checked out, hauled the luggage out to the car—Beck had left his bag with Reed's—and picked up a bag of doggy kibble. Kimberly had insisted on paying for everything. Now I was pacing between the truck and Rania's convertible, fretting over what the hell I was supposed to say to Carlton. Dammit, I had to stop thinking of him as Carlton. It wasn't his name.

The anger built as Will parked, and by the time he turned the engine off, I was ready to castrate my ex. What had he done with my necklace? If he'd sold it, I'd... I'd... I didn't know, exactly, but fulfilling my birthright seemed like an attractive option. Where was he? I peered through the back window and saw Beck next to a sorry-looking dog, and my heart lurched, but with fury bubbling through me, that story would have to wait.

There he was. In the trunk, lying behind the back seats. I yanked open the hatch, only to get lifted off my feet by an arm around my waist as Beck slammed the lid back down with his other hand. Damn, the man could move fast.

"Easy, sprite."

"Don't you 'sprite' me. And let me go!"

"Not if you're going to assault a man in the middle of the hotel parking lot."

"He deserves it."

"Maybe so, but we'll talk about that somewhere without an audience."

"I need to know what happened to my necklace."

"We're not doing this here, Nicole. Do you want to ride with me or Rania?"

Stupid question. "Rania."

I hated leaving without answers, but I could grudgingly admit that asking a bound man questions right outside an upmarket hotel might attract the wrong sort of attention.

Beck sighed. "Did you get the dog food?"

"It's in your truck. How did you end up with the dog, anyway?"

"She didn't like Kenneth Corwin either."

***

Twenty minutes later, our little convoy pulled over on the cracked asphalt outside a boarded-up diner. A sign advertising seniors' discount still swung back and forth, squeaking in the breeze, right next to a "For Sale" board. Apart from the occasional car going past, the place was perfectly secluded. Now could I get some answers?

I jumped out of the car before Rania turned the engine off, and Kimberly hurried behind me to catch up. This time, I got the trunk of the SUV open and slapped Corey Harmon once, twice, three times before Beck got to me.

"You selfish prick! Where's my necklace? What did you do with it?"

I'd wound my arm back for another go when Beck caught my hand. "That's enough."

"Really? You think? It wasn't your stuff he stole. It wasn't you that he ran out on. Where the hell is my necklace?"

"He doesn't know."

What?

"Well, what did he do with it?" I leaned into the

trunk. "Did you sell it? Did you? Who to?"

"I didn't take it, babe."

"Don't you dare call me your babe."

It was worse than being called sprite. I wrenched my hand out of Beck's grip for good measure.

"Beckett tells me you didn't get my note," Corey said.

"Note? What note? There was no note."

"I left it on the table downstairs. Next to your textbooks."

"No, you didn't. There was nothing there."

I visualised that spot in my mind. It had been the first place I'd looked for my missing phone, and I was absolutely certain that I hadn't seen any note.

"Yeah, there was. Like, a whole essay explaining the situation, and it said at the bottom that I'd mail you a cheque. I'm really sorry, babe, but I was in a tight spot when I took those things. I figured you never watched the TV much yourself, or called anyone, and I knew the professor would lend you his laptop to finish your paper or whatever. And I'm gonna pay you back when I can."

A tear rolled a wet, salty track down my cheek. "Where's my necklace?"

"I swear I didn't take that."

"Then where is it?"

"There was only one other person in that house."

It took a moment for his insinuation to sink in, and I almost choked.

"Lulu? You're accusing *Lulu*?"

"Think about it—who else would take the note as well?"

"You're crazy! And you're a nasty, deceitful thief."

Will touched me gently on the back. "We're not sure he's lying. Not about this."

"Of course he is."

But Reed shook his head too. "Met a lot of liars in my time, Nicole. It'd be easier for all of us if Harmon was being dishonest, but..."

"How? How would it be easier?"

Beck gave a tiny shrug. "Because between the three of us, we could get him to tell us anything we wanted."

At the edge of my vision, Corey shuddered and lost a few shades of colour. Who was I supposed to believe? My ex-boyfriend, a self-confessed thief; two men I barely knew and Beck, a man with a tendency to be economical with the truth; or Lulu, my best friend of four years? Not since my mom died had I felt so utterly helpless.

"Lulu would never do that. She even filed a police report, for goodness' sake."

"Did you see the report?" Reed asked.

"No, but she told me she did."

"So you don't know for certain?"

"This is insane. Lulu was the one who lent me a new purse and went with me to Jive to look for you. Why would she do that if she took my necklace herself?"

"To cover her tracks," Reed said.

"What if I'd found Corey? Then what?"

"Uh, without wanting to sound insulting, she probably figured you weren't that good of a detective."

Okay, so that was a fair assumption, but it still didn't address the biggest question.

"Why would Lulu steal from me? What motive could she possibly have?"

It was Corey's turn to answer. "I think she owes

somebody money. I overheard her on the phone before I left. And I swear when I drove off on that Wednesday morning, Lulu was watching from the window. I accidentally slammed the door on my way out, and you know what a light sleeper she is."

"Didn't you put something in our cocoa? A sleeping pill? I swear you did."

"Uh, maybe. But she only drank half of hers."

I sat down with a bump. Yes, on the asphalt. My legs simply wouldn't hold me up anymore. Two weeks, and my entire world had fallen apart. If this was true, I'd lost three of the four people I'd been closest to in the world, and yes, I was including Beck in that because although our time together had been brief, I was caught up in a heady, intense swirl of what-might-have-beens. And let me tell you, if Corey's betrayal had shaken me and Beck's half-truths had hurt, Lulu deceiving me would tear my heart out.

"How do I know? I don't know anything anymore."

Kimberly crouched beside me. "Did Lulu ever give any indication that she might be having financial problems?"

"Uh... Uh... She was always tight on the rent. And these last few months, she's been selling all her stuff. But she said she just hated clutter!"

Plus she'd cut down on going out unless a guy was paying, and she'd downgraded our cable package to get rid of the movies, but I thought that was because she watched nothing but reality TV at the moment. How could I have missed all these signs?

"This police report..." Reed said. "I've got a buddy on the force, and he's got contacts everywhere. If we can confirm nothing was filed, are we happy to assume that Lulu's our culprit?"

Will and Rania murmured their agreement, and Beck nodded. Even Corey chimed in, still lying on his side in the trunk.

"I guess that makes sense. I know for sure it wasn't me, anyway."

"Give me a minute, and I'll make the call."

Rania and Kimberly sat on the ground with me while Reed moved a short distance away, then the dog scrambled out of the car and wormed her way onto my lap, licking my tears away with a sandpapery tongue.

"Hey, hey, that's all slobbery."

But she didn't stop, just wagged her scrawny tail and pushed a wet nose into my hand, working that special brand of magic possessed by every dog. How could anyone stay sad in the face of such sweetness?

"Okay, okay, I get it. You're cute." And skinny too. Every rib showed, and her hip bones stuck out like handles. Bald patches marred what should have been a smooth ginger coat, and she was covered in lumps and scabs. Then there was her horrible limp... I should have been furious with her old owner, but at that moment, I was running out of anger to go around.

Focus on the dog, Nicole.

Her energy helped me to my feet, and I found the bag of food in the back of the car along with a bottle of water. An empty coffee cup made a makeshift bowl for my new friend to drink from, and boy was she thirsty. By the time Reed came back, she'd slurped the whole lot.

"Anything?" I asked.

"He's looking into it. We should get going, and hopefully he'll call while we're on the road."

"Get going where?"

Beck came into view. He'd mostly been avoiding me until that point. "I need to get Harmon back to Sacramento."

"Which part of 'Rex will kill me' don't you understand?" Corey asked.

"Which part of 'your mom's about to lose her house' don't *you* understand?"

"Just give me a week. Then I can pay my attorney and he can negotiate a deal."

"That's not how this works. You missed every court date."

"Because I was busy working."

"And by working, you mean engaging in criminal activity."

"Yeah, well, I can't pay an attorney on what I earn serving drinks in a bar, can I?"

This was the most animated I'd ever seen Corey. Usually, he never put much effort into anything. And I was undecided. Before, when I thought he'd taken my necklace, I'd have served him up to Rex on a platter myself, but now? Having been on the receiving end of Scarface's wrath, I'd feel weirdly guilty if any harm came to Corey, even if I did still hate his guts for taking my laptop.

But before I could make any kind of argument either way, my phone rang, and I froze. Because it was playing "This Girl is on Fire," which my possibly former best friend had set for a joke the day she got a particularly bad case of sunburn. It had downloaded to my new phone when I synced my data.

Lulu was calling.

CHAPTER 33 - NICOLE

"WHAT SHOULD I do? *What should I do?* Should I answer it?"

I held the phone out as if it were red hot, and Beck peered at the screen.

"Great timing," he muttered.

"I don't know what to say to her."

If I didn't answer, she'd want to know why not. And if I did, and I sounded as nervous as I felt, she'd question that too. And since we hadn't heard back from Reed's friend yet, there was still an outside chance Lulu was completely innocent in all this.

"Nothing that could make her panic. If she suspects we're onto her, she might run before we can get back to San Francisco and ask her some questions."

I took a deep breath, my finger hovering over the green icon. *Just act normal, Nicole.*

Then the phone stopped ringing.

Kimberly gave a high-pitched giggle. "I guess that's a good thing?"

A stay of execution, so to speak. One that lasted all of five seconds before the phone rang again. I knew Lulu—if she tried calling twice, either it was life or death or her favourite contestant had just gotten voted off whatever reality show she was watching that day. Either way, she wouldn't quit until I answered.

"Hi."

I switched the phone to speaker and tried to sound upbeat, but my voice was hollow, disconnected from the rest of me.

"Nicole." Lulu's voice was weak, breathless. Not at all like her. "They took me. Damien—"

She ended on a squeak, and my heart began racing. What was going on?

The next person to speak was a man with a heavy accent.

"*Sí*, I have your friend. And I'll exchange her for the man you know as Carlton Hines. You have four days to find him and bring him to me, or I'll assume you've failed."

If Lulu was breathless, I was suffocating. I tried to inhale, but the air wouldn't go into my lungs.

"What?" I gasped.

"Four days. Carlton Hines."

"Bring him where?" Beck asked.

"Ah, is that the bounty hunter?"

"Yes."

"Well, if you can stop fucking Miss Bordais for long enough to do your job, perhaps you could help her?"

"You didn't answer my question."

Beck's tone was cold. Ice cold. I'd never heard him speak like that before.

"I'll check in each day. When you're ready to deliver Hines, I'll give you directions."

"How do we know you'll let Lulu go?"

"That's a risk you'll have to take. What's life without risk? It keeps things interesting. Four days, and the clock is ticking."

The line went dead, and if it hadn't been for Beck's

arm snaking around my waist, I'd have slithered to the ground again.

"Who the hell was that?" Reed asked. "What was that accent?"

"I— I—"

"That was Rex," Corey informed us. "The accent was Honduran. And no way are you handing me over to that maniac. He'll peel my skin off my body and use my tongue as a pincushion."

"I can understand why he'd want to do that. You talk too much."

"Hey, you'd protest too if some renegade wanted to turn you over to a known killer. And don't think he won't shoot the messenger. My buddy Shane was supposed to deliver a package of IDs, and one of Rex's henchmen fired a gun at him. The whole lot of them are unhinged."

Scarface. And he'd killed Macy that night as well. "The same man tried to strangle me. I... I... How *dare* you put us all into this position? I should be in my lab right now, researching telomerase activators." And speaking of labs... "Why did Lulu mention Damien? What's he got to do with this?"

"Could he be working with this Rex guy?" Reed asked.

"Damien? A criminal? That's crazy. He freaked out last year when he got a parking ticket."

"Didn't Lulu say he went over to your place recently?" Beck asked. "Remember she called while we were driving through Arizona?"

Snippets of that conversation came back. The way she'd called him Danny at first, and his later denial that he'd been there at all. Cold dread settled in the pit of my stomach.

"That was them scouting out our house, wasn't it? Preparing for this?"

"Yeah. Knowing what we know now, I'd say it probably was. Do you have his number? I've got a contact at the phone company who can trace his location just in case."

"Yes. Yes, I have the number."

I fumbled my phone out of my pocket, and Beck caught it when it slipped from my hands.

"PIN number?" he asked.

"One-two-three-four."

"Sprite, you need to change that."

"Spare me the lecture. Please." I gave my head a little shake as some of my senses returned. "What are we even doing? We need to call the police."

Corey snorted out a laugh from his position in the trunk. "The police? Are you kidding? Because half the cops in San Francisco are scared of Rex, and the other half are on his payroll. Why do you think I ran instead of handing over the information I have?"

"You said you were coming back," Beck reminded him, and Corey fell silent. "You were lying about that too, weren't you? Do you realise your mom's gonna lose her house? I'm not kidding."

"I planned to send her money to rent a new place. Look, I just don't want to die."

"Well, we have to do something," Kimberly said, the voice of reason. "We can't leave a woman to suffer, even if she did steal Nicole's necklace. And while you"—she nodded at Corey—"are a self-centred asshole, we can't in good conscience let Rex commit another murder."

"So what does that leave?" I asked. "It's not as if we

can take on Rex ourselves."

Silence fell, a deafening quiet that seeped into my lungs and weighed them down. Was this a nightmare? Would I wake up soon? Because I didn't do drama. This couldn't be my life. My life was straightforward, routine, slightly dull if I was honest. No, this had to be some parallel universe I'd accidentally ended up in, a strange simulation that took my hopes and fears and amplified them into a horror story.

Only last week, a SWAT team had raided the home of a Los Angeles drug dealer to rescue a kidnapped actress, and the resulting massacre had made the national news. Words like "overconfidence," "underprepared," and "incompetence" had been bandied about. What if Lulu ended up in the middle of another bloodbath? She'd still been my friend. I couldn't just pretend the last four years hadn't happened.

I pinched myself, but nothing changed. So I tried harder, harder, until Kimberly gently took my hand in hers.

"It'll be okay. We'll fix this."

"How? How will we fix this?"

"I can do it," Beck said softly.

"Do what?"

"Rescue Lulu."

"Now *you've* lost your mind. Everyone's lost their damn mind."

"Doing shit like that was my job before I got injured. It wouldn't be the first time I've snuck into a house full of heavily armed men who want to shoot me. Yeah, if we can find out where Lulu is, I reckon I'd stand a reasonable chance of getting her out of there, and then we can find your necklace too."

"A reasonable chance? *Reasonable*? So there's also a chance you could get captured yourself? Or injured? Or killed? I don't want my necklace back if it means risking your life."

My heart lurched as the words left my mouth. No, I didn't want Beck to get hurt. Come to think of it, why was he even here? Surely he should have hightailed it back to Sacramento to collect his bounty as soon as he captured Corey?

He shrugged. "By rights, I should already be dead. I've been living on borrowed time anyway."

"No. No, no, no!"

Weirdly, it was Corey who agreed with me. "She's right, buddy. One man against at least fifteen? It's a suicide mission."

"Two against fifteen."

We all turned to stare at Rania.

"That used to be my job too."

Will shook his head. "No way, Nia. You fought so hard to get away from all that."

"I'll never get away from it. Can't you see what's happening to the world? The darkness is like a cancer, and it's spreading."

"You're not risking your life."

"Do you have a better idea?"

"Three against fifteen," Reed said, and Kimberly gasped.

"You can't."

"What I can't do is let these two go in alone. And Rania's right. Crime rates are sky high, and the cops are fighting a losing battle. Not just here, but everywhere. There aren't enough prisons to hold all the criminals."

"Same in the UK," Will said. "Except they've started privatising the prison system. Companies put up the capital, and then the government rents the spaces. Our taxes are going through the roof. It's not only the criminals who are making money out of this crisis."

"Are you planning to kill Rex?" Corey asked.

"I'm planning to get Lulu," Beck said. "But if Rex starts anything, I'll defend myself."

"Oh, he'll start something, all right. But I guess that's my best hope. If he's out of the picture, I can serve my sentence in peace then get on with the rest of my life. So I guess I'll help, but I'm not picking up a gun."

"Help how?"

"With information. I can tell you who you'll be up against, and also where to find Rex."

"And then you'll go quietly to jail?"

"If that's what the judge decides."

"If you insist on going ahead with this, I can act as a lookout," Will offered. "Although for the record, I think you're insane, and if anything happens to Rania..."

She laid a hand on his arm. "It's my decision to do this, Will. There are so many times I could have done something to help people and didn't, but now it feels like the wheels of fate are turning, pushing me to act. Pushing all of us to act. Us finding each other the way we did, there must have been a purpose to that."

"Then you're not doing it alone. I don't know the first thing about guns, but I'll help in any way I can."

Kimberly folded her arms. "I don't believe this. Nicole, tell them to stop being stupid."

"Me? What makes you think they'll listen to me?"

"Because Beckett's the ringleader, and he's gaga

over you."

After the cold shoulder I'd given him? I didn't see how he could be, but when I looked at him, he gave me a sheepish smile.

"What's it to be, sprite?"

Talk about pressure. But this was the kind of decision I should have been making for years, wasn't it? Life or death, and I'd shied away from every single one.

A day ago, it would have been so much easier. I'd have wanted to save Lulu, no question, but I couldn't deny that my judgement had been clouded a tiny bit by how she'd treated me. My fingers moved automatically to the patch of bare skin where my necklace should have sat. Either she or Corey was a thief, and I didn't trust either of them right now.

Then there was Beck. As the initial sting began to dull, I'd looked at his revelations with fresh eyes, and the mishmash of jumbled thoughts flying around in my head became clearer. Figuring that I'd get justice for Anna was a fair presumption to make when he'd never met me. After all, wasn't that my purpose? Yes, he could have owned up sooner, but I understood how that conversation might have been a difficult one to broach. Who wanted to tell the person they liked about their crazy ex? Certainly if I could've snapped my fingers and made Corey disappear, I would have.

"I'm so sorry," I told him. "All that stuff I said before. The way I treated you. I wish I could take it back."

"You were stressed."

"We're all stressed. It was no excuse. I'm... I'm not really used to this teamwork thing."

Beck opened his arms, and I tucked myself against

his side, one hand pressed against his chest as he hugged me tightly. In the middle of a crisis, his heart beat slow and steady, unlike mine, which was dancing the samba.

"Hold on," Corey said. "Are you two...?"

There were limits to teamwork. "Butt out."

If we hadn't had an audience, I'd have been tempted to kiss Beck, but we did, so I settled for squeezing his ass instead. That earned me a smile.

"Now that we can have a conversation without yelling, you need to make a decision. Do you want us to go in after Lulu?"

"I wish we could leave it to the police. Reed, can your friend check another report for me?"

"What report?"

"We told them Rex's henchman murdered a girl behind the Jive bar in San Francisco. If they haven't begun looking into that, then I'll have to assume they won't act to help Lulu either."

Extrapolation of data. Something my science brain could handle.

"I'll ask the question."

"And if they've ignored the tip, you want us to act?" Beck asked.

I bit my lip as I nodded, terrified that by trying to save one flawed friend, I was risking four other lives as well. Sometimes in this world, there were no good choices.

CHAPTER 34 - BECKETT

REX HAD GIVEN us four days, and it took us most of one to travel to Abbot's Creek, taking it in turns to sleep and drive. I moved Harmon from Reed's trunk to my back seat so I could question him about Rex's operation on the way. We also got confirmation from Reed's buddy that Damien's phone was in the lab, so at least we could rule him out of proceedings.

Why Abbot's Creek? Yeah, Harmon asked that question too, because he didn't want to go anywhere near jail while Rex was still breathing. And after hearing his stories, I had a better understanding of why. If even half of them were true, Rex was one sick motherfucker.

But we needed weapons. I had a semi-automatic with me and so did Reed—apparently he carried it everywhere, even on vacation—but we'd require more than that to take down a gang that had its roots in the Honduran underworld. Those guys weren't amateurs. Honduras was the murder capital of the world right now.

I had an AR-15 and a hunting rifle at home, but that wouldn't be enough either. No, we'd need to talk to my Uncle Ernest. Not Tammy's husband but her and Mom's older brother. Normally, I tried to avoid him because once he started lecturing on the Second

Coming and the Apocalypse, he could carry on for hours, but Ernest had weapons. Everything from a home-made flamethrower that scared the bejeezus out of me to a rack of well-oiled assault rifles. He also had a bomb shelter complete with air filtration system, enough food to feed a small town for a decade, plus so much stockpiled fuel I was surprised the government hadn't invaded yet. And somewhere, I strongly suspected, he had a tinfoil hat too.

Since we were coming into town, I'd taken over behind the wheel while Nicole sat beside me with the dog between her feet. According to Harmon, the mutt didn't have a name beyond "Hey you!" so Nicole had called her Smartie.

I rested a hand on Nicole's thigh, mostly out of relief that I could do that again without her breaking my wrist, but also because Harmon was watching. He might have been cooperating, but the guy was still a dick.

"You okay, sprite?"

"I'm just glad I'm not driving now."

She'd been terrified of the truck, but she'd still taken a turn on the bigger roads. Out of all of us, she was the least resilient, and I hated that she'd been dragged into somebody else's conflict. Hated that she was one of the Electi, which was the worst career mismatch I'd ever seen, even worse than my sister's brief stint handing out flyers for Tito's Rib Shack. She got all the free ribs she could eat, but she was a vegetarian.

"You did well."

She made a face. "I drove too slowly."

"We're almost there, and that's all that matters."

"At least we know we're doing the right thing now."

We did. Reed's contact—his buddy Wyatt back in Maryland—had called in favours and found out that firstly, Lulu had never reported the theft of her and Nicole's stuff, and secondly, nobody had matched our anonymous tip about Caracortada with Macy's murder. For fuck's sake. We'd literally given them the crime-report number.

Doing this ourselves was the best way, the path with the greatest chance of success, and I'd be lying if I said I didn't feel the same buzz I used to get in the Rangers simmering through my veins. Not because I was trigger-happy, but rather because I was a big fan of justice and the satisfaction of achieving it.

"Welcome to Abbot's Creek," Nicole read as we passed the town limits. "Population five thousand, two hundred and three."

"Five thousand, two hundred and two human beings plus one crazy-ass bitch."

Harmon chortled from the back seat. "Sarah Renwick? They let her out of prison?"

"Unfortunately."

"Then there's hope for me yet."

Nicole twisted around to look at him. "Stop talking, *Corey*."

I put on the turn signal and took a left. Our first stop was Eric's place to drop off Smartie. In between panicking about impending fatherhood and building flatpack furniture, Eric had promised to take her to the veterinarian and make sure she ate well until somebody picked her up afterwards. Ideally, that somebody would be me, but Nicole had promised to get her if I couldn't.

"Keep your head down," I warned Harmon. "My

cousin's a bond enforcement agent too, and if he sees you, I doubt he'll be quite as understanding as me."

"And if you try to escape, I'll chase you to the ends of the earth and shut your balls in a nutcracker," Nicole told him. "I already have the nutcracker."

That's my girl.

Harmon flattened himself into the rear footwell, and I tossed a blanket over his head for good measure then headed for the front door. Predictably, Eric had a thousand questions, but I sidestepped them by telling him I found the dog meandering along the road in a remote area. It wasn't a complete lie, and I didn't have time for a discussion on Smartie's origins.

That part of the trip was relatively painless, but then we had to visit Uncle Ernest.

"He'll probably aim a gun at us to start," I said to Nicole. "Try not to be alarmed. He rarely fires it."

"Rarely?"

"He's not keen on door-to-door salesmen. And if he offers you a jar of his pickled beets, my advice is to take it then toss it in the trash later because he gets offended otherwise."

"Take the beets. Got it."

"And I should probably take this moment to reassure you that not everyone in my family is like Uncle Ernest. In fact, Aunt Tammy swears he must've been beamed down by aliens."

"Your aunt believes in aliens?"

"Just forget I mentioned that part."

***

"Not a bad shot, is she?"

When we first arrived, Uncle Ernest's distrust of foreigners had led him to greet Will and Rania with suspicion, but now Rania had blasted the centre out of the bullseye, that suspicion turned to a grudging admiration. Damn, she was good, even though she claimed to be out of practice.

And she moved like a cat. Smooth and silent, creeping around Uncle's makeshift range on light feet as Will watched with a mixture of surprise and alarm. Me? I watched with relief as she and Reed discussed tactics and compared guns.

I'd played down the danger of the rescue mission for Nicole's sake, and although I had training and experience on my side, my fitness wasn't what it had once been and getting in and out unscathed would still be a hellishly difficult task. Knowing I had competent backup let me breathe a little easier.

We'd be using handguns, untraceable pistols with the serial numbers filed off and Uncle's custom-loaded ammunition. I didn't ask where he got all this stuff. I didn't want to know. He'd also provided us with a top-notch radio system, a police scanner, night-vision goggles, camouflage clothing, an industrial-sized first aid kit, and a roll of fucking tinfoil.

"Yes, she's a great shot," I told Uncle Ernest.

"I'll finish helping your girl to load the beets into your truck." How many jars was he giving her? "And that young man you've got shackled in the back seat says he needs to use the bathroom."

One advantage of Uncle being a few grains short of a full load was that he didn't ask questions when we showed up with Harmon handcuffed into my vehicle by his ankle. No, Uncle just offered him coffee like any normal person and gifted me a proper pair of leg cuffs that were "elliptically contoured so you can keep him shackled for longer, see?"

But Harmon still needed to be let out occasionally to take care of bodily functions. "I'll deal with him."

I didn't trust him not to disappear if I turned my back, but he did seem to be cooperating, so when we got back to my place to grab dinner and make our final plans—not to mention dispose of a crateful of beets—I let him loose in the living room with the promise that I'd shoot him in the foot if he tried to run.

"Pizza's here," Kimberly announced as the sound of a car crunching over gravel drifted through the open window. "I ordered extra chicken wings as well. And ice cream."

While she went to the door, the rest of us began shuffling papers to make room for the food. The whole coffee table was covered in pictures and diagrams, and most of the floor too. Will's buddy had got us a grainy snapshot of Rex, a surveillance photo by the looks of it, and the guy looked surprisingly normal. Nondescript. Around forty, smiling, wearing a suit and tie. The kind of man who hired sick fucks like Scarface to avoid getting his hands dirty.

According to Harmon, Rex lived in a mansion in Marin County, and Google Earth showed a sprawling structure surrounded by a high wall, the grounds dotted with trees and bushes that would give us cover as we approached. And better news—the property backed onto a forest. Even though I was more used to urban warfare in places with too much sand, I'd spent a lot of time training in the US as well, which meant creeping through trees in the dead of night had become second nature. Moving slowly, that was the key.

A small building next to the front gate suggested the presence of guards, but we'd confirm that when we got on site. With three days left, we could comfortably take one day to snoop around and still maintain the element of surprise.

While we made our move, Nicole, Kimberly, and Corey would camp out in Joel's apartment. There was still a likelihood that Rex was watching the house Nicole shared with Lulu, and when I sent Joel over there to check the situation and feed the rats, he reported the front door had been splintered around the lock then wedged closed, and the place was a mess inside. Worse, he'd been followed when he left, although he'd lost the tail with some swift footwork on the Muni.

And if anything happened to us, Joel would... No, I shouldn't be thinking that way.

The meal had the feeling of the Last Supper, except Judas was missing. We'd last heard from Lulu two hours ago when Rex called to remind us the clock was ticking and graciously allowed her to sob for Nicole. Part of me hoped we'd get in and out cleanly on this rescue mission, but the other half hoped he'd give me an excuse to put a bullet through his frontal lobe.

Were we totally prepared? No. But as my old commanding officer used to say, if we waited until we were one hundred percent ready for every job, nothing would ever get done. We'd have to go in at eighty.

Nicole shuffled closer on the sofa until our thighs touched. We weren't quite back to where we'd been before, but at least she seemed to have forgiven me for keeping secrets from her. I'd learned my lesson now.

I'd never leave her in the dark again. But until I got the Sarah situation sorted, we couldn't move forward either, and I dreaded dealing with Psycho Barbie even more than facing Rex.

Criminals were greedy, bloodthirsty, and reasonably predictable. A deranged woman scorned? Wild like nothing else on earth.

"Are you gonna eat that slice of pepperoni?" Nicole asked.

"Not if you want it."

She leaned in closer to whisper in my ear. "Are you trying to win my affections with pizza?"

"Is it working?"

"Yes."

I was about to put my arm around her when Will got up so fast the pizza box on his lap landed on the floor.

"Hey, who's that?"

"Who's who?"

"I swear there was someone outside the window."

I was hot on his heels as he crossed the room, but when we peered out, the only movement came from the old orange tree on the other side of the yard blowing in the breeze.

"What did he look like?"

"She. Blonde. Fine features. That's all I saw before she vanished."

Fuck. How many fine-featured blondes would be spying through my window on my first day back in town? There was only one. How cosy had I looked with Nicole? I sure hoped Sarah would think the relationship was platonic, but her wiring wasn't exactly up to code.

"Is everything okay?" Nicole asked.

No more lies. "That might have been Sarah."

"But we've only been here for a few hours."

"Welcome to the world of obsessive stalking. We'll have to check she's not tailing us before we get to San Francisco."

Nicole slipped her hand into mine and squeezed. "I'm so sorry this is happening to you."

"Isn't that my line?"

That got me a weak smile in reply.

This had to be tearing Nicole apart. All the lies, the betrayals, the danger. Mom always said I had a protective instinct, and I wanted to shield Nicole from everything, but two things stood in my way—Sarah, and staying alive long beyond Monday.

CHAPTER 35 - BECKETT

WHOEVER SAID CRIME didn't pay was either a liar or not very good at committing it. The first time I saw Rex's home through its tall metal gates, there was a Porsche in the driveway. During the course of yesterday, it had been joined by a Ferrari, a Lamborghini, and a Range Rover, and now there was a Bentley parked outside. The back of the house told the same story—the swimming pool, the tennis court, and the perfectly manicured garden said breaking the law was a very profitable enterprise.

But while Rex was a master at committing felonies, fortunately for us, he wasn't so good at securing his property. The cops in his pocket and his formidable reputation had led to complacency, to gaps in the motion arcs of his security cameras, to tree limbs overhanging his walls, to guards who spent more time checking their phones than watching for intruders. He thought he was untouchable.

Our surveillance yesterday suggested sixteen people inside, plus Lulu, a little worse than Harmon's initial estimate of fifteen. But three of those people were maids and a housekeeper, and then there were a couple of chicks in bikinis whose sole purpose seemed to be lying by the pool and looking pretty. Hopefully, those five would bug out at the first sign of trouble.

That left the two men sitting in the gatehouse and another seven in the mansion, plus Rex and—we suspected—Scarface, who Will had glimpsed arriving late last night in a black Mercedes. Unless they'd gone out over the back wall, they hadn't left.

We'd try to bypass them all.

"Ready?"

Two whispers in the affirmative came from Rania and Reed.

"Is everything still clear?" I asked Will.

"All clear out front."

Early this morning, he'd worked his way into a bush a hundred yards away with Uncle Ernest's military-grade binoculars. Apart from a steady stream of ants, nobody had disturbed him.

We'd chosen just after dawn to make our move. Light enough to see, early enough for Rex's men to be sleepy after their late drinking session the night before. One of the assholes had gotten so shit-faced he fell into the pool, and the two bikini girls fished him out, giggling, and dragged him onto a sun lounger.

"Go on three, two, one..."

I was coming from the west, skulking along behind the triple garage while Rania climbed over the back wall to the north and approached along the side of the pool house. That left the east for Reed, who planned to gain entry to the house through a downstairs window the housekeeper had left open. Rania would climb up a fancy metal trellis to a second-floor balcony while I picked the lock on a side door. I'd had enough practice over the years that the leather gloves I was wearing would hardly slow me down. We'd all come in civilian clothes, not the camouflage outfits Uncle Ernest had donated to the cause, because nothing screamed "up to no good" like skulking through the woods dressed like an ad for a military surplus store. Our only concession to our true purpose was to cover our faces when we reached the edge of the property—black scarves for Reed and me, and a dark red one for Rania.

Once inside, I'd check the first floor with Reed, and if we didn't find Lulu there, we'd head upstairs to meet Rania. At least we weren't going in blind. We'd started off with Harmon's hazy recollections from his one and only visit to the mansion plus a scribbled layout, then somehow—I didn't know the details and I wasn't sure I wanted to—a friend of Will's had obtained the architect's detailed floor plan and emailed it over.

If I had to put money on where Lulu was being held, I'd guess at a small room between the library and the dining room that the architect had marked as storage. No doors, no windows, and it wasn't close enough to the bedrooms for her struggles to disturb anyone's sleep. The walk-in closets were an outside possibility.

"No sign of her in the living room," Reed whispered. "But there's a big guy asleep on the couch and a second in an armchair, so tread carefully."

"She's not in the smallest bedroom," Rania said.

Only five more for her to check.

I prowled through the house, careful not to let my footsteps make a sound on the tiled floor. The decor was surprisingly tasteful. Either there was a Mrs. Rex somewhere or he'd hired an interior designer, because I couldn't imagine any man caring whether the tassels on the drapes matched the rugs.

The loudest sounds were the distant ticking of a

clock, the faint *sssh* of the AC, and my heart pounding against my ribs. Once again, I was deep in enemy territory, and this time, I didn't have the might of Uncle Sam backing me up.

A door opened ahead, and I ducked into the half bath beside me, except luck wasn't on my side. The fucker needed to take a leak.

I surprised him from behind the door with a chokehold. Desperate fingers clawed at my arms, my hands, my face, and I adjusted my grip to press on his carotid artery. He tried to reach behind to return the favour, but all he got was a fistful of scarf. The guy let out a gurgle as he collapsed to the floor, and I blew out a quiet breath as I zip-tied his wrists and ankles and stuffed a sock into his mouth. How much noise had we made? I needed to move fast in case anyone decided to investigate.

No footsteps came running, and I pulled my scarf back over my face as I hurried down the hallway. Light footsteps sounded ahead, and this time they carried on past as I ducked into a side room, the quiet squeak of rubber on tile accompanied by the rustle of fabric and a female voice singing softly in Spanish. The housekeeper or one of the maids. We'd discussed subduing the women if they crossed our paths, but ultimately decided against it unless they saw us first. The risk of someone else noticing our presence increased every time we stopped to gag and bind a person.

"Two bedrooms clear," Rania announced as I crept into the hallway again.

The library was ahead on my left, and I paused to look inside. Over by the floor-to-ceiling windows, another of Rex's men was sprawled out on a daybed with a blonde draped across his chest, minus her bikini. That was hanging from a floor lamp.

"There's a commotion happening outside," Will said in my ear. "Two men just ran east across the garden." A pause. "I can't see what's going on, but somebody's shouting. Something about an intruder?"

"All quiet here," Reed said.

Rania followed up. "And here."

I was ready to back out of the room when I spotted a bare foot sticking out from behind a desk, and a smear of reddish brown on the pale skin made me stop. Was that...? Yes. It was blood. I moved to get a better look. I'd only met Lulu once, but there was no mistaking her mascara-streaked face. The motherfuckers had stripped her to her underwear and tied her to a chair. It must have tipped over as she tried to free herself.

"Got her. In the library," I told the others, then tiptoed forward with a finger to my lips.

Lulu's eyes widened, but she got the message. Fuck. Every inch of her was scraped or bruised, and from the way she trembled, I wasn't sure she'd even be able to walk. No matter. I'd carry her out of there if I had to.

The knife from my belt sliced through the rope with little effort, and Lulu leaned on me as I helped her to her feet. Reed appeared by my side and took some of the weight.

"Go out through the side door," I whispered. "It's the fastest way, and probably the safest too."

Getting an injured woman through Reed's window would probably make a noise, plus the housekeeper-slash-maid had gone in that direction.

"I'm leaving too," Rania said in my ear.

One important lesson I'd learned in the military was that no matter how much time and effort you spent planning an operation, something always went wrong. The trick was minimising the damage once the problem occurred.

Today, that hiccup happened as we tiptoed along the hallway outside the TV room. First a door slammed, then a loud scream tore through the air. A woman's scream that made every hair on the back of my neck prickle.

"Fuck," I muttered under my breath as Lulu tripped over the edge of a rug. I tightened my grip on her arm in time to stop her from hitting the deck. "Rania?"

"That wasn't me," she said over the radio. "I'm on the balcony."

Then who the hell was it?

I looked at Reed, and he looked at me. No way could we walk away if another woman was in trouble. It wasn't in my nature, nor his judging by the steely glint in his eyes.

But we still had to take care of Lulu.

"Get her out of here. I'll go back."

"I can—"

"Do it."

I was already turning, ears following the sound of heavy footsteps running through the house towards the atrium. Thankfully, Reed thought the better of questioning me and wrapped an arm around Lulu's waist.

"Stay safe, brother."

"Rania, you leave too."

"But—"

"Go."

With people moving all over the house, I slipped back into my favourite bathroom for a few moments while I waited for the dust to settle. The guy I'd incapacitated hadn't moved, and he glared at me with hate-filled eyes. Had they kidnapped another girl? The only females we'd seen were staff and the bikini girls, and none of them had shown any sign of being held against their will. And the scream had definitely been help-me-I'm-terrified as opposed to give-it-to-me-harder.

I slipped out into the hallway again, and now I heard voices. The Spanish-accented tones of Rex's men versus our mystery woman's high-pitched hysterics.

Or *was* she a mystery woman? Something about that pushy, I'm-right-and-you're-wrong delivery seemed worryingly familiar.

Ah, shit. That insane bitch. I peeped through the doorway to the atrium in time to see Sarah at her crazy worst. Somehow, she'd gotten a gun off one of Rex's men, and now she had it pointed at a middle-aged guy who stood at the bottom of the stairs in silk pyjamas, hands in the air. Was that Rex? I'd only seen one blurry photo, but it sure looked like him. Another goon had a gold-plated pistol aimed at Sarah's head, but his hand was shaking so badly he'd be lucky if he hit her at all. Another five men had that deer-in-headlights look. I'd come across their type before—tough on the streets where they could throw their weight around, cowards when they got into a situation they didn't know how to handle.

"Don't move or I'll shoot!" she screamed. "Nobody messes with my man!"

I had the gold-plated-gun guy's head in my

crosshairs. One squeeze of the trigger and I could remove him from the equation. But a tiny part of me was tempted to walk away, to let them do whatever the fuck they wanted to Sarah because she'd ruined Anna's life and mine too. Hell, on more than one occasion, I'd been tempted to shoot her myself.

Except I didn't get that chance. She glanced across and saw me, and instead of using her one functioning brain cell and shutting the hell up, she gave me a beaming smile. "Ooh, there you are, honey."

Too late, I heard the sound of a revolver being cocked behind me.

"Don't turn around. Walk forward."

The man's harsh whisper cut through me like the Grim Reaper's scythe. Talk about difficult positions. The only thing keeping me alive was the fact that he couldn't get a clear shot at Sarah with me in the way, and if he killed me, she'd be able to shoot Rex before I crumpled to the floor.

"Shoot her instead, and I'll let you live," the man said.

I might have taken that deal if I'd believed him. But assholes of his ilk had no honour, and I'd be dead before Sarah's body hit the fancy rug. We had a stand-off.

"Can't do that."

"Let him go!" Sarah screeched. "Or I'll blow this man away. I swear I will!"

"Call her off," the man with the gun told me.

"I can't. She never listens to a word I say."

"Women. They are all the same. They should learn to do as they're told."

No, that'd never happen, and right then, I was

grateful for their autonomy. Because Rania's bullet slammed into the gunman's head with perfect accuracy and enough force that when his dead finger twitched on the trigger, he missed me and shot the wall instead. Sarah screamed and fired at pyjama guy, then her chest exploded in a cloud of crimson as the goon with the fancy gun served his master one last time. I killed him with a double-tap to the head before he could take another breath.

My ears were ringing as I stepped forward into the carnage. "Nobody else move unless you want to join them. One at a time, lie on your fronts. You on the left —start first."

Slowly, they complied. Now that their boss was out of the equation, they were rudderless, and nobody else wanted to die.

I turned to glance at the man on the floor behind me, and my tension eased a notch when I saw a vaguely familiar face staring up at me through one glassy, blood-spattered eye. Scarface, now minus his scar since the exit wound from Rania's bullet had blown away the entire left side of his head.

"Is that Sarah?" Rania asked, nodding past me.

"Yes."

"Rania?" Will sounded frantic. "What are you doing in there?"

"Tidying up."

She moved closer and fired one more round into Sarah's head. Stood back. Waited. It took me a moment to realise what she was doing—her duty. The duty I'd once hoped Nicole would perform. If there was any thread of life left in Sarah, Rania's actions would have set Anna free.

"Sorry. She was already gone."

Shit. All that pain, all that heartache, and I'd still failed. Anna was stuck in Abbot's Creek for good, an eternal victim of Sarah's madness.

Rania watched our backs while I secured the rest of Rex's men with flex cuffs, but the other occupants of the house kept a low profile. That was the problem with building an army out of lowlifes and scum—none of them stayed loyal. All they cared about now was saving their own skins.

Which meant we were free to leave. Guns in hands, we retreated the way I'd come in, back through the forest to my truck, and only once we were relatively safe did I manage to speak to Rania properly.

"Everything that happened... In there... Sarah... Thank you."

"Don't worry about it. We're a team now, right?"

"Right."

"And Sarah was crazy."

"Was" being the operative word. She was gone, and try as I might, I couldn't feel upset about that. For years, I'd been looking over my shoulder, waiting for her to fuck up my life yet again, and now I was free. Free to breathe easy again. Free to sleep at night. And free to make a move on Nicole if she'd have me.

"Yeah, she was."

Chapter 36 - Nicole

I COULDN'T LISTEN.

No, I mean it. I really couldn't listen to the rescue attempt because Beck had told Joel that under no circumstances was he to give me or Kimberly the radio earpiece. He'd been sitting in the same armchair for the last half hour, the TV on quietly in the background as I wore a hole in the carpet.

"Can't you sit down?" Corey asked. "You're making me dizzy."

"How can I possibly be making you dizzy? I'm walking in straight lines."

"Whatever. It's annoying."

What did I ever see in that idiot?

"Don't worry about Beck," Joel told me. "That asshole's got more lives than a cat."

"What about Reed and Rania?" Kimberly asked. "Waiting for them to rescue somebody else is actually worse than waiting for them to rescue me."

And she should know, seeing as she'd actually gotten kidnapped by a madman earlier in the year. And while the idea of being abducted left me cold with fear, my nerves couldn't take much more of the waiting either. Stress was a strange beast—nothing tangible, but with the power to choke up every cell in your body and turn it into a rigid, shuddering mess. A ball of negative energy that festered and grew, pushing outwards until your sanity finally burst.

Kimberly handled the pressure by making shapes out of paper clips. She'd brought two boxes full, and now the coffee table was full of twisted metal animals, a Noah's Ark of anxiety. Corey tapped his foot constantly, and my own tension nearly made me hurl his damn shoe across the room.

"They've found Lulu," Joel announced. "Well, Beck has." Twenty seconds passed. A minute. "Reed's bringing her out."

"What about Beck and Rania?" And why had Joel gone all tense? That frown didn't look encouraging. "What's wrong? Is something wrong?"

"Just relax."

Why did telling somebody to relax always have the exact opposite effect? I ground my teeth together, then bumped my shin on the coffee table because I was distracted. A pile of paper clip animals landed on the rug, and Kimberly cursed under her breath.

"No, I won't freaking relax! What's happening?"

Even though Joel was wearing a close-fitting earpiece, I still heard the bang, or rather, the bangs. The unmistakable sound of gunshots coming from a mansion in Marin County. So did Kimberly, and every bit of colour drained from her face.

"Just tell us what's going on," she demanded, scrambling up to clutch at my hand.

"I'm not sure," Joel admitted.

"How can you not be sure? You must know something."

His pause turned into an eternity, a gaping chasm of time where my heart raced and my breathing stopped altogether. Then the corners of Joel's lips twitched.

"They're okay. Beck and Rania are both okay."

"Then what were the gunshots for?"

"I don't know. But they're coming back. Just sit tight until they get here."

***

Half an hour passed before Beck walked in with Rania, Reed, and Lulu, and I still hadn't worked out what to say to him. The fear that he might not make it back had been replaced by a new horror—the realisation that today, he'd return to Abbot's Creek with Corey, and I wouldn't have any reason to see him again. Beck, not Corey. I didn't care if Corey took a walk off the edge of the Empire State Building.

What did a girl say in a situation like this?

I had no idea, but then Beck saved me the trouble by hurrying straight past and into the bathroom. A weak bladder? Or was he just avoiding me? Either way, that left me with Lulu, and I didn't know what to say to her either.

"Uh, I'll get you a blanket or something."

Her legs were bare under Beck's jacket, which came to mid-thigh, and she'd wrapped her arms around herself, holding the edges of the leather tightly closed. Dried blood crusted around the edges of her nose and mouth, and it was streaked down her legs too. What had they done to her? I didn't want to care, not after what she'd done to me, but I couldn't stop my heart from lurching.

Suddenly, a piece of gold didn't seem so important

anymore.

I'd barely gotten two steps towards the bedroom when Joel appeared and wordlessly handed me a fleecy blanket. He looked as out of his depth as I felt.

"Here." I wrapped the blanket around Lulu's shoulders, but it slipped off. A tear rolled down her cheek, and what could I do but hug her? Beside me, Kimberly was already in Reed's arms, and Rania was making a slight detour with Will in the Porsche to get rid of the weapons before they came back.

One tear became a hundred, then Lulu gasped as she spotted Corey sitting on the far side of the room.

"Carlton's here."

"Don't worry about him at the moment."

"I can't believe you found him."

He rose to his feet. "Because now you can't keep claiming I stole Nicole's necklace, right?"

An asshole to the last, that was Corey. "This isn't the time."

"Really? You think? Because I'm about to go to jail. It's karma, that's what it is. I did something stupid, and now I'm getting locked up for years. Lulu stole and lied, and she got kidnapped. This is, like, payback from beyond the grave."

"I'm not sure the universe works like that."

"I didn't used to believe in all that other-worldly mumbo jumbo either, but there are too many coincidences. I had a lot of time to think about this shit while I was in San Francisco."

And yet he still hadn't realised how self-centred he was. Couldn't he see how much Lulu was hurting? I probably knew more about the metaphysical than most, and while I was only fifty percent sure karma existed, I was one hundred percent certain that assholes did. Corey wasn't earning himself any points right now.

I tried to block him out.

"Lulu, why don't you sit down? Did they... Did they do anything to you?"

We both knew what I meant. She was half-freaking-naked, after all.

"Not that way. The guy in charge would sit on a chair with me at his feet and whisper that he was saving me for himself. How he'd make me cry and beg." She coughed, dry and rasping. "I thought... I thought..."

"Don't think. It's over now, and he can't hurt you. Do you want something to drink? Or should we take you to the hospital?"

"No!"

Her fierceness surprised me. "No to a drink, or no to the hospital?"

"The hospital." She slumped into the chair Corey had vacated. "I'm never going to the hospital again. That's how I got into this mess in the first place."

"Huh?"

"Carlton's right. I stole and I lied, and I'm so, so sorry."

"You took my necklace?"

She nodded. "It was that damn nut allergy. When I went into anaphylactic shock and you took me to the emergency room? I don't have insurance anymore, and it cost over twenty thousand dollars. I had to borrow it all, but then I couldn't afford the repayments, and the credit card companies were gonna send me to collections, so I borrowed some money from this guy I met, but when I couldn't pay him back, he...he..."

She dissolved into tears, and with dawning horror,

everything made sense. All the little jigsaw pieces slotted into place. The way Lulu had stopped eating out. Her selling almost everything she owned. Hunting for a better-paying job. Desperation, all of it.

"You owed money to a loan shark?"

She nodded, and Kimberly let go of Reed for long enough to hand her a tissue.

"But... But you were looking at new iPods. And you bought all the drinks when we went out to Jive."

"I wasn't going to actually buy a new iPod. I just didn't want you to realise how broke I was."

"I didn't take the iPod either," Corey muttered.

"Why didn't you tell me all this?" I asked Lulu.

"Because I didn't want you to worry. You had that big research proposal going on, and all those hours in the lab, and you always budget everything to the last cent because you're so damn organised. I guess I didn't want to look stupid either."

"So you took my necklace instead? How was that better?"

"I just freaked out! When I woke up before you and realised what Carlton had done, I came to tell you, but then the necklace glinted and I thought it was like a sign, you know?"

"A sign? That's so messed up, Lulu."

"I wasn't thinking straight. This guy, he was calling me twenty times a day, and I figured if I just borrowed the necklace for a few weeks, I could 'find' it later and you wouldn't even know."

"You *borrowed* it? But you helped me to look for Corey."

"I never thought we'd actually find him."

"Where's the necklace now?"

"In a pawnshop in Bernal Heights."

The tension whooshed out of me like air out of a burst balloon. We'd found it. I sagged backwards, just in time for Beck to straighten me up again with an arm around my waist.

"Is this the necklace you're talking about?" he asked. "It's been in a pawnshop all this time?"

Lulu nodded, and a fresh wave of fear rolled through me. "What if they sold it?"

"Not allowed, sprite. They have to keep it for thirty days under California law, and we're not past that yet. Which pawnshop? I'll take you to buy it back."

Lulu gave us the address, and the place was only ten minutes from our house. All the panic, all the tears, and it'd been so close.

"I don't have the money yet," Lulu said. "But I'll get it, I promise."

"How? How will you get it? What are you gonna do? Start selling Amway?"

She huddled up smaller, and now she wouldn't meet my eyes.

"Not Amway." Her voice dropped to a whisper. "Those dates I was going on? They weren't all dates."

Oh my gosh. She'd been... She'd been selling *herself*?

"No!"

"What else did I have left?"

How blind had I been not to see the difficulties she'd gotten herself into? I'd been caught up in my little bubble at the lab, ignoring everything but science while the people around me were in trouble. Lulu, Corey... Yes, Corey was an asshole, but I hadn't noticed his problems either.

This was so screwed up. *Everything* was screwed up.

What should I do? I felt so, so sorry for Lulu, but she'd still lied to me. I could forgive her, but could I ever trust her again? And Beck... Where did I stand with Beck? He'd avoided me when he first got back, but now I was plastered against his stomach. I wrapped my hand over his much larger one, and his arm tightened.

"I don't know what to do," I whispered.

Kimberly came to the rescue. "Go with Beck. I'll take care of Lulu, and Reed'll watch Corey."

"But..."

"Just go. We're a team now, the way we were always meant to be."

CHAPTER 37 - NICOLE

"WE NEED TO go to the bank first," I said to Beck as we climbed into his truck.

Lulu was right when she said I budgeted carefully. I put my savings into fixed-term accounts to get the best interest rates, and the next wasn't due to mature for another month. According to Lulu, the necklace had raised three thousand dollars, so I'd need to beg the bank manager to let me access the money early so I could get it back.

"No, we don't."

"Yes, we do. I don't carry three thousand bucks in my wallet."

"I'll give you the money."

"What? You can't do that."

"I'll get six thousand dollars when I turn Corey in, and since I wouldn't have found him without your help, half of it's yours."

"But—"

"You earned it."

This man, he was everything. Kind, brave, generous, and not as annoying as I'd once thought. But how did I make my feelings clear? While other girls in high school had fooled around with boys and learned what made them tick, I'd been hanging out in the science lab. My understanding of the Y chromosome was on more of a molecular level. How was I supposed to tell Beck I'd fallen for him without scaring him off? He sent so many mixed signals, and I struggled to interpret them.

He mistook my hesitation-slash-panic for something else.

"Don't worry, there's no strings attached. Once we've got your necklace, I'll take Corey back to Abbot's Creek. Bet you'll be glad to see the back of us, huh?"

"Can I come?" I blurted.

Now Beck turned to look at me. "You want to spend more time with your ex?"

"No, I want to spend more time with you."

"Time doing what?"

Good question... Anything. Everything. Riding him like a sex-starved cowgirl.

"Uh, you know."

"I don't. I think you should explain."

Why was it always so difficult to find the right words when it mattered? With Corey, it had been easy to fall into a pattern of mediocre dinners and lousy sex because I didn't much care, but Beck was different. I wanted Beck to be my future.

"There's this... How do I explain? There's this...this *thing*, and it scares me, and I didn't want to like you, but I do, and I have no idea how to say anything because you make my brain go all fuzzy."

"Then how about you shut up and kiss me instead?"

I looked up into his eyes and saw the sparkle had come back, but I barely had time to process that before he dragged me across the centre console and into his lap. Then some sort of demon took over me as I clawed at his back and sucked his damn face off. Freaking hell, the man could kiss. Just the right amount of tongue and pressure and heat and hands, hands that wormed their way inside my shirt and cupped and squeezed and, oh hell, if he didn't ease up, we'd be in danger of getting arrested for public indecency.

Finally, he backed off an inch, and I sucked in air. I was shaking. Why was I shaking?

And why was I sitting on a baseball bat?

"Is this really happening?" I mumbled.

"It's happening. We've got two errands to run, and then you're mine."

His. I liked the sound of that. Possessed, but this time in a good way.

"I'm already yours."

As we drove, Beck told me what happened at Rex's mansion. How Rex and Sarah had ended up dead, and how Rania came to the rescue by shooting Scarface. *Rania*. I felt connected to her on a level I didn't understand, but at the same time, she scared me. Rania was everything I wasn't—tough, brave, and street-smart. Deadly.

"Are you okay with it?" I asked Beck. "When you came back, you seemed kind of detached. The way you headed into the bathroom..."

"I had some asshole's blood in my hair. Didn't want to get that anywhere near you. You've been contaminated by this shit enough already."

Really? That was it? Phew.

"This is almost over. And it hasn't all been bad. Life's about balance, and if Corey and Lulu hadn't tried to screw me over, I'd never have met you or Rania or Kimberly. For me, the heartache was worth it."

Beck brought my hand to his lips and kissed my

knuckles. So damn sweet.

"Worth it for me too, sprite."

***

Five hours later, I didn't bother to wave as Beck escorted Corey into jail. Yes, my ex had partially redeemed himself in the hunt for Lulu, but his snide comment on the trip to Abbot's Creek about Beck stealing his girl made me want to kick him in the balls. Instead, I'd smiled sweetly because there'd been enough violence over the last twenty-four hours.

"Don't flatter yourself, Corey. I just used you to save buying batteries for my vibrator."

He shut up after that.

How long did it take to get a body receipt, as Beck called it? Half an hour? An hour? I rummaged through my purse—well, Lulu's purse—for some gum and a hairbrush, because tonight, Beck had promised to take me on a date. A nice dinner, he said, anywhere I wanted. But there was only one thing I wanted to eat, and I was hoping I could persuade him to skip the restaurant.

My necklace glinted in the mirror, back in its rightful place once more. The owner of the pawnshop had been disappointed when Beck handed over his debit card because apparently his wife had taken a liking to the piece.

"Sure you don't want to sell it?" he asked.

"I'm sure."

"My Roberta says it's real spiritual."

If only they knew. "It belonged to my mom."

"Well, if you ever change your mind..."

"I won't."

Movement caught my eye, and I looked up to see Beck jogging towards the truck.

"Twenty minutes," he said as he slid into the driver's seat. "That's a new record."

"I'm impressed."

"Have you thought about what you want to eat?"

"Endlessly."

"And?"

"Take a guess."

"Italian? Chinese? Mexican?"

"Nope. Closer to home."

"American?"

"Getting warmer."

"There's a burger joint two streets away, but they don't make their fries crispy enough. How about a steak? There's a good steak place on the other side of town."

"That wasn't quite what I had in mind."

"You're gonna have to help me out here."

I looked pointedly at his crotch. Waited a beat. Another. Then grabbed the handle above the door as Beck floored it out of the parking lot.

"Hey, slow down! There're cops around."

"They're all inside, celebrating the capture of a long-time FTA. Did I ever tell you my favourite thing to eat is pussy?"

Crude, yes, but I didn't care. Not when Beck hauled me out of the truck and carried me into his house. Not when he tossed me onto his bed and tore off my clothes. And certainly not when he made me scream and clamp my thighs around his head. Holy hell, I'd never let go that way before. I clapped my hand over my mouth in horror.

Only for Beck to laugh. "Don't hold back. My nearest neighbour's eighty years old and mostly deaf."

"Honestly, I've never screamed like that, not ever."

"I'll take that as a compliment."

He crawled forward, letting me take just enough of his weight to feel the delicious hardness waiting for my attention. His kiss tasted of both of us, and once I might have found that icky, but Beck was introducing me to a whole new side of myself that I hadn't known existed. If I never left his bed again, I'd be happy.

"This may sound crazy..." I started.

"From you? Never."

"Shut up. I think... I think I'm halfway in love with you. Obviously, I have no other terms of reference, so I'm not one hundred percent—"

"Is this where you give me the science talk about margins of error? Because I'm not listening."

"Look, I've never done this before."

"Me neither. But I'm all the way in love with you, and now I'm just waiting for you to catch up."

Oh. Oh! Beck loved me? I felt all weird and prickly, but a strangely pleasant prickly. "I don't know what to say."

"So use your mouth for something else instead."

That I could do, but a sudden attack of nerves got the better of me. Beck wasn't Corey. What if I got this wrong? My fingers fumbled with his belt buckle, and I gulped when I finally saw his cock close up. Freaking hell. Someone had supersized him. When I wrapped my hand around it, my fingers didn't even meet.

"Nicole?"

"Mmm?"

"We'll go slow, okay?"

He understood. Beck always understood, and halfway became three-quarters. I could easily love this man.

By using both hands and my mouth, I managed to get a groan out of Beck, but before I could taste him properly, he sat up and lifted me forward. He wanted me to ride him? Because I'd always been more of a missionary girl despite my earlier thoughts. Miss Unadventurous, that was me. But this was Beck, so I swallowed the panic needling up my spine, rolled on a condom, and slowly, slowly lowered myself onto him.

"You okay?" he asked.

"Full."

"Tight. Fuck, that feels good. Give me a minute, would you? When you move, I'm gonna come so damn fast."

I leaned forward to kiss him, and this was more than just sex. It was a meeting of souls, as corny as that may sound. Beck was the man I was meant to be with. The man fate had chosen for me.

When I did move, my orgasm crept up on me, so sudden I cried out again as Beck grunted and released. I was gone. His. Nothing would ever pry me away from him. And to my utter embarrassment, that feeling of relief made me cry as I buried my face in the crook of his neck.

"What's wrong?"

"Nothing. Everything's right."

"I should probably mention at this point that I don't totally understand women, so if I do something wrong, then I apologise in advance."

"I love you."

His arms tightened around me, and my world became whole.

"Love you too, sprite."

***

After a night with Beck, a proper night where I didn't have to worry that I was clinging to him like an overachieving limpet, a chirp from my phone brought me crashing back down to earth in the morning.

Kimberly: The loan guy came to your house last night. Reed answered the door and got him to back off for now, but we don't think he'll give up. What do the rats eat? Lulu's only just gone to sleep, and I don't want to wake her to ask.

Beck tilted the screen to see. "Shit. We'll have to deal with that. How much does she owe?"

"I don't know, but those guys charge stupid amounts of interest, don't they?"

Six thousand dollars, to be precise, six thousand dollars on top of the ten Lulu had borrowed. By the time we got back to San Francisco, she was awake, sitting in the living room with big dark circles under her eyes and her knees drawn close to her chest.

"We cancelled her 'date,'" Rania whispered when we walked in. "Some guy kept calling to complain she didn't turn up last night."

"Thank goodness. Are *you* okay? Beck told me what you did."

She shrugged. "One day, I'll be able to leave all that behind, but it seems that day hasn't arrived yet."

"I don't know how I'll—we'll—ever be able to thank you."

"You would have done the same."

"How? I'm not brave like you. I have no idea how to shoot a gun."

"Neither does Kimberly."

"But she's so smart. And kind. And so organised—I mean, she runs her own business making people happy."

"If the need arose, you'd be brave. I know it. You're smart too, just in a different way, and you can help us all by carrying on with your research. I'm as curious as you are to find out how our powers work, and I know Kimberly is too. She..."

"She what?"

"She's terrified of passing the curse on. She always figured if she didn't have biological children, it would end there, but my mother always told me that if that was the case, my soul would pass on to a new person, somebody random. That the curse would never die."

"My mom told me that too. That's why I've been trying so hard to find a way to control it. I mean, it was hard enough to learn about this from family, but can you imagine if you had this ability and you didn't get any explanation at all? If you just had ghosts yelling at you to kill people day in, day out?"

"Exactly. So the most important thing for you to do is to get back to your lab."

"Will you let me have DNA samples? I promise I won't publish any of the test results."

"Of course. Just tell us what you need."

"First, I need to help Lulu to fix up her mess. I know you probably think I'm crazy after what she did, but I can't simply abandon her."

Rania reached out to hold my necklace between her

thumb and forefinger, studying it as it caught the light. I wore it on a blue cord rather than a chain so the metal didn't get scratched, and it gleamed as brightly as the day my mom first hung it around my neck.

"It's good that you still have compassion. We'll lend her the money. She can repay it whenever she's able."

Oh my gosh, I nearly fell over. "Are you serious? You and Will?"

"We talked about it last night. Lulu's situation impacts on you too, and neither of us wants you to have any more trouble when you should be focusing on your research and your time with Beck. You're together now, aren't you?"

My cheeks heated as I nodded. "As of last night."

"I thought so. He looks at you like you're his world now."

I glanced across at him. "Everything's changed so much this month."

"And it'll only get better. You'll see."

CHAPTER 38 - NICOLE

"SO WE'LL MEET you at seven?" Kimberly asked over the phone as I walked towards the lab building. "Where do you want to eat?"

"Seven, yes. Why don't you surprise us?"

Us. There was now officially an us. Beck and I were still working out the logistics, but we were definitely together. He'd been in my bed for the three nights since Lulu's rescue, and yesterday, I'd caught him googling to check that rats and dogs could live together happily in the same household—an important consideration, he said, since he now had two pooches. Thankfully, Smartie adored Gibby. Eric had sent a picture of them curled up together in the same basket in between emailing endless photos of his new baby.

George and Tempi had already given Beck their seal of approval. Tempi loved to lick Beck's ears, and George ground his teeth in a way that might have seemed strange to non-rat owners, but was a sign of affection, honest.

Life was gradually getting back to normal. Or should I say, the new normal. Last night, the others had all come over for dinner at the professor's. Reed had surprised me by offering to cook, and the Mexican feast he'd made was far superior to anything I might have attempted. According to Kimberly, he liked to get creative in the kitchen, and she left him to it because the only thing she was good at making was a mess.

Darlene had been in her element with three people to talk to—she'd been a real social butterfly before her death—and dinner had taken on a jovial atmosphere with a bottle of champagne the professor had been saving for a special occasion and even some party poppers.

We had not only meeting each other to celebrate, but also the fact that one of San Francisco's most notorious gangsters had been removed from the picture. The story of Rex's death had made the evening news. The anchor tried not to sound gleeful as he read from the teleprompter, informing us that Rex had been shot in the face in what appeared to be a hit by a rival gang—because, folks, who else would be crazy enough to bust into his house?—then died alongside two of his henchmen and, sadly, a young woman who might have been a kidnap victim. Knowing what we knew about Sarah, we raised a glass to that last part too.

I'd miss the others when they left, but Kimberly was only five hours away by plane and Rania promised to visit again before the end of the year. And we still had two days to go before they went home. I needed to spend today in the lab because I desperately needed to catch up with some of the work I'd fallen behind on thanks to Corey, but Beck had promised to pick me up so we could all go out after Kimberly, Rania, and their guys got back from their trip to the Golden Gate Bridge. In the meantime, he'd promised to fix my sticky bedroom window so it actually opened again.

And secretly, I couldn't wait to get back to the lab. Now I had two extra blood samples to work with, and the possibility of discovering our secret left me buzzing, so much so that I'd set an alarm on my phone to remind me to leave at six. Otherwise, the risk of pulling an absent-minded all-nighter was very real.

"Okay, I'll get Reed to find somewhere good," Kimberly said. "He's brilliant at coming up with restaurant suggestions. Did I tell you about the weird little shack thing he found in Utah?"

"I don't think so."

"They served the best ribs ever. Honestly, I didn't even care when I dripped sauce on my second-favourite top. We should go there someday."

"Really? Like a road trip?"

"Yes, with all six of us next time?"

Before I met Beck, I'd never even have dreamed of going on a crazy adventure like that, but now the thought of embarking on another made me smile. "I'd love to."

"I'll start organising it as soon as the next few weddings are finished. I've got a busy two months when I get back."

"Do you want me to help with the planning?"

"Not if it takes you away from the lab. I can't wait to see what you find."

I couldn't help laughing at her eagerness because it mirrored my own. Kimberly and Rania were my soulmates in every way that mattered.

"I'm heading there right now."

***

In the lab was where I felt most at home, surrounded by microscopes and electrophoresis equipment and all the bottles and beakers and flasks that combined could unlock the secrets of my being.

Damien was already there when I arrived—the real Damien this time, not the fake one Rex had sent to visit Lulu. Will and Reed thought Rex must have gotten Damien's name from the university's website in order to fool her.

Speaking of Lulu, we were still sharing a house, although the atmosphere was strained. She was being overly cheerful, insisting on doing all the chores and grocery shopping, which felt more awkward than nice. She'd even cleaned out the rats' cage and weeded the tiny front yard, and not once had she mentioned the lock Beck had fitted to my bedroom door.

I promised myself I'd give it a month. A month to see if I felt any less tense each time I walked into my own house. If not, I'd start looking for a new place to live.

"I hear you had an adventure?" Damien said.

"Oh?"

How much had the professor told him?

"Your trip to Vegas? Did you win much?"

Yes, I hit the jackpot. "Not really. But I, uh, I met a new guy."

"Ooh, congratulations! Aren't you glad now that you dumped the worm you were living with?"

Seriously, had I been the only person not to realise Corey was an asshole? At least he was in jail now.

"I didn't dump him, remember? He ran out on me. But you're right—it was for the best."

"Such a dick move. Do you want a coffee? I'm just gonna get one for myself."

"Are you going to that place by the admin

building?"

"Where else? Nobody froths the milk like they do."

"In that case, could you get me a latte and one of those banana muffins?"

It was good to be healthy, right? I rummaged in my purse for money, but Damien waved my offer away.

"My treat. You can get the next one."

"Sure. Where's the professor?"

"Running late. He said something about a headache."

A headache? Or a hangover? He'd been trying to do the moonwalk at one a.m. this morning.

When Damien closed the door behind him, that was the first moment I'd truly been alone since I met Beck, and as I puttered around preparing reagents, loading them into syringes for precision, and organising my workspace, it gave me some much-needed time to think. I still had one decision to make. Beck had mentioned his ex-girlfriend—a victim of Sarah—and the one problem we hadn't managed to solve was her being trapped on earth. And now that Sarah was dead, Anna would never be free.

The question was, should I volunteer to speak to her? It would be awkward, for sure, but maybe I could give both her and Beck some comfort if I offered to act as a go-between. I'd talk to him about it. Or perhaps I should see what Kimberly thought of the idea first?

The door clicked, and my taste buds cried out for coffee. Funny, I'd never liked it much until, as an undergrad, I'd discovered the magical properties of caffeine.

"Did you remember the sugar?" I asked, looking up.

Except it wasn't Damien standing in front of me,

and the man didn't have a cup of coffee in his hand. No, he had a piece of thin rope.

And a scar slicing through the left side of his face.

What? How?

The malevolent sneer on his face told me he hadn't come to offer a surprise research grant. My heart pounded against my ribcage as I took a step back, then another and another until I hit the workbench behind me.

"Uh, are you lost?"

I could only hope. How was Scarface in the professor's lab? Spirits couldn't move, and his body was in the damn morgue. Or was it? He certainly looked real.

"No, Nicole Bordais, I'm not lost."

Oh hell, oh hell, oh hell.

My phone was in my purse, and even if I could reach it, I'd never be able to dial 911 in time. And the handle for the fire alarm was way across the lab. When would Damien be back? The line for coffee got awful long in that place, and beads of sweat popped out on the back of my neck as I imagined him stumbling in a minute too late and tripping over my lifeless body.

Worse, Scarface would get away because everyone in San Francisco thought he was dead. *Beck* had told me he was dead, so how could he possibly be here and *breathing*?

"I... I don't understand."

"Of course you don't, little girl. You got in way over your head. But let me explain you this. When a man attacks my family, he has to expect retribution. Your boyfriend broke into my boss's house and shot my brother, and now I will kill you in return." Scarface grinned, and that scared me more than anything. "I'll even enjoy it."

"He didn't shoot your brother!"

That was Rania. I mean, it had to have been, right?

"Liar! I saw him in the house where my brother died."

"You were there?"

"If I had been, he would have left in a body bag. No, there were cameras, and two minutes before the gunshots, your boyfriend walked along the downstairs hallway. Now, let us see how he likes losing someone he loves."

I opened my mouth to scream, but before any sound came out, Scarface was on me, spinning me so he could loop the rope around my neck from behind. A fingernail tore out of its bed as I clawed at his arms, but it didn't make any difference, and the rope got tighter, tighter, tighter.

My life couldn't end here. No way. Not when so much had changed for the better. I grabbed a conical flask and smashed it over his head, but since all it contained was distilled water, that only made him angry.

"You little bitch. I like it when women struggle, did I tell you? Maybe I should've fucked you first."

He adjusted his grip, and warm blood trickled down my neck as the rope sawed into my flesh. The bright lights of the lab started to dim, and instead of wishing for life, I began to wish death would hurry up and take me quickly because my lungs were on fire.

One. Last. Chance.

My fingers scrabbled across the wooden bench and clasped around a syringe. What was in it? I couldn't remember, but I didn't care. If I could just get him in the eye with the needle...

I reached behind me. Stabbed.

Missed his eye and hit flesh instead. His neck?

Fuck.

I depressed the plunger, and he let out a roar, yanking the rope harder, tighter, angrier.

Then the lights went out.

CHAPTER 39 - NICOLE

"AYEEEEEE!"

DAMIEN'S SCREECH could have woken the dead, and for a moment, I thought it might have. Then I realised the lab reeked of coffee, and I knew I must be alive since ghosts had no sense of smell.

"What...?" The word came out as a croak, and my throat burned. I tried again. "What...?"

No better.

"OMG! Is he dead?"

I flopped over onto my belly and somehow made it to my knees. Then immediately wished I hadn't. Holy fuck.

What the hell had been in that syringe?

Oh. Yeah. Concentrated hydrochloric acid. One component of the reagents I'd been mixing, except now it had eaten Scarface's neck away from the inside out. That, children, was why you always took proper precautions when handling chemicals. I leaned to the side and vomited.

"What the heck happened?" Damien squealed. "We've gotta call the cops!"

Good idea.

I still couldn't speak. The pool of blood and acid was congealing on the floor, but I crawled a little farther away, just in case. Was it really over now? I mean, Scarface wasn't breathing. I'd killed a man.

It occurred to me that I should be more upset, but I struggled to care. Scarface had killed Macy, he'd attacked me, undoubtedly he'd been involved in kidnapping Lulu, and he'd have killed Corey if we hadn't stepped in. No, he deserved everything he got. Macy was free. I was free. And I was willing to bet that cities from Tegucigalpa to San Francisco had a few less spirits inhabiting them today. My only regret? That I didn't get the chance to see his black soul rise up and leave his body the way Rania told me they did. The scientist in me got curious about things like that.

A gasp came from the doorway.

"What happened?" Professor Fairchild asked. "I oversleep one time—*one time*—and now there's a dead body in my lab? Who left it there? I think we need a permit for that."

"He... He tried...to kill me."

"Oh. Oh dear." The professor turned to Damien. "Well, have you called the police?"

"Not yet."

"Better do that, then." He stopped to check out Scarface's body. "Was that acid?"

"Yes."

"Fascinating. Just fascinating. We all know what it can do in a Petri dish, but this is something else. Are you okay, Nicole? Here, let me help you up."

I steadied myself on his arm as I clambered to my feet, knees still trembling.

"He just walked in. I didn't even—" Pain sent me into a coughing fit. "Didn't even hear him coming."

"Shh. Sit down, and don't try to speak until the ambulance gets here." The professor's voice dropped to a whisper. "Is this something to do with...you know?"

I nodded, and even that hurt.

He gave Scarface's body a sharp kick with one leather wingtip. "Asshole."

Chapter 40 - Beckett

FUCK.

I'D ONLY just found Nicole, and today, I nearly lost her. Twice, I'd fucked up. Once in Rex's mansion when I'd let Scarface's brother pull a gun on me, and a second time when I made a wrong assumption about who Rania had killed. And Corey had warned me. He'd told me two of Rex's men were brothers, and I'd been too dumb to consider the connection.

Twice, the Electi had fixed the problems I'd created. First Rania, then Nicole, and I was so damn proud of my girl.

I wrapped my arms around her as she curled up on my lap in the professor's living room. His place had seemed like the best place to regroup after this morning's drama and the police interviews that followed. We all stuck to the same story—that Scarface and Nicole had crossed paths when he was looking for her ex-boyfriend, and we had no idea why he'd come back other than his threat to rape her.

The professor, for his part, seemed to be taking the corpse in his lab remarkably well. Nicole said he'd fallen apart after his wife's death, but today, he'd directed the police and made sure Nicole was kept as comfortable as possible under the circumstances until I got there. I kind of understood his behaviour. I'd seen—

and been responsible for—a whole cemetery full of bodies during my time in the army and slept like a baby afterwards, but if it had been Nicole lying cold on the tile instead of Scarface, I'd never have forgiven myself. It would've been like losing Anna all over again, but worse, because Anna had been a casual thing and I'd already lost my heart to Nicole.

"I'm so sorry, sprite," I whispered for the hundredth time.

"Stop saying that. Nobody could have known."

"I should've checked the corpse at Rex's better. And guessed about the hidden cameras. Anything but left you exposed."

"If you'd been with me this morning, he'd just have waited for another opportunity."

"What if there's another brother out there? Or Rex has a cousin? I'll have to be your damn shadow."

"We won't leave her alone in the lab," the professor promised, walking in with coffee. "Either Damien or I will stay with Nicole at all times."

"You think that'll help if someone runs in with a gun? There's a mass shooting every damn day in the United States, sometimes more, and it's only getting worse. Campus security's shit. Anyone can walk in and out because the card reader's faulty and people keep wedging the door open. Plus the fire escape doesn't latch properly, and the first-floor windows open wide enough for a person to fit through. I noticed all that the first time I was waiting for Nicole, and I bet there are more issues too."

Waiting for Nicole. That sounded much better than spying on her.

"Really?"

"Yes, really."

"I'll have a word with the university board."

"Doesn't it feel like something weird's going on?" Kimberly asked. "The way the three of us have had dramas recently, I mean."

Rania spoke up, regarding us with watchful eyes. "It's fate. We were meant to find each other."

"Fate would be if we'd bumped into each other on the subway or taken a vacation at the same resort. This is something else. Something bigger."

I feared Kimberly was right. Three very special women, and they'd all been victims of madmen in the last year? What were the odds of that happening?

"Like a push to fulfil our purpose?" Rania asked. "It feels as though we're playing cosmic chess, but without fully understanding the rules."

"And one of the pieces is missing."

"What are we going to do about that? Wait and hope the stars align, or actively look for our fourth sister?"

Now Will spoke up. "We've got three investigators on the team. My vote is yes, we look for the missing member of the Electi."

"Nicole needs to carry on with her research," Kimberly told him.

"Agreed. So it's a two-pronged attack. Nicole digs into your past while we look at the present."

Although I wasn't officially an investigator, I might be able to assist, and I wanted to be a part of whatever they were planning. I told myself it was just to help Nicole, but the paranormal had fascinated me ever since the day I died in the hospital. Recent events had only boosted my curiosity.

"Actually, I've already started the search. Before I found Nicole, I was looking for one of the Electi to help me with Anna. I've got files and files full of information."

"What sort of information?" Will asked.

"I've spent years scouring the internet for any mention of people talking to the dead. Ninety percent of it's bullshit, but every so often, I'd come across an account that sounded genuine. Plus out-of-body experiences, people describing phenomena that sounded like the spirit guide I saw, and the occasional medium who seemed to be more than a charlatan."

"Did you follow up any leads?"

"A handful of possibles. I've been sifting through them one by one for months, and I've eliminated the first twenty-seven."

"Then we'll take that as a starting point and expand on your search. My pal RJ'll help with the computer stuff, and Reed's sister's dating a cop who's in on the secret. He'll be useful too."

Reed nodded. "We'll find her. Together, we'll find her."

"And I'll speak to Anna," Nicole said. "If you still want me to, that is."

There were so many reasons I loved this girl, and that was just one more. "I think she'd very much like the company."

Epilogue - Nicole

TWO MONTHS LATER, my life had changed completely again, but this time for the better.

"Is here okay?" Beck asked, settling George and Tempi's giant new cage onto a table in the living room, which was easier said than done with two pooches skittering underfoot.

"Perfect. Hey, Smartie, come over here."

She was a different dog now. Licky, waggy, and a constant trip hazard, although she was so freaking sweet we had to forgive her for that last part. She still had scars around her neck from an ill-fitting collar, but her fractured leg had healed, and now that the cast was off, she was free to run around the house and garden as much as she wanted to.

Yes, the garden. We had a new home, courtesy of Kimberly. She said, and I quote, "No psycho roommate's going to interrupt your research again," and insisted on becoming our new landlord. And I mean *insisted.* She told us she'd buy a house, and if we didn't live in it, then it would sit empty until we gave in. Her contribution towards my work, she called it. Apparently, she'd gotten a huge divorce settlement from her ex-husband plus a trust fund from her father that she rarely touched, and she wanted to do something constructive with the money rather than leaving it to sit in the bank.

So there we were, and when I said "we," I meant me and Beck. Living in a three-bedroom detached house that she refused to tell us the cost of, complete with a tiny apartment over the garage for Lulu. Our relationship wasn't close like it once had been, but I couldn't abandon her completely, not after everything she'd been through, and we'd salvaged a tentative friendship.

The professor had lobbied the university board to improve campus security, and following a sit-in protest by a group of social-media-savvy students terrified that they could be the next victim of a trespassing rapist, the powers that be had given in and agreed to hire three new guards to patrol the area.

And who was in charge of security at the lab building? I'll give you a clue—I got to accompany him home and peel him out of his new uniform every night. Even though Beck was vastly overqualified for the position, he insisted—there was that word again—on taking it because he wanted me to be safe. One step up from being a nightclub bouncer, he said.

And he'd rented out his place in Abbot's Creek to move to San Francisco permanently with Gibby and Smartie. Now I had a man who'd sworn to protect me, two new pets, my soul sisters, friends in Will and Reed, and an amazing new home. If three months ago, someone had asked me what my dream was, this would have come pretty close.

***

"Are you sure you don't mind doing this?" Beck asked.

"It's weird, but it's kind of my job."

Today, we'd driven to Abbot's Creek, ostensibly to visit Eric and his new crying, pooping, farting machine, but also so I could talk to Anna. Beck had shown me a picture of her, a beautiful blonde with long hair and perfect teeth, and I'd felt vaguely intimidated until I remembered that he'd told me he loved me four times last night alone.

And Anna was a ghost of her former self.

"I just need to know if she wants anything. How else can I make her life—her death—more bearable?"

"Like what?" The truck drew to a halt. "Wait. Where are we?"

I'd been expecting the charred remains of a building or perhaps a rubble-filled lot, but this...this was beautiful. A tiny park with trees and benches and flowers tucked in between two houses. It even had a children's play area in one corner.

"Anna's home. When I realised she was stuck here, I spent most of my savings buying what was left of her old house and having it torn down, then I turned it into a garden for her. She always loved the outdoors, and kids too."

He'd done all this for a ghost? Out of love? Guilt? Both were powerful motivators, and he'd used them to create something quite lovely. Beck *felt*. From the tips of his fingers to his mind to his heart, he understood and empathised in a way I sometimes struggled to do. And that only made me love him more.

"That's the nicest thing I've ever seen."

His cheeks went a tiny bit pink. "I worried you'd think it was dumb. Over the top."

"We each have to help them in our own way."

I was still at it with the anonymous tips, and with Beck around to provide cover while I had my other-worldly conversations now, I'd managed to report the details of three murders so far this month. We kept an eye on the news and travelled to crime scenes after our volunteering stints at the animal shelter on Saturday mornings. A macabre sort of hobby, if you like.

"I'm not even sure whereabouts she is," Beck said.

"Over by the sundial."

I saw Anna from the window before I even got out of the truck, watching us with alert eyes. She'd died of smoke inhalation, that much I could tell, because she was still pretty, just a little grey around the edges. A spirit's appearance got captured as they died, and she'd breathed her last before the flames touched her. Now she looked ethereal as the dappled sun filtered through the leaves above.

I climbed out of the truck and walked towards her, Beck following.

"Hey."

"He found you? Beck really found one of the Electi?"

"He told you about that?"

"So many times, he said he was looking, but then he stopped visiting, and I figured he'd given up. I'm Anna, by the way. But I guess you already know that?"

"And I'm Nicole. Beck's told me all about you, but we should start at the beginning."

Beck dragged over a bench so we could sit together. Well, pretend to sit, in Anna's case, since she'd have passed right through the sundial if she'd done anything but play-act. And Anna turned out to be one of the easier spirits to deal with. As happy in death as she was in life, it seemed.

"So you're together now?" she asked, peering at our joined hands after we finished telling the tale of our recent adventures. "You and Beck?"

"We are."

Her perky smile got wider. "I always hoped he'd find the right person, although it's kind of weird the way it happened."

"Weird doesn't even begin to cover it. And I'm so, so sorry that you're stuck here."

"Honestly, I was sceptical about the whole Electi thing anyway. Who goes around killing people because of some ancient prophecy in this day and age?"

"So you're not upset?"

"I'd be lying if I said I wouldn't rather be free, but Beck's made this place nice for me. Fall will be here soon, and that was always my favourite time of year. All the vivid colours and kids playing in the leaves, and at least I don't feel the cold anymore."

"Is there anything else we can do for you? I feel bad that Beck won't be around so much."

"Maybe cut back the trees beside the road? It'd be good to see the sidewalk again."

I relayed the message to Beck, and he nodded. "Consider it done."

Back in the truck, I slumped into my seat. Why was it always the nice ones that hit me the hardest? Spirits like Anna had no business being trapped in eternal limbo, and I cursed the person who'd come up with that stupid rule. If the Electi had the power to see ghosts, why couldn't we also release them?

"You okay, sprite? Did Anna say something to upset you?"

"No, not at all. Quite the opposite, in fact."

He let out a breath. "She always was sweet."

"And that's the whole problem. It sucks not being able to help people like her, people whose killers are already dead. We have to come back and visit, okay?"

"I was hoping you'd say that. You're right—it sucks. And it's strange, don't you think? That whoever created you and this elaborate system of supernatural justice didn't cater for that eventuality?"

"Yes, it *is* strange. But my mom never knew of a solution, and it seems Rania and Kimberly don't either."

"What if something happens when the four of you get together?" He reached across to touch my necklace. "Maybe this is a part of it? Your mom said it was important, right? And we don't yet know why."

"I guess anything's possible."

I only hoped we got the chance to find out for sure.

WHAT'S NEXT?

The Electi series continues in *Demented*...

Iris McGivern never envisioned spending her twenties locked up in a psychiatric hospital, but there she is. Stuck with bad food, rude staff, and rules, rules, rules. The place is interminably dull. At least, it is until the murders start. Oh, sure, management claims the deaths are accidents, but Iris knows better. How? Because she can speak to the victims.

Newly qualified psychiatrist Marcus Hastings never aspired to work in a secure unit, but his student loans won't pay themselves. And he hates to back away from a challenge, even if that challenge is a delusional blonde who talks to birds, squirrels, and occasionally thin air. Fascinating, in a purely clinical sense, of course.

When fate throws them together, will Iris escape with her life? And will Marcus escape with his sanity?

For more details: www.elise-noble.com/demented

And if you also enjoy romantic mysteries without supernatural elements, why not give my Blackwood series a try? The story starts in *Pitch Black*...

What happens when an assassin has a nervous breakdown?

After the owner of a security company is murdered, his sharp-edged wife goes on the run. Forced to abandon everything she holds dear—her home, her friends, her job in special ops—she builds a new life for herself in England. As Ashlyn Hale, she meets Luke, a handsome local who makes her realise just how lonely she is.

Yet, even in the sleepy village of Lower Foxford, the dark side of life dogs Diamond's trail when the unthinkable strikes. Forced out of hiding, she races against time to save those she cares about. But is it too little, too late?

Pitch Black is currently available FREE.
For more details: www.elise-noble.com/pitch-black

If you enjoyed *Possessed*, please consider leaving a review.

For an author, every review is incredibly important. Not only do they make us feel warm and fuzzy inside, readers consider them when making their decision whether or not to buy a book. Even a line saying you enjoyed the book or what your favourite part was helps a lot.

WANT TO STALK ME?

For updates on my new releases, giveaways, and other random stuff, you can sign up for my newsletter on my website:
www.elise-noble.com

Facebook:
www.facebook.com/EliseNobleAuthor

Twitter: @EliseANoble

Instagram: @elise_noble

If you're on social media, you may also like to join Team Blackwood for exclusive giveaways, sneak previews, and book-related chat. Be the first to find out about new stories, and you might even see your name or one of your ideas make it into print!

And if you'd like to read my books for FREE, you can also find details of how to join my review team.

Would you like to join Team Blackwood?

www.elise-noble.com/team-blackwood

END-OF-BOOK STUFF

Phew, this book made it on time. For a while, I thought it was gonna be late because right now, I'm fucking exhausted. I have a weird working arrangement where I play accountant for six months out of twelve, and the way the schedule shook out this year, I've ended up working four of those months together. Which means every other scrap of spare time is spent writing and editing and proofing and sleep comes a poor third place.

Fun fact: I drink a LOT of coffee, but it's all decaf. I haven't touched caffeine in seven years, but times like this really test my willpower.

It's been a miserable few months too—before Christmas, Taura the sugar glider died, in January, Trev the horse had to have a tumour removed, in February, the other sugar glider, Fairfax, died, and in April we lost Bella dog. But although my heart hurts, I'm grateful to have had all these animals in my life. My world would be a lot less colourful without them.

Switching back to books, I finally got to write a story about a bounty hunter. I've wanted to ever since my dad bought me my first Stephanie Plum novel a long, long time ago. If you haven't tried that series, then I'd definitely recommend it. Just don't drink coffee while reading because you might snort it out of your nose. #TeamRanger

If you've read the blurb for Demented, you can guess what's coming up next. Or can you? There's a nice twist left in this series, but you'll have to wait for a bit to find out what it is ;)

In the meantime, you'll get Indigo Rain, the next Blackwood UK book, which fulfils another of my writing ambitions. Yup, there's a rock star in it. Or rather, four rock stars. Originally, Ethan in White Hot was gonna be a rock star, but I changed my mind on that because he's too well-behaved. So, it's fallen to Alana Graves to deal with Indigo Rain and their bad habits, with a little help from Emmy and Zander.

Happy reading, and talk to you again soon, hopefully when I'm awake.

Elise

Thanks so much to my beta readers for this book—Quenby, Jeff, Renata, Terri, Lina, Musi, David, Stacia, Jessica, Nikita, and Jody—and my proof readers—John, Debi, and Elizabeth.

And thanks as always to Abi for the cover (including Nicole's many shirt changes!) and to Nikki for editing. One day, I'll manage to do proper timeline before I start writing a book.

Lithium
Carbon
Rhodium
Platinum
Lead
Copper
Bronze
Nickel
Hydrogen (2021)

The Blackwood UK Series
Joker in the Pack
Cherry on Top (novella)
Roses are Dead
Shallow Graves
Indigo Rain
Pass the Parcel (TBA)

Baldwin's Shore
Dirty Little Secrets (2021)
Secrets, Lies, and Family Ties (2021)
Buried Secrets (2021)

Blackwood Casefiles
Stolen Hearts
Burning Love (TBA)

Blackstone House
Hard Lines (TBA)
Hard Tide (TBA)

The Electi Series
Cursed

Spooked
Possessed
Demented
Judged

The Planes Series
A Vampire in Vegas
A Devil in the Dark (TBA)

The Trouble Series
Trouble in Paradise
Nothing but Trouble
24 Hours of Trouble

Standalone
Life
Coco du Ciel (2021)
Twisted (short stories)
A Very Happy Christmas (novella)

Books with clean versions available (no swearing and no on-the-page sex)
Pitch Black
Into the Black
Forever Black
Gold Rush
Gray is My Heart

Audiobooks
Black is My Heart (Diamond & Snow - prequel)
Pitch Black
Into the Black
Forever Black

Gold Rush
Gray is My Heart
Neon (novella)

Printed in Great Britain
by Amazon

60127611R00218